ACCEPTING HIS MATE

TAMSIN LEY

with

AURORA SHIFTERS

A Production of

Twin Leaf Press

UNTAMED INSTINCT

CHAPTER ONE

Adrian crouched among the cottonwood leaves, claws digging into the bark as he surveyed the dead moose in the clearing below. He'd been waiting here in his mountain lion form for several hours and was eager to move on, but had to be certain the carcass had been deserted before he drew closer to investigate. He'd received numerous reports of abandoned animal kills over the last few weeks, and his supervisor at the ranger station wanted whoever—or whatever—was doing the poaching to be tracked down.

Scattered throughout the Wrangell-St. Elias Park, the previous sites had been old before Adrian reached them, the evidence around the carcasses obscured by smaller predators and decay. This site seemed fresher, the stench of rot less intense, although flies swarmed over the bull's hide and stubby, velvet-covered antlers. If the killer was human, they weren't out for trophies. And they definitely weren't doing it for meat. Someone or something was killing for fun, and they were slowly moving closer to human-occupied lands.

Adrian's tail twitched angrily, and he let out a grunt of resignation before dropping nimbly to the ground. The scent of rotting flesh grew stronger as he approached, and flies rose in a cloud, exposing gashes writhing with fresh maggots.

He circled the moose, estimating it had been dead slightly longer than twenty-four hours. Clawed paw prints, almost twice the size of his own, scarred the earth around the kill. He lowered his muzzle and sniffed, tail lashing. The familiar musk of a grizzly filled his nose. *Shifter grizzly*. He released a hiss of displeasure. The last thing the shifter community wanted was a rogue member drawing attention to the national park. Randall, Adrian's tough-as-nails wolf supervisor, would not like this.

Fuck, Adrian didn't like it either. Mountain lions weren't unheard of in Alaska, but rare enough to cause a ruckus among humans if sighted. The vast wilds of the park were his refuge—his *territory* in the mind of his mountain lion. The local bear shifters would want to take care of a rogue grizzly themselves.

Adrian exposed his canines and turned away, prowling through the trees toward his ranger cabin to call his supervisor.

Just out of sight of his cabin, he shifted and retrieved the uniform he kept in a hollow tree, shrugging into his clothing before emerging into the clearing. His cabin was a small log building nestled next to one of the many rock faces jutting from the mountain, roof covered in thick moss and a small porch screened in from mosquitoes. One of the more popular trailheads started nearby, and a small message board fluttered with notices campers left to each other at the end of his overgrown driveway.

Inside the two-room cabin, a few small windows shed dusky light over the sparse furnishings. Passing the small front area with a table, a propane fridge, a wood stove, and an old sofa, he moved to the bedroom where a king-sized bed took up almost every inch of space. He retrieved his cell phone from the nightstand and moved to the corner of the front room where he got the best reception. He kept an old ham radio in the shed for when the notoriously spotty cell service didn't work, but he couldn't talk to Randall about shifter business over the radio. Thankfully, the phone showed two bars today. He dialed the main ranger office.

"This is HQ," a woman's nasal voice answered.

"Cherry, it's Adrian. I need to talk to Randall."

"Oh, hi, handsome!" Her voice brightened. "We haven't heard from you in a while. How've you been?"

Adrian bared his teeth and reminded himself to be polite; Cherry was human. "Doing fine."

He hated social niceties, which was why he'd become a ranger in the first place. This remote location suited him well, and he only ventured into town when he needed supplies. Most of his duties allowed him to patrol the trails alone, talking to the occasional hiker and reporting any problems. Several times a year he had to oversee search and rescue operations when a hiker got lost, but more often than not, he found the missing person before a full team even arrived.

"You doing okay on handouts?" Cherry chirped back.

He glanced toward the door where a stack of papers had gathered a layer of dust. He was supposed to pass them out to tourists, but since he avoided people, he used very few. "All good. I just need to talk to Randall."

"You betcha."

The phone clicked. A few heartbeats later, the supervisor's voice came on the line. "Adrian, what's up?"

"I've got a lead on the poacher. I found a spike-fork moose abandoned yesterday, and there's fresh grizzly sign all over the place. Smells like a shifter."

"Shit. Don't tell me the infection's moved to our territory."

"What infection?"

"Rogues." The sound of fingernails against beard stubble scratched over the phone line. "Two rogue wolves and a moose were put down in Anchorage over the winter, then a black bear outside Valdez this spring. No rhyme or reason to why. Council sent out a memo a while back. Don't you read your emails, Adrian?"

Adrian glanced at the dust-covered laptop under the nightstand. "Not like I have wifi out here, Randall. I'll catch up next time I go into town."

Randall made a frustrated noise over the phone. "Well, if a shifter's behind these abandoned kills, it's likely a rogue. File your report then go handle it ASAP."

"Me? Isn't this Den business?" Although the Council oversaw shifter law, local shifter groups liked to take care of their own business.

"Not this time. A travel blogger already posted about the kills. We need to get ahead of the news before it goes viral. Take your rifle."

"I'm a ranger, not a SWAT team, Randall."

"This is your territory. I need you to handle it. There could be hikers in danger."

"Fuck." Adrian grimaced. "What if he shifts before he dies?" It was one thing for a ranger to take down a dangerous bear. Quite another if a human body showed up killed by a ranger's bullet. And in a face-to-face fight, a mountain lion couldn't stand up to a full-grown grizzly, especially a shifter gone rogue.

"Make your first shot count."

"I hate this shit." Hanging up, Adrian pocketed his phone and grabbed his rifle before heading back outside. He'd file a report when he got back. Best to get on the trail while it was still relatively warm.

He started up his ATV, its disused engine letting out a disgusting belch of smoke. The damn thing cut off his ability to hear or smell anything, which made his mountain lion bristle in discomfort. *I know, me too.* But he couldn't carry his rifle while in feline form.

Stowing the weapon in the mounted case on the front of the ATV, he rolled out of the cabin's clearing toward the trailhead parking lot.

CHAPTER TWO

$\mathcal{D}$arcy stopped her Subaru and eyed the overgrown path. According to Google, this dirt road should lead to a trailhead parking lot, but it looked like if she drove any farther, she might end up "parked" more permanently. Her all-wheel drive had managed the old, rutted road, but the path was getting narrower, with branches rubbing her door panels. *Did I take a wrong turn?*

She glanced in her rearview mirror. There had been a space wide enough to turn around a short way back. Putting the car in reverse, she carefully maneuvered through the brush, backing into a flat area that looked like it would make a nice campsite.

The overcast sky filtered dimly through the thick canopy of trees, and she hadn't seen a soul since turning into what had started out as a fairly decent dirt road. She rolled down her window and breathed in the verdant forest air. *This looks like as good a place to start as any.*

Her interview with the coven was the day after tomorrow, and she'd come in search of herbs to make an eloquence potion. This would be her last-ditch effort to overcome the stutter that ruined every spell she tried to cast. Poor Aunt Willow still had a patch of white hair behind one ear from one of her lessons. Darcy'd tried to buy an eloquence potion from the local apothecary shop, but it turned out it only worked for the person who made it, and the effects would not be permanent. But she didn't need to be *good* at incantations, only steady enough to pass the coven's apprenticeship test.

Cutting the engine, she reached over to the passenger seat to retrieve her copy of *Wild Edible and Medicinal Plants of the Pacific Northwest.* She was more familiar with gardens than wilderness, but her mom had sent her to summer camp every year of her childhood, and the forest didn't daunt her.

Tapping her phone, she opened her GPS app and pinned her current location so she could find her way back, then tucked it and the book into a reusable grocery bag alongside a small trowel, a pair of purple and yellow gardening gloves, and a compact rain poncho. She looked around as she stepped out of the car, taking in a circle of stones around an overgrown fire pit. The mossy log seats around it obviously hadn't been disturbed in quite a while, and knee-high saplings and brush filled the clearing.

Locking the car even though she doubted she needed to, she headed toward what looked like a trail on the uphill side of the clearing. According to her book, wild rhodiola rosea grew on rocky slopes at high altitudes.

She set off between the trees, scanning the surrounding plants for signs of fleshy rhodiola leaves. A thick layer of dry leaves and twigs crunched under her feet, birds sang overhead, and in the distance a woodpecker tatted out a rhythm. She let out a contented sigh, running her fingertips over the smooth gray trunk of a quaking aspen as she passed.

A scraggly thicket of salmonberries crowded the trail, and she sampled a few, letting the sweet juice coat her tongue. A mosquito buzzed her ear, and she reached into her bag for her homemade insect repellant. She wasn't yet much good at magical potions, but she had a decent grasp of essential oils, and her minty-citrus concoction not only worked, it smelled good. After dousing herself, she tucked the small spray bottle away and continued on.

The path grew steeper, making her calves burn as she climbed until she reached a sharp turn. To her right, the trail paralleled the top of a rocky ridge, but about fifteen feet below, she spotted a clump of rosette shaped leaves. *Rhodiola?* She stepped toward the edge to get a better look.

The ground beneath her feet collapsed. Too startled to even scream, she bumped and slithered helplessly down the incline on her backside, coming to a stop among a rain of pebbles and dust.

More stunned than hurt, she sat up and pushed her strawberry blonde hair out of her face before struggling to her feet. Other than a few scrapes and a racing heartbeat, she wasn't hurt, thank the Goddess. Next to her, scaly rosettes of rhodiola crouched staunchly among the rocks. Amidst the dust, her minty-citrus scented insect repellant had become cloying. She pulled the crushed bottle from her bag and wrinkled her nose. Oily residue covered everything inside. She wiped her phone and the book on the leg of her jeans. At least she'd be insect-free for a while.

Along the cliff face behind her, a scoured swath of dirt and stone showed her path down the steep incline. It was a wonder she wasn't seriously injured. She peered both directions along the wall. Not one spot looked possible to climb.

"Fuck," she muttered. Her stutter never affected her curse words.

She turned back to the rhodiola. *Might as well make the most of the situation before I try to climb back up.* She pulled out her book to make sure the photos matched, then put on her gardening gloves and shoved a clump aside to get at the root. The plant seemed to grow directly from a crack in one of the large stones. If she could've used store-bought herbs, she would've, but for this potion, the rhodiola root had to be freshly gathered within seventy-two hours after a full moon.

Jabbing the pointed end of her trowel into the crack, she tried to pry it apart, but the tool scraped uselessly against the stone. She tried several angles, but the ground refused to give up its hold on the plant. Standing upright, she glared toward the overcast sky in frustration.

As if the heavens were laughing at her, a fat raindrop hit her square on the forehead. *Great.*

She wiped at the moisture with the back of one wrist, moving on to another nearby plant. All she succeeded in doing was breaking a fingernail down to the quick and snapping a few stems off at ground level. "I need these damn roots."

How could this be so hard? Her trowel didn't give her enough leverage against the rocks. She would have to come back with a full-sized shovel and try again. At least she knew where the rhodiola was now.

Stuffing her trowel and gloves back into her bag, she pulled out her phone to mark the spot on her app.

No reception.

She held the phone overhead and paced a few feet in either direction, waiting for a signal. The app refused to come up. Maybe the rock wall was blocking her. *God, what a day.*

Well, as long as she didn't stray from the wall, she wouldn't end up walking in circles. Eventually, she'd get reception again. Or at least find a relatively easy spot to climb and get back to the trail.

Phone in hand, she began walking along the base of the cliff.

Adrian stopped his ATV next to a blue Subaru Forester and cut the engine. What was a car doing so far off the road? He dismounted and circled the vehicle. Judging by the tire tracks, it'd only been here a few hours. A single set of footprints—a woman's, he'd guess by the size—headed straight toward a game trail that led to the moose kill site. He'd need to hurry if he wanted to catch her before she reached it.

He shouldered his rifle and started off, yearning for the ease of his mountain lion form. Where the trail veered to follow a ridge, a swath of fresh dirt marred the edge. Cautious of an undercut, he edged closer and peered over the drop-off. That landslide was definitely not the product of a controlled descent, but he didn't see a body. He called out, "Hello, anyone down there?"

Only wind rustling the leaves responded.

Sniffing the breeze, he tried to detect if the woman was still nearby. A delicious odor wafted toward him, masking all other scents and making his inner feline wriggle. *Catnip?* How strange.

Since the footprints ended here, he would have to investigate. He clambered down using his hands and feet. Descending as a mountain lion would've been easier, but approaching a frightened hiker as a predator was never a good idea, let alone one as rare as a mountain lion.

At the bottom, the strong essence of catnip made his feline instincts claw for attention. Reigning in his desire to shed his clothing and roll around on his back, he found the scuff marks of the woman's shoes and followed her trail.

Loose sand and random boulders made walking difficult, but the trail of catnip led him forward even when the footprints weren't clear. At a large tree, several limbs had been freshly broken, as if the woman had tried to climb up.

The scent of catnip was stronger here, as well as the delicious scent of female. Floral with a hint of sweet black tea, it reminded him of his early days with his mother, before his mountain lion had emerged, before the pack rejected him. A mountain lion didn't belong among wolves. He was what they called a "sport," an offspring with unexpected traits inherited from a long-ago ancestor.

The female scent in the area made his uniform trousers feel uncomfortably tight. *Mate*, his mountain lion purred. Adrian's balls agreed, but his head knew better. The catnip had to be messing with his senses. While he appreciated human females, he'd never met one who made him want to claim her. He was thinking about claiming this one sight-unseen.

And the heady scent was powerful, driving him forward even more than his duty to protect a hiker.

Ahead, another tree had four deep gouges staining the papery white trunk with lines of sap. *Claws*. This was a fresh bear marking. Adrian sniffed the air, senses muddied by warm female and dizzying catnip. The grizzly shifter had been here. Had made this mark. But something was off about the scent, a cloying, ashy odor that made bile rise in Adrian's throat. Randall's warning about an infection returned.

Running his tongue over his lengthening canines, Adrian unslung his rifle and unlocked the safety. The female ahead was in danger. *My female,* his cat rumbled. Adrian couldn't deny the instinct. He picked up his pace to a run.

Darcy had changed her mind; she hated nature. From now on, she was sticking to cultivated herbs for her potions. No more of this wild herb bullshit.

How far had she walked? The sun poked feebly through the cloud cover, making it feel as if evening was approaching, although her phone said it was only two o'clock. The cliff was just as high as before, and she still didn't have a cell signal.

Her chest tightened. No one knew she was out here, not even Aunt Willow. No one would miss her until she didn't show up for her coven test in two days, and even then, they'd probably assume she chickened out.

"Fuuuck!" She batted at a spider web blocking her way and glanced once more at the steep cliff face. Thinking she might be able to shimmy along a branch to reach the cliff top, she'd tried to climb a tree a ways back, but the lower limbs had been too spindly to support her weight.

She whimpered as her ankle twisted for the millionth time on a loose rock. Ahead, the trees gave way. Maybe she could get a cell signal there. She limped forward, breaking into a clearing full of chest-high bushes interspersed with blackened prongs of what had once been trees.

Pulling out her cell again, she checked her signal. Not even half a bar. She groaned and turned once more to the cliff. How could there not be a single place she could climb? Maybe she should turn back and try the other direction.

Something grunted behind her. She spun, facing the sea of bushes.

A massive, dark shape with a wide head rose among the foliage about a hundred feet away. She took in its small ears, beady eyes, and huge paws. Her heart slammed against her ribcage.

A bear.

She wanted to scream, but her voice stuck in her throat. Was that a black bear or a grizzly? She'd grown up in Anchorage, and was technically an Alaska girl, but had never come face-to-face with the state's mightiest predator. All she knew was that for one kind of bear you fought back, and the other you played dead. Before she could decide which to do, the bear opened its mouth and roared.

"Oh, fuck!" She stumbled backward, feet slipping on the rocky slope. She fell to her ass against the stony ground, phone clattering from her hand.

The bear dropped to all fours and charged toward her with unbelievable speed, feet thumping against the earth like a drum.

Darcy screamed again, feet churning uselessly against the rocks. She grabbed a handful of pebbles and threw them as the bear broke from the shrubs a few feet away. Flinging her arms up to cover her face, she glimpsed a golden shape streaking in from the side.

It slammed into the bear, bowling it sideways and tumbling into the bushes. A wide swath of brush flattened in their wake. Darcy lowered her arms, gaping at the entangled creatures. The second beast was almost as large as the first, its long, golden tail lashing as it snarled and clawed the other predator. *Do we even have mountain lions in Alaska?*

The animals circled each other, fangs bared, ears laid back. Lunging forward, the bear struck with one giant paw. The big cat sprang straight up, out of the way. He landed on the bear's shoulders, sinking his fangs into its neck.

With a deafening bellow, the bear reared, shaking the lion off. The lion twisted and landed on its feet. Facing off, they circled again, snarling and lunging.

I have to get out of here. Darcy pushed upright, palms stinging and sticky with blood from where she'd fallen against the rocks. A jolt of blinding pain shot up her ankle, and it suddenly refused to take her weight. Breathing shallowly, she leaned one palm against the cliff and hop-stepped back the direction she'd come.

The mountain lion appeared to be driving the bear away, pursuing it toward the trees at the other end of the slope. Darcy had no idea how she'd been lucky enough to have two predators decide to duke it out with each other instead of have her for a snack, but she wasn't about to complain.

She tripped over a root, collapsing to her hands and knees. The sound of battle had ceased, and for a moment, she held still listening. Was it too much to hope they'd forgotten she was here? Maybe she should just crawl away so they wouldn't see her over the bushes. She lifted her head, aiming for the tree line.

Her gaze connected with the tawny golden eyes of the mountain lion. He crouched less than an arm's length away, muzzle stained crimson and one ear torn. She jolted backward, toppling onto her backside like a crab. *This is it. The end.* No one would even find her body because the lion would drag her off and eat her.

The lion prowled forward, a deep purr vibrating the air. His golden eyes mesmerized her, and her heart thundered so hard, she couldn't breathe. She found herself unable to look away.

He stepped forward slowly, gracefully, until his front paws straddled her. She was forced to lie back to avoid bumping noses. Barely breathing, she lay beneath him, the heat of his body radiating against her.

"N-nice kitty," she whispered.

He continued purring, lowering his face to rub his cheek against hers.

She cringed, expecting fangs. Only the rough prickle of his whiskers rubbed her skin. With trembling hands, she pushed his head away, the tawny fur lush and soft against her palms.

The big cat responded by purring louder. His golden eyes held an intelligence she hadn't expected. Why wasn't he tearing into her? Could he be somebody's pet? She dug her fingers into the thick fur and the tight fear in her chest eased a bit.

A long rough tongue snaked out to taste her throat, sending a surprisingly sensual shiver through her. She lay perfectly still as the lion moved down her body, snuffling and licking and rubbing. Was he marking her? She knew nothing about mountain lions.

He lifted a wide paw and placed it on her belly, kneading gently without baring his claws. Her skin quivered under the touch. He nudged his head up the inside of her thigh until he reached her center, hot breath penetrating her jeans.

She gasped, belly tightening around unexpected butterflies. *Oh, God.* She'd never had a fetish for animals, but this lion…

The cat lifted his head, intelligent gaze connecting to hers. He seemed to be considering. After several heartbeats, the air between them shimmered. The cat's features grew hazy, muzzle flattening and ears receding. The furry hide smoothed, and the limbs lengthened. Within moments, the beast was replaced by a tawny-haired, golden-eyed man kneeling between her legs. His hands were planted on the ground on either side of her thighs, every naked square inch of him rippling with muscle.

In a voice like a roll of thunder, he asked, "Why do you reek of catnip?"

When Adrian had seen the grizzly, his mountain lion seized control before he could even aim his rifle, charging forward in catnip-driven recklessness. Now his clothing was shredded and he was drunk on catnip, inches from the most enchanting woman he'd ever encountered. Bits of leaves and sticks snarled her strawberry blonde hair, and her wide blue eyes met his. "What a-are you?"

Her stuttered words caused a surge of emotion inside him, a possessiveness he was not used to feeling. *Mine.* He wanted to lick every square inch of her. To rub his own scent across her curvaceous body. To fill her with his seed and make her his in every way possible. His mountain lion was growling *mate* over and over in his head. It had to be the catnip. The potent scent blocked even the rank stink of bear, confusing his senses, making his head swim as if he'd been roofied. He couldn't even detect what kind of shifter she was. Was she in heat? Why else would she have perfumed herself in catnip and come to his territory?

He crawled up her body, bringing his mouth within range of hers. Securing one of his knees between her legs, he pressed his thigh hard against the heat of her crotch, thinking about how she'd feel wrapped around him. "Are you looking for me?"

She shook her head, both palms braced flat against his chest. Her jaw trembled. "I-I don't even know what you are."

He searched her blue eyes but found no guile. As he focused, the acrid smell of her fear carved a path through the other smells, sobering him. "Then why the catnip?"

"I-insect repellant. The b-bottle broke," she choked out, her attention shifting beyond his shoulder. "Is the bear gone?"

The bear. He lifted his head toward the crushed trail of alder bushes. A grizzly would normally have been more than a match for Adrian's mountain lion, but the scent of the terrified female had given Adrian a ferocity he'd never thought possible. The rogue now lay with his throat ripped out. At least any human stumbling upon the dead bear would assume it had died in a fight with another predator. He pressed the tip of his tongue against the fangs that kept trying to emerge and shook his head. He hoped Randall had been wrong about a rogue infection.

He'd figure that out later. Right now he had this female to deal with. "The bear's no longer a threat. What's your name?"

"D-Darcy."

"Darcy." He let her name roll off his tongue, drinking her in, fascinated by the way her lips moved. His mountain lion refused to disentangle himself from her. "I'm Adrian."

Her pretty throat moved with a swallow, and she slid one hand from his chest to touch the stubble on his chin, as if doubting he was real. "What kind of witch are you?"

Shivers raced through him. That was the smell he couldn't place. Ozone. She'd been near a witch recently. He said, "I'm a shifter, not a witch."

"Oh," she said on an exhale, her sweet breath fanning his cheek. The acrid scent of fear shifted and a high, fleeting whiff of arousal reached him.

He turned his head to nuzzle against the inside of her wrist. It was taking everything he had not to succumb to his desire to claim her here and now. *Damn catnip.*

Lips still brushing her skin, he asked, "Why are you out here in the forest alone, kitten?"

"Harvesting r-rhodiola." Her voice had a rough breathiness he found irresistible.

He rubbed against her wrist and felt dampness against his thigh where it remained between her legs. God, he wanted to taste her. He slid his cheek to the crook of her arm, tongue flicking against her tender, sensitive skin.

She gasped, and the scent of her arousal grew, but so did the acrid scent of fear. "Are you going to eat me?"

He wanted to tell her yes, in the best way possible. Woozy from catnip, he pulled himself under control and lifted his mouth from her skin, forcing himself to stand. "I would never harm you."

Her eyes grew rounder as her gaze flickered down his body. "W-why are you n-naked?"

Her adorable stutter was more pronounced as she obviously tried not to look at his crotch—and failed miserably. Part of him liked the attention, but it was making it difficult to stay off of her. He kept picturing her plump, red mouth around him. He glanced around for something to cover himself while he growled out, "Kind of difficult to wear clothes as a mountain lion."

She returned her attention to his face, a pink flush rising to her cheeks. "W-would you like to borrow my rain poncho?" She pulled a bag from her shoulder and produced a cheap green emergency poncho.

"Thank you." He accepted the packet and shook out the thin plastic before wrapping it around his hips like a kilt. A huge tent rose over his crotch. He gestured downward. "I can't do anything about that. It has a mind of its own."

A giggle escaped her, breaking the tension between them. Her smile was like a sunrise, and a giddy sensation welled up inside him. It reminded him of the stories his father used to tell about meeting his mother. How the pack had never felt like home until he'd bonded with her.

He clamped down on the memory. Packs were for werewolves. Mountain lions lived alone.

"Come." He offered her a hand. "I'll show you back to your car."

"You know a way back up the cliff?" She put her delicate palm into his, and he pulled her onto her feet.

"Of course. This is my territory."

She took one limping step and stumbled against him, her full breasts soft against his arm. A purr rose in his chest. She was round and soft in all the right places, yet solid enough to be a worthy mate. *Mine.* The word flitted through him again.

"I t-twisted my ankle," she said.

Without waiting for permission, he swept her into his arms. "I'll carry you."

She gasped, clutching his neck. "I'm too heavy!"

"You aren't heavy." In fact, she felt like a feather in his arms, fitting perfectly against his chest. He strode along the cliff to where a stream cut a trail, heart beating faster than carrying her warranted.

CHAPTER SIX

Darcy clung to Adrian as he stalked toward the trees. He smelled of pine, wood smoke and hot-blooded male, and the heat of his naked chest against her made her insides clench with need. Now was not the time or place to feel horny, but damn if this guy wasn't some sort of sex-god. *No, he's a shifter.* She'd never met one, but the other witches talked about shifters as if they were barely controlled animals who argued until they drew blood. How could she have mistaken him for a witch? *Not only does my stutter ruin every spell, I can't even tell shifters from witches.* She felt like the stupidest witch on the planet.

They reached a tiny stream trickling down the cliff, and her stomach lurched as he leapt upward from ledge to ledge without breaking his stride. *Damn, he's nimble.* His gait barely even jostled her aching ankle.

She forced herself to loosen her chokehold on him. Mountain lion, mountain man, this guy was hot.

His nostrils flared, and she wondered if he could smell her pheromones. Which only turned her on more. *What the hell is wrong with me?* You'd think she was a cat in heat.

His chest vibrated with a growl. "Don't do that."

She looked into his face. "What?"

"I can smell your arousal. It's as distracting as catnip."

Oh, shit, he *could* smell her. And that only made her core clench tighter. She looked away, focusing on the trail ahead to avoid his gaze. She didn't want to stutter out some lame excuse and embarrass herself any more than she already had. *Stupid sexy shifter.*

They reached the top of the ridge and he threaded his way through the trees with unerring confidence. "Why are you looking for rhodiola?"

She swallowed, gathering her words on her tongue before speaking. "I'm making a potion."

"You're making it?" He bent his face closer and inhaled deeply, which was weird but also kind of sexy.

"Yes," she said with more confidence than she felt.

A frown creased his brow. "You don't smell like a witch. Not exactly."

His words created a hollow in her chest, an echo of all the times her mother told her she had no natural talent for witchcraft. If it wasn't for Aunt Willow, Darcy wouldn't even know a coven existed. Not that she had a hope in hell of getting them to teach her anything, not at the rate she was going. She had no idea how she would get her hands on some fresh rhodiola root between now and her test day after tomorrow. Her throat hurt with the effort of controlling words tangled by emotions. "What d-do I smell like, then?"

His lip twitched, revealing a sharp canine that made her heart race. "I'm uncertain."

"Well, I'm n-not a shapeshifter, that's for sure."

He raised one eyebrow. "Would that be so bad?"

She bit her lip, realizing she'd just insulted him. "N-no."

His nostrils flared, but he didn't remark, swiveling to avoid catching her feet against a long evergreen bough.

The trees soon opened into the clearing where her car was parked. Next to it sat an ATV with a Forestry Service logo on the side. Adrian set her on the ATV's padded black seat.

"This is y-yours?" She'd imagined him as a wild mountain man, not a Forestry official.

"I'm a ranger." He dropped to his knees in front of her and slid his calloused hands behind her calf, drawing her leg toward him. "How's your ankle?"

Rockets of anticipation shot up her leg to her insides. How could he continually have such a carnal effect on her? She cleared her throat, preparing to tell him it was fine, but then he rotated her ankle, and she yelped.

"Sorry. It doesn't look broken, but it's definitely sprained." He'd been gentle, but damn, that hurt. He stood and rummaged through a box on the back of his ATV. "I have a bandage in here somewhere."

Even though her ankle throbbed, she was mesmerized by his lithe grace. His arms were well-proportioned muscle, bulging and flexing as he moved, and the broad cobra shape of his back made her want to run her palms along his ribs to his narrow hips and gorgeous ass.

He returned with a first aid kit, and with surprising dexterity and gentleness removed her shoe and sock. Every time his fingertips brushed her skin, it was as if her whole being cried out for more. As he wrapped her ankle, she could almost think he'd cast a spell on her. Except shifters didn't cast spells.

He finished and rose. The poncho tented over the front of his hips remained as pronounced as ever, and part of her wished she hadn't asked him to cover himself.

"Thank you for your help," she said, pleased when she didn't stutter.

His golden eyes seemed to glow in the dim forest light. "You're welcome. Can you drive?"

"I th-think so." She pushed herself onto her good foot, but before she could take another step, he'd scooped her up again.

"Keys?"

She dug awkwardly in her bag and retrieved them. He carried her to the driver's side door and gently lowered her feet to the ground, maintaining one arm around her waist for support. She unlocked the car and opened the door, but instead of sitting, she turned and wrapped her arms around his neck. He'd saved her, but for all she knew, she'd never see him again and she wanted to do this before she lost her nerve. Raising herself on the toes of her good foot, she kissed him solidly on the mouth.

Much to her surprise, he slid one hand up her back to cup her neck, keeping their lips together. The firm tip of his erection nudged her belly, drawing the butterflies in her stomach downward. He tasted so good, lips softer than she would've imagined. He moved them slowly against hers, sliding his tongue into her just once before pulling away.

Confidence boosted, she let out a slow breath and opened her eyes. "W-would you like to come to dinner at my house? It's the least I can do."

Wow, that had been a long sentence. More words than she usually strung together at once. And she'd barely stuttered at all.

To her relief, he smiled, showing a tiny bit more teeth than most people showed, but his hands were a warm comfort on her hips. "I'd be delighted."

He said yes! Flustered and excited, she plopped down in the driver's seat and jabbed the key into the ignition. Her trusty Subaru started right up. There were so many things she needed to do to get ready. Her house was a mess, for one thing, and she needed to wash her sheets. Plus, she was out of mascara. She hoped the Trading Post had some.

He rested one forearm on the top of the open door, showing no inclination to step back and close it. Had she forgotten something? She met his gaze, and his eyes sparked with a feral desire that made her insides tighten.

"I can probably track you down by the trail of catnip, but it would be much easier if you gave me your address, kitten."

Heat filled her face. She'd never had a pet name before, and he kept calling her kitten in a way that made her want to roll over and show him her belly. Or her naked pussy. Geez, the guy gave her a one-track mind. She stammered out directions, and he nodded, closing the car door and stepping out of the way.

She bumped her way down the rutted road, watching the rearview mirror until he was hidden by brush. Then it hit her. What the hell did you feed a mountain lion for dinner?

drian watched the Subaru disappear and stood listening to the fading engine until he was certain Darcy'd reached the road. With the allure of catnip gone, he took a moment to reassess the emotions roiling through him. Her kiss had surprised him, started a fire inside him that could only be quenched by her—preferably her warm wet pussy around his cock. He'd scratched his carnal itch a time or two with human females, but never imagined himself with a mate. *She's my mate.* His mountain lion was certain of it.

But she claimed she was a witch. Could a shifter even claim a witch? Interbreeding sometimes happened—his mountain lion was proof of that, and in high school he could recall several scandalous rumors of a young pack-mate getting caught making out with a vampire.

But supernaturals generally kept to their own kind, and claiming a mate was far more serious than a high school crush. For the first time in a long time, he missed belonging to a pack, missed the glint in his oldest brother's eyes when he'd shared naughty rumors with the younger siblings.

But that had been before Adrian knew he was different. Before his feline had revealed itself and forced Adrian into solitude, unable to accept a pack-Alpha's bond. *Now you want a mate?*

The mountain lion inside of him rumbled assent.

Adrian could only shake his head. He loved a lot of things about his mountain lion, but its unpredictable nature was not one of them. Once he got Darcy out of his bloodstream, they'd see what his lion thought.

Removing the clingy plastic poncho from around his waist, he tucked it into the box on his ATV and pulled out his spare uniform. He needed to retrieve his phone and rifle, then file his report. The sooner he got that out of the way, the sooner he could get to Darcy's.

He followed the trail back to the cliff and descended to where he'd shed his clothes. There was little left of his uniform, but he gathered his keys, phone, and rifle before investigating the corpse. The grizzly lay as he'd left it, sprawled in the dense shrubbery, brown furry throat matted with blood. The musky stink of the shifter was even worse after death, but there was also a note of something else, that ashy scent he'd noted before. *Illness?*

Adrian felt a twinge of regret over the shifter; rogues usually had a sad story leading up to their descent into madness, often events beyond their control. He took several photos, making note of the distinguishing white patches of fur, one on the base of the bear's skull and another just behind its left shoulder-blade. Both were over what a hunter would consider kill spots, as if the bear had been marked for death. *Odd.* Hopefully, the marks would help the shifter's den-mates identify the body quickly and provide closure for loved ones.

Out of respect, he placed a few broken shrubs over the body to conceal it from prying eyes and headed back toward the ridge. As he reached the base, he noticed a squat stand of wild rhodiola not too far away. Wasn't that what Darcy'd been gathering? He didn't recall seeing or smelling any herbs on her except the catnip. She might appreciate a few roots if she hadn't managed to gather any.

Glancing around to be sure no one was nearby, he shimmied out of his clothing and shifted, using his claws to make short work of the rocky soil around the plant. After unearthing several roots, he shifted back and dressed before climbing up to his waiting ATV.

Back at his cabin, he called Randall. "We don't need to file an extermination report with the Forest Service," he added. "There were no bullets involved. You can tell the Den to come claim their dead."

A beat of silence. "What the hell, Adrian? You took on a grizzly while shifted?"

"I got the drop on him while he was attempting another kill." For some reason, Adrian didn't want to mention Darcy. His emotions around her were too raw, and for now, he wanted to keep her to himself. It was enough that he'd done his duty with the rogue. "There was definitely something wrong with him, though. He smelled and tasted like ash."

"You were supposed to use your rifle. We don't know what's causing this outbreak. Now you could be infected."

Adrian gritted his teeth. "I feel fine." He thought about the ashy taste the bear had left in his mouth. "I'll let you know if I get any symptoms."

"Very funny, Adrian. A rogue isn't going to report himself going rogue. Seriously, there will be a lot of questions. The Council will want an inquisition."

An inquisition meant he'd have to show up at the local bar where the shifters held their meetings. "You know I hate going into town."

"It'll give you a chance to catch up on your emails," Randall said, sarcasm dripping from his words. "Keep your phone handy so I can reach you."

"Fine." All Adrian wanted to do was hang up so he could get ready for dinner with Darcy. He'd deal with rogue infection threats later. "Oh, and the grizzly had some white markings that might make it easier to identify him. I'm forwarding you some photos from my phone."

"All right." Randall sighed. "Good job, by the way."

Adrian grunted and hung up, then went to the stream behind his cabin to scrub up.

Darcy stopped by the Trading Post to pick up something for dinner. The small store didn't have a lot of selection, but Karl, the owner, carried meat in the freezer. Men and mountain lions were both bound to like a steak, right?

A metal shelf bisected the small grocery, and the pegboard wall behind the register held an assortment of hardware and auto parts. A glass case full of Native artwork supported a cash register where Karl's gray head was bent over a book.

"Hi, Karl," she said as she entered, hobbling on her injured ankle.

He set his book down. "What happened to you, sweetie?"

"A sp-sprain." She stopped at the counter, glancing toward the freezer cases in the back. "D-do you have steak?"

Karl rose and headed toward the storeroom door. "Let me check. I stopped keeping the expensive stuff up front 'cause it kept getting stolen." He disappeared into the back room.

Darcy examined the pegboard, checking the price on the long-handled shovel hanging there, but found it hard to focus. *He rescued me from a bear!* The witches in the coven would never consider befriending a shifter, let alone asking one on a date, but Darcy couldn't stop thinking about Adrian's golden-eyed gaze and the way his mouth had felt when she'd kissed him. And he was obviously attracted to her. The erection he'd sported the entire time they'd been together couldn't be denied —he'd even joked about it, which she found remarkably endearing.

She remembered she needed mascara and limped over to the shelf bins where Karl stocked a few bargain-basement cosmetics. The bell over the door jangled, and she looked up at a woman in a billowy blouse with a long auburn braid. *Aunt Willow.* Her smile died. Darcy'd been seventeen when Mom died, and Aunt Willow had stepped in as a surrogate, teaching her about witchcraft and attempting to correct her stutter. But neither magic nor physical therapy had helped.

Darcy definitely didn't want to get caught up in conversation with her aunt right now, but it was too late.

"Darcy? What happened to you?" Aunt Willow's gaze darted to Darcy's bandaged foot. "Are you injured?"

"J-just s-sprained." Only two words, but she stuttered them both. Talking to Aunt Willow always seemed to make the problem worse.

Her aunt advanced, pursing her lips in disapproval. "Well, it's nothing a little spell won't fix."

With a quick glance toward the back where Karl could be heard moving around, Aunt Willow leaned over and brushed her fingertips over the bandage, speaking some barely audible words. The pain in Darcy's ankle turned to ice, then disappeared as if it had never been there.

Standing upright once more, her aunt crossed her arms over her ample bosom. "There. Quite simple."

Darcy's throat tightened at the subtext—that she must lack the willpower to succeed. "Th-thank you."

"You look like you've been rolling around at the zoo." Aunt Willow's red manicured fingernails snatched a bit of moss from Darcy's hair. "And you smell like you fell in a vat of horse liniment. No wonder the coven is on the fence about you."

Nausea filled Darcy's belly. She hadn't even taken the test yet. "Th-they are?"

"Don't worry. I assured them you won't follow in your mother's footsteps."

Mom had been a coven member during her early years, but had divorced herself from her fellow witches and moved to Anchorage before Darcy was born. Darcy hadn't even met her aunt until the funeral, and no one would tell her why mom left.

Willow leaned closer, glancing over her shoulder to be certain Karl wasn't in earshot. "But when you show up in public like this, you make me look like a liar."

Heat filled Darcy's face. Her aunt was determined to restore the family's reputation by getting Darcy into the coven, and Darcy was terrified about letting her down.

Karl reappeared carrying a frozen vac-pack of meat. "Hey, there, Willow."

Darcy thrust two twenties at him and took the package, ignoring his call that she'd forgotten her change as she rushed from the store. What was she thinking? She shouldn't be taking time for a date when she should be working on her potion. But she'd failed to gather the rhodiola, and although there was still plenty of Alaskan summer daylight, the rain had begun in earnest, pounding hard against her windshield as she drove toward home. *I'll head out first thing tomorrow.* And this time she'd take a real shovel. Maybe she could convince Adrian to help her.

She pulled to a stop on the gravel driveway of the house she was renting, dodging puddles as she sprinted for the front door. Her wet clothes still smelled like insect repellant, and she tossed them in the washer before heading to the shower and lathering herself twice. At least her strawberry blonde hair no longer looked like a frayed broomstick, but her encounter with her aunt had her on edge. She couldn't shake the negative energy.

Performing a quick sage smudge around the living room made her feel slightly better, so she seasoned the steaks and scrubbed a couple of potatoes. She was growing a few heads of lettuce among her herb pots on the porch, and stepped into her Crocs to go outside and pick a salad, glad the rain had slowed to a misty drizzle. Someday, she wanted to have a house with a garden and a shed to dry her herbs, but for now, her pots worked. Running a frond of rosemary beneath her nose, she decided to use some for the steaks.

The rumble of an engine drew her attention as a dark green Ford pickup rolled into view. *Adrian?* He parked in the street and stepped out of the truck, looking handsome and well-groomed, broad shoulders straining ever so slightly against the white button-down shirt. He'd been gorgeous when naked, but Goddess, he rocked the clothing look, too.

Holding something in one hand, he prowled toward the porch. "Hello, kitten."

She loved the pet name, and the way his eyes reflected the light, making him seem dangerous and sexy. "C-come inside."

She led the way, stepping out of her shoes in the entryway.

He closed the door and thrust a plastic grocery bag toward her.

She accepted it and peered inside. Two perfectly gnarled roots lay twined together. She let out an awed breath. "Rhodiola?"

"My mountain lion wanted to bring you a dead rabbit." He untied his scuffed work boots. "I thought you might appreciate this more."

She hugged the roots to her chest. *Goddess, this guy is too good to be true.* Now she could focus on making the potion instead of spending tomorrow wandering around the forest. "You just saved my ass again. Thank you."

He set his boots next to her Crocs and faced her. "Next time you want to go walking in the woods, call me. I'll give you an escort."

The fluttering in her stomach intensified. "I b-bet you say that to all the girls."

His eyes glowed in the light coming through her living room windows. "I don't talk to other girls."

Feeling light and warm, she carried the roots to her kitchen. "Do you want wine?"

A tiny smile flitted across his mouth and he tilted his head. "No catnip?"

Her insides fluttered with uncertainty. "D-do you want catnip?"

He grinned and shook his head. "I'm only teasing. Wine would be great."

God, he was stunning when he smiled. She could barely catch her breath as her stomach flip-flopped. Glad to have something else to focus on, she poured two glasses and handed him one.

He took a sip. "Your home is nice."

"Thanks." She dampened some paper towels and wrapped the rhodiola before placing it into her crisper drawer. Tomorrow, she'd make the potion. But tonight, she was going to thank this hunky ranger for his help, even if it meant making small talk. "D-do you live here in town?"

"No, I live in a ranger cabin out in the park."

"Are there other m-mountain lions living in the park?"

A sardonic smile curled his lip. "I'm the only one I know of."

"Oh." She frowned. "I thought shifters had packs."

Adrian's smile transformed into a fanged grimace. "Packs are for wolves."

Startled at the scary transformation, she sucked in a breath. "S-sorry."

His face softened, and he sighed. "My parents are from the pack in Gakona."

She gaped. "W-wolves? But you're... How'd that happen?"

"If a bloodline is impure—if it has another shifter type in its ancestry—a different shifter type can be produced. The mountain lion form is recessive. The pack didn't want me."

"They rejected you?" she asked softly, knowing exactly how he felt.

He licked his lips and looked into his glass. "It's for the best. Mountain lions prefer solitude."

Darcy took a deep gulp of wine. "But you're here. With me."

He lifted his chin. "You're... different."

Usually to her, different meant bad, but he made it seem like a good thing. "I'm n-not really a witch. That's why I need the potion."

He canted his head. "How's a potion going to help? I thought you either were a witch or you weren't."

Closing her eyes and picturing the words before she spoke, she said, "My m-mom was a witch, and so's my aunt. My stutter ruins my spells. The p-potion will cure it." Goddess, she hoped that was true. "At least long enough to p-pass the coven's tests."

"But isn't the potion itself magic? If you can make it, that seems like it should be proof enough."

She shook her head. "They have specific tests for apprentices. Not just any human with a spark of magic can join."

"And what will joining the coven give you?"

"M-mentors."

"You mean teachers?" He raised his eyebrows. "Can't your aunt or your mom just teach you?"

"M-my mother is dead. And my aunt tried. But m-my stutter…" she trailed off, waving one hand as if that explained everything.

"I'm sorry." His gaze on her remained steady, not like he expected her to speak, but as if he understood. He wasn't finishing her sentence for her, just listening and letting her set the pace. She wasn't certain if that gave her more confidence or less.

Uncomfortable with the turn of conversation, she retrieved the steaks from the fridge. "Do you like b-bar-b-be—" She took a steadying breath. "Barbecue?"

He nodded once. "Rare, please."

Of course he wants rare. Smiling, she carried the steaks toward the balcony.

CHAPTER NINE

drian followed Darcy outside onto the small porch, admiring the sway of her ass in her jeans and the way her green tee shirt hugged her curves. She said she wasn't a witch yet, but she'd certainly bewitched him. The coven's tests weren't fair if they would penalize her for stuttering.

The porch was barely ten feet across and filled with pots of various herbs. A small folding table held a tabletop propane grill. From here, he could see the edge of her neighbor's house across the street, but trees mostly blocked the other widely-spaced homes. Even so, the sounds and smells of nearby people were almost overwhelming. Next door, a baseball game played on the television, and somewhere nearby a rhubarb pie had just come out of the oven. Part of Adrian missed having a community, but his mountain lion would never put up with having people this close all the time.

Darcy's deliciously floral scent mixed with the herbs on her porch helped ground him amidst the whirlwind of sensory input. He set his wineglass on the porch rail and moved in close behind her while she adjusted the flame to preheat the grill.

She shut the lid and turned, colliding with his chest. "Oh!" Her luscious mouth fluttered into a hesitant smile. "Excuse me."

"You're beautiful when you smile." He used one finger to brush a wisp of hair out of her eyes.

Arousal spiked the air and a delectable flush infused her pale freckled skin. Bending, he feathered his lips over hers. She responded warmly, accepting his tongue when it dipped into her sweetness. He delved one hand into the soft hair at her nape, pulling her deeper into the kiss, while his other hand rested gently on her hip.

As he languidly explored her mouth, her nipples grew hard against his chest. Damn, he wanted her naked so he could sample all of her.

Children's voices cut the air as two youngsters biked past on the dirt road. Darcy pulled away, glancing that direction before turning once more to the grill. "This should b-be hot now."

Was he moving too fast? He didn't know and didn't care. He'd been with a few women, humans, to satisfy his needs when the opportunity arose, but he'd never been as driven to have one as he was now. His cock was more demanding than his stomach at the moment. He pressed himself against Darcy's backside before she could place the meat on the grill.

She sucked in a breath, hand hovering above on the grill's lid. Her back arched as her ass contacted his erection. She leaned back until her shoulder blades met his chest. He could feel her rapid shallow breaths as she awaited his next move.

He was happy to oblige. Sliding both palms flat over her ribcage until his fingers met atop her belly, he secured her against him. She let her head fall back against his shoulder, allowing him access to her neck. Did she realize how damn sexy that was, yielding to his beast in the most primal of ways? His canines ached to come out, to place his claiming bite upon her shoulder. He dipped lower and put his lips against the skin just above her shirt collar, letting the tip of his tongue flicker against her skin.

Her entire body trembled. She slid both hands behind her, locating the line of his throbbing shaft through his slacks. Aching for more, he groaned, pumping his hips forward to catch her hands between them for a moment. She stroked his length, drawing him to excruciating hardness. He cupped her heavy breasts, thumbs finding her nipples and massaging them through her bra.

Nuzzling the nape of her neck, he imagined what it would feel like to take her from behind. She was making tiny noises of pleasure, and when her fingers fumbled at his belt buckle, he almost bit down then and there. *No, not like an animal.* He wouldn't claim her, only enjoy a night of pleasure if she would grant it. Anything more permanent was not possible, not for a loner like him.

He turned off the propane and pressed his mouth close to her ear. "I want you."

She nodded.

That was the only consent he needed. Spinning her to face him, he cupped her face in both hands and kissed her properly. Deeply. Possessively. Their tongues fought back and forth until she panted against him, her deft fingers opening buckle and zipper until his cock sprang free. She encircled him with a firm grip.

Aware of how exposed they were on the porch, he grasped her wrist, ceasing her movement. "Where's your bedroom, kitten?"

She blinked as if disoriented, then smiled. Taking his hand, she led him inside. "I th-thought you'd never ask."

Heart pounding, Darcy led Adrian through her living area to her queen-sized bed. She'd only been with a few guys, but none of them had ever made her feel the way Adrian could in only a few minutes. Her panties were damp—which she was certain he already knew—but she lay back on the bed, propped onto her elbows, and slowly opened her legs.

His tongue slid along his lips, giving her a glimpse of long canines. Those teeth should frighten her, but for some reason they only turned her on more. His features seemed unable to decide if he was a cat or a man, his face marked by lines of fur. She found him fascinating. Gorgeous.

Above his open fly, a fine line of dusky hair pointed from his navel to an erection the size of which she'd never seen. Wanting to taste him, she reached out and wrapped one hand around his shaft, drawing him close.

He grunted, hips flexing. Her fingers didn't quite meet as she encircled his girth, but she slid her grip up to the pulsing tip, letting her thumb run over a bead of pre-cum glistening at the slit. He growled with desire. Or was it a snarl?

She took the head of his cock in her mouth, rolling her tongue around the smooth velvet knob as she reached around to push his pants down his hips. He tasted masculine and sweet, and she opened wide to draw him in. Unable to take all of him, she encircled the base of his shaft with her hand and squeezed.

He groaned, threading both hands into the back of her hair and trembling with restraint as he obviously resisted the urge to thrust deeper. She worked his length, sucking and licking, curling her fingers around his heavy balls until he groaned and pushed her back against the bed. He slid the hem of her tee shirt upward, grazing her skin with his heated palm. His eyes seemed to glow with an almost feral light, and he lowered his face to her bared abdomen.

Taking a long inhale, he blew it out, raising goose bumps where his breath fanned her skin. His stubbled cheek met her bare abdomen with an electrifying jolt. Heat raced from her bellybutton and settled on her clit.

She gasped, back arching. *Holy fuck, he's good.*

His big palms unhooked her bra and cupped her breasts as he grazed his chin against her. She could feel him humming. *Purring.* He swiped his tongue in a broad path up to her ribcage.

She slid her hands to his mop of thick, tawny hair and groaned. His tongue continued lapping against her skin, driving her mad. Making her squirm.

He moved downward, supporting her lower back and drawing her against him, licking, sucking, nipping. The heat between her legs ached to feel that mouth. He neared the waistband of her jeans and growled, "Let's take these off."

She mutely nodded. *Oh, yes.* He could do anything he liked as long as he didn't stop with that tongue. Releasing her grip on his hair, she flicked open the button and lowered the zipper even as he tugged at the waistband. Before she knew it, she was down to her panties.

His pants had been discarded at some point she didn't remember, and he planted a bare knee firmly between her spread legs, placing both broad palms atop her thighs. His skin felt searingly hot against her, and she trembled, pussy tightening and legs widening.

She swallowed, enraptured by the pure magnificence of him, and tugged at his shirt. "I want to see you."

With dexterous fingers, he flicked open the buttons and shrugged free, exposing golden skin rippling over broadly muscled shoulders and abs. Heat flooded her panties.

His thumbs traced lazy circles against her inner thighs, making it hard to think straight. His pine forest musk reached her, and she wanted him like she'd never wanted another man. She looked into his tawny gaze, drowning in desire.

He smiled, attention trailing down her body to her panty-clad crotch. "I'm going to eat you."

Her chest tightened in alarm yet her hips automatically flexed upward, as if he'd just stroked her cleft.

In a swift move, he slid both thumbs beneath the thin crotch of her panties and with a snap, tore the fabric loose. Then he plunged his face between her legs. It was as if his entire mouth engulfed her pussy, long tongue circling her lower lips and sending a wave of dizzying desire through her. She made a strangled noise and tilted her head back, both hands tangling in his hair as he licked and stroked her until she was on the edge of climax.

She rocked her hips against him, catching a rhythm with his tongue against her clit. The quivering in her belly was growing almost painful, a rippling wave hovering just below the surface. Then his tongue penetrated her, going deep into her channel and stroking a spot that turned the sensation into a roaring wave.

With a cry, she convulsed around him. He didn't relent, pumping his tongue in and out of her until he'd lapped up every drop of her orgasm. She melted against the comforter, barely able to breathe.

He gave her pussy a final satisfied lick and then prowled up her body to hover above her, face-to-face. She could feel his breath on her, smell herself on him. Normally she'd shy away from her own odor, but mixed with his musk, it fanned her desire again. His huge cock rested against her inner thigh, a rod of heat she wasn't sure she could handle, yet wanted more than breath itself.

She looked into his eyes and gasped, "Take me."

He growled, flexing his hips until the swollen head pressed against her entrance. With maddening slowness, he filled her, stretching her tired muscles around him, easing forward in small in-and-out strokes that had her panting by the time he was fully seated inside her. She wrapped both arms around his lean waist. His skin felt like velvet, and she crept both hands over the solid mounds of his ass, pulling him closer, deeper.

He withdrew for a beat, chest heaving as he stared at her face. Then he slammed back into her. She cried out, riding the waves of her pleasure as he pounded out a rhythm as primal as the earth, stroking in and out, filling her, consuming her. Another climax built within her, promising more pleasure than the first.

This was perfect. Absolutely, mind bogglingly perfect. She felt the prick of his teeth against the top of her shoulder and she wanted the pain, craved it in a way she couldn't explain. She tilted her head, giving him more room.

"Harder," she begged.

He snarled, abs flexing powerfully as he rocked his hips, cock throbbing as if growing even bigger inside of her.

"Ohhh!" she moaned, her orgasm cresting. "Yes, do it!"

His teeth at her neck clamped down, and what should've been shockingly painful only intensified her pleasure. As his cock pulsed and his pace slowed, warmth pooled onto the bedding beneath her ass.

She gulped air, body trembling and satiated. Her hair was sticky against her neck and the smell of blood filled the air. She reached up, fingertips tracing the tender bite mark. Surprisingly, she didn't mind.

He caught her hand and lifted it, brows pinched. "You okay with this?"

She met his eyes, thinking he was the most perfect being she'd ever met. "I-I liked it."

"But will you tomorrow?" His frown remained firmly in place, sparking a thread of alarm in her.

"What do you mean? I'll heal."

"I claimed you." His eyes glowed with light that could only be magic.

The pit of her stomach flip-flopped. *Claimed? As in, bound us as mates?* "But I'm a witch."

Adrian rose, running a hand over his hair and pacing. "Fuck."

She sat up and pulled the edge of the comforter over her torso, heart slamming against her ribs as her sex-muddled thoughts cleared. She'd been bitten by a shifter. What did that mean for her magic? She'd never heard of a shifter witch before. As far as she knew, you could only be one or the other. "But I want to be a witch."

He paused his pacing and stared at her, then bent and snatched up his pants. "I have to go."

"W-wait!" She scrambled forward, following him into the living room with the comforter wrapped around her. How could he dress himself and walk at the same time? She could barely keep the comforter from tripping her, and he was already shoving his feet into his boots. "Why are you leaving?"

He spun to face her, his features tight and hands clenched at his sides. "You're perfect and amazing, but you don't want me and I can't take a mate. I will fix this, I promise."

With that, he flung open her apartment door and dashed to his truck.

Darcy pressed her hand over the wound on her shoulder, stomach churning as she listened to his tires kick up gravel. He'd left her. He'd marked her and left her. *Goddess, I'm so stupid.* Just because he'd saved her life and brought her gifts, didn't mean she could trust him with her body. Or her heart.

She closed the apartment door and retreated to the bathroom. In the mirror, the blood looked garish trickling down her pale freckled skin, but there was less of it than she'd feared. Grabbing a washcloth, she cleaned the wound. It had stopped bleeding, but would probably leave a scar. *A mark.* How was she going to explain this to her aunt?

Shifters and witches didn't mix. Period. Would the coven still accept her if they knew?

She closed her eyes and searched herself for a hint of shifter power. What would that feel like? She knew she had to go to the glacier and drink from a magical Source to acquire a shifter form, but would she sense it if an animal spirit was waiting for her? She tried to picture a gorgeous golden female mountain lion, but felt no different from before. *Even shifter magic avoids a girl with a stutter.*

Gritting her teeth, she glared into the mirror and repeated the words of one of her most recent speech therapists. "No. N-negative. Self-talk."

Adrian said he was going to fix this. Maybe there was a way to erase the bite. If not, she just had to hide the mark. which shouldn't be difficult. This was Alaska; between the bugs and the cold, it wasn't like she was prancing around in strapless sundresses, anyway. The coven never needed to know.

Besides, wasn't a claiming supposed to bond mates together? The way Adrian had rushed out of here, he obviously didn't have any warm fuzzies for her.

Regardless of how empty she felt with his absence.

*A*drian didn't have a Pack or a Den or a Pride to turn to for advice like other shifters. Other than Randall, who he preferred to keep at arm's length, the only shifters he knew personally were his parents in Gakona. They were the last people he wanted to turn to, but he'd do it if there was a way to reverse this.

Tires throwing up mud, Adrian rounded the corner onto a dirt road spotted at regular intervals by long driveways. Between the thick trees, he could glimpse secluded houses, yards full of abandoned vehicle parts, a chicken coop...

God, I fucked up. He hadn't meant to bite Darcy, but when she demanded "harder," his feline instincts took over. His mountain lion wanted her, wanted to make her his, regardless of what Adrian's head was saying. He'd driven into her like a rutting beast, and his fangs had come out without a second thought. Now all he could think about was touching her again, tasting her again, holding her close the rest of the night. But that instinct wouldn't last. He knew himself better than that, and he'd want his space again, eventually. He wasn't a social creature.

Plus, she was a witch—or wanted to be.

"Shit shit shit." He pounded the steering wheel. He'd fucked up her life. If the claim could be reversed, he needed to figure it out now, before it became permanent.

He parked across the street from his parents' driveway and stared down the narrow lane to the pale yellow ranch-style house. It looked exactly as it always did during his random drive-bys over the years, with his mother's orange and yellow nasturtiums overflowing the half-barrel planters at the base of the concrete pad porch and filmy lace curtains drawn across the big living room windows. What if they turned him away?

He hadn't spoken to his family since they'd discovered he was a mountain lion and sent him to Anchorage to foster with a lion Pride when he was fifteen. A "boot camp for wayward shifter teens" they'd called it. Fuck that. He wasn't a savannah lion, he was a mountain lion, and his parents hadn't even known the difference. Pride or Pack, he didn't belong. After a few weeks of getting bullied by the Pride's Alpha, he'd run away.

The next few years Adrian lived on the street, avoiding Child Protective Services and attending class at King Career Center. His teacher had been a shifter, a black bear, who seemed to understand Adrian's need to be alone and do things for himself, and had helped Adrian get his diploma and secure this job with the Forestry Service after he turned eighteen.

Now, Adrian took a calming breath, got out of his car, and walked stiffly toward his parents' front door, stepping over the crack in the concrete he and his brothers used to pretend would curse you if you touched it. The inner door was open, and the scent of Mom's moose-burger casserole floated through the screen.

His hand hesitated over the door latch. *This isn't home anymore.* He couldn't just walk in unannounced. He didn't belong.

A familiar silhouette moved into view behind the screen and his father's voice scratched out, "Adrian?"

Dad wore his State Trooper uniform, his hair grayer but still the same neat trim he'd had as long as Adrian could remember.

Adrian's throat tightened. "Hi, Dad."

"You finally decided to visit."

"I..." He swallowed thickly. "I need your help."

"This have anything to do with that rogue shifter today?"

Adrian stiffened. "You know about that?"

"Randall keeps the shifters at the station up to date."

Of course. Wrangell-St. Elias bordered his parent's pack territory. Adrian just hadn't expected Randall to be in communication with his dad. But he shouldn't be surprised. The shifters who worked for the state were almost like a pack in and of themselves, regardless of their animal forms, and kept the shifter Council updated on shifter affairs.

But now wasn't the time for resentment or privacy. Adrian needed answers. "The rogue's not why I'm here."

"We just sat down to dinner." Dad pushed open the screen as he called over his shoulder, "Alice! Come see who's here."

Adrian remained frozen on the porch. He felt like he'd gone back in time ten years, a gangly fifteen-year-old waiting for Dad to punish him for ditching school or fighting. How was he supposed to confess he'd fucked up yet again? "I can't stay."

Mom's plump figure elbowed past Dad to fling her arms around Adrian's neck. "Adrian! We've been waiting for you forever."

Had she always been this tiny? He awkwardly patted her back. "Waiting for me? What do you mean?"

Behind his parents, Kepler appeared, his face unreadable. His brother wore ratty jeans and a black tee shirt that said RTFM. "We heard you were living in the park."

Guilt rose in Adrian's chest. As the two youngest, he and Kepler had been as close as litter mates growing up, and since returning to the area, Adrian had considered reaching out several times. But he never knew what to say, and then so much time passed, contacting Kepler only became more awkward.

Adrian nodded stiffly at Kepler. "Good to see you, man."

"Come, eat." Mom latched onto his hand, dragging him toward the dining room with the scarred wooden table he'd done his homework on as a kid. She pulled out his usual seat and turned to look at him all teary eyed. "I'm so glad you're here."

Adrian sat down while Mom set another plate in front of him, feeling off-balance under their unexpected welcome. She and Dad had sent him away. Hadn't wanted a mountain lion. Now they were acting as if he was a prodigal son.

"Why *are* you here?" Kepler sat in his place across the table and crossed his arms. "You obviously want nothing to do with us."

Adrian looked his brother in the eyes. "I'm sorry I didn't call you, Kepler. But I wasn't welcome here."

Mom gasped. "Why would you say that?"

Adrian clenched both fists under the table, claws protruding against his palms. How could she not know? "You sent me to live with fucking lions!"

Mom's eyes were glassy with unshed tears. "You hated the pack. We only wanted to show you other options."

"I also talked to one of the bear Dens," Dad added. "But I thought you might prefer cats, even if they were the wrong kind. There weren't any mountain lions to foster you."

"We were struggling," Mom added. "You don't understand how many strings your dad pulled to keep you out of juvie."

How many times had he been suspended for fighting? Adrian had always been too willful and only followed instructions when they suited him. Only his years living among humans had forced him to take control of his aggression, which was easier if he stayed away from people. Even now, his instincts screamed at him to flee. *I'm not here to hash out my past.* He had more pressing problems. "I appreciate that. Really. But right now I need to know if there's a way to nullify a claiming mark."

Mom gasped, eyes brightening. "You found a mate?"

"Why would you want to annul a mark?" Dad's gray eyebrows furrowed.

Adrian sighed. "I made a mistake and I want to fix it."

"Why is it a mistake?"

"She's… not a shifter." The admission sent a flush of embarrassment through him.

Mom loaded his plate with casserole as if he was still a child. "Shifter or not, if your animal chose her, then she's the one. It's fate, Adrian. Are you worried she won't be a lion?"

"Mountain lion," Adrian corrected. He didn't want to answer questions, he just wanted a simple answer. But his family always talked things to death. Tried to convince him he was wrong. He wasn't wrong about this, and he didn't have time to argue. "I don't want her to become a shifter at all. I can't take a mate."

"You can't cut and run on a mate like you did with your family." Kepler sneered. "That shit's sacred."

"All right." Dad patted the air as if calming a puppy. "Let's just back up a minute. If your mountain lion chose her, why do you keep saying she's not your mate?"

"Having some needy female around all the time would drive me insane. I detest people. I can barely stand myself."

"Is she needy?" Dad asked.

Adrian realized he was misrepresenting Darcy. Sure, he'd helped her, but she wasn't what he'd call needy. He admired the way she was pursuing her witchcraft despite the coven's bullshit requirements. But he couldn't tell his family that. Bad enough he'd claimed a human; he didn't think he could face their judgment if they knew he'd claimed a witch.

He picked up his fork and pushed chunks of moose burger around his plate. "I'd just prefer to keep my space. I made a mistake."

Kepler glared across the table. "Ever consider your mistake might be running away? Again?"

His brother's words stung, but Adrian would make things up to him later, after he got through this mess with Darcy.

Mom put her hand on Adrian's arm. "Even mountain lions aren't meant to be alone all the time. Having a mate isn't about being social. It's about sharing common goals and putting someone else first. Give things a chance."

He pulled away from her touch and rose, pacing the small dining area as if it was a cage. He just wanted to go back to the way things were. But his mountain lion wanted to go back to Darcy's. Fuck, he needed to get her out of his head. "She doesn't want to be a shifter. I fucked up. I need to reverse the claim."

A knowing look infused Dad's face. "Is your problem that you don't want a mate, or is it that you want to protect this woman?"

Scowling, Adrian resumed his pacing. How the hell was he supposed to know? It felt as if he had a barbed hook in his heart. All it would take was a tug and Darcy'd pull him back to her side.

Dad followed Adrian's pacing with his eyes. "She doesn't have to become a shifter, but a claim can't be reversed, only replaced by another one."

Adrian's steps faltered, his claws and fangs straining to emerge. Even thinking about someone else with Darcy made his blood boil. He took shallow breaths, unable to form words as a growl rose from his throat.

"Listen, son," Dad continued. "You came here for my advice, so here it is. I say stick it out and give things a chance. She may surprise you. You may even surprise yourself."

Adrian stared at his feet, at the interlocking pattern of blue circles on the floor. He absently realized the linoleum was new, replaced since he'd been here last. Could he give things a chance with Darcy? He'd bitten her, changed her life forever. He rubbed his forehead. After the way he'd left, she might not even talk to him again.

"She doesn't have to become a shifter?" Adrian said it more to reassure himself than as a real question.

"If she doesn't drink from the Source, she'll stay as she is. The only thing that has changed is that you've bonded to her."

Kepler crossed his arms. "Adrian doesn't give a shit about bonds."

Meeting his brother's eyes, Adrian realized he'd done to Kepler exactly what he was now doing to Darcy. Abandoning someone important. Whether Darcy wanted him or not, he was bonded to her. He was part of her life. "All right. I'll give this a chance."

CHAPTER TWELVE

*E*yes swollen from crying, Darcy rolled over in her bed and stared at the twilight sky outside her window. *He didn't even say thanks for the evening.* Granted, she didn't know Adrian well, but the way he'd left seemed out of place for the heroic man who'd risked his life for her and brought her gifts. Not all mates were fated, that much she knew, but for some reason, being with Adrian had felt special, not just an accident.

She shook her head violently back and forth over the pillow. If it wasn't for the ache between her legs and the tenderness on her shoulder, she might imagine Adrian had been a dream. A hot, primal, mind-blowing dream. But she needed to let it go. He obviously had.

The best way to stop thinking about Adrian was to stay busy, and she had plenty to do. She still needed to brew the potion for her upcoming apprenticeship test. She flung back the bedcovers and threw on some ratty sweatpants and a tee shirt.

In her kitchen, she brought out her mortar and pestle, the small propane burner she used for distillation, and several beakers and flasks. On her first attempt, the base elixir turned muddy instead of the clear gold it was supposed to be. She let out a shuddering breath. *Stay focused.* This had to be perfect—there was no room for mistakes. She dumped it, scrubbed everything, and started again.

Her second attempt overheated and cracked the beaker, spilling scalding liquid all over her countertop. She jumped back to avoid being splattered, sending her jar of pearl dust crashing to the floor. Fine white grit scattered across the linoleum, mixing with the ruined potion and bits of glass.

"Fuck fuck fuck!" She needed pearl dust for the potion.

A gagging odor rose from the mess, not unlike ozone and burning garbage. Goddess, her neighbors were going to report her for cooking meth or something. She raced to open the windows, letting in the cool morning breeze. Flinging open her front door, she gasped—Adrian sat on the stoop, knees drawn up, elbows resting on top of them.

He lifted his chin and looked at her. "Hey."

He came back!

He regarded her calmly, just as gorgeous in the pale dawn light as she remembered, all tawny-skinned and broad shouldered. Self-conscious, she glanced down at her disgusting sweat pants then back at him. "H-how long have you b-been out here?"

He rose as if pulled by magic strings, his golden eyes wild with determination that made her heart pound. "I didn't want to disturb you. May I take you to breakfast?"

The walls around her heart softened. He wanted to take her to breakfast? This was more like the Adrian she'd first invited to dinner. *Did he come up with a way to reverse the claim?* Her pulse felt like it was about to choke her, but she nodded. "I'll ch-change."

Wrinkling his nose, he peered past her into the apartment. "I'll wait out here."

Leaving the front door open, she swapped sweats for a teal green blouse with a high neckline that hid the bite on her shoulder and a matching peasant skirt, then followed Adrian to his pickup.

He opened the door for her like a gentleman, tucking her skirt against her legs after she climbed in, hand lingering a little longer than necessary at the back of her calf. Butterflies filled her stomach as his gaze traveled up her thigh and body to meet her eyes. "I seldom eat out. Where do you suggest we go?"

She directed him to a tiny café favored by locals. It was smaller than the lodge frequented by tourists, and she got the impression he'd prefer as little traffic as possible. And when they finished eating, the nearby apothecary would be open and she could purchase more pearl dust.

Morning light slanted through the café's windows across the four empty tables. An old man with barely three wisps of hair on his head sat near the café's register drinking coffee and reading a paper. A dark-haired waitress who looked like she was still wearing smudged eyeliner from a party last night looked up from wiping the counter. "Seat yourselves. I'll be there in a sec."

Adrian took her hand and led her to a booth table nearest the back exit. Such a little gesture shouldn't make her feel so happy, especially since he was about to tell her how to reverse his claim, but his touch made her smile. She sat, and he slid into the seat across from her, picking up the laminated menu. He perused it in silence while Darcy snuck glances at him over her own menu. Every time their eyes met, the butterflies in her stomach tried to take off. This was feeling less and less like a breakup breakfast. It almost felt like a date. *Is this a date?*

The waitress poured them coffee, and they both ordered sausage and cheese omelets. Darcy wasn't sure if she could eat, but coffee sounded great.

Adrian offered her the tiny pitcher of cream. "You take cream?"

"Thanks."

He poured a generous amount into her cup, then used the rest in his. Avoiding her gaze, he perused the menu again. He seemed as nervous as she was, and she found the idea endearing. Maybe this wasn't a breakup after all. Gaining confidence, she extended her leg until her foot met his beneath the table.

He lifted his chin, eyes flashing with unmistakable desire. Could this be the mating bond she'd been unable to find earlier? They barely knew each other, but her soul felt pulled to his. Normally, she wasn't much of a talker, but there was only one way to figure all this out.

She drew in a breath and asked, "Are we g-going to talk about last n-night?"

"I'm sorry, but there is no way to remove the claim."

Well, that was straightforward. She let out a shaky breath, surprised to discover she was less upset than she'd imagined she'd be. At least he'd come back and been honest with her.

He set his coffee down stoically. "Just so you know, I'm going to suck at this."

"At what?" She gulped out the words.

His gaze met hers. "A relationship."

Her heart skipped a beat. *He wants a relationship?* No one had ever said that to her before. She felt all warm and fuzzy inside. "Talking over breakfast is a g-good start."

"I like to be alone. A lot." He said it like he expected her to get up, brush her hands together, and walk away.

Thinking of how much time she spent alone studying to join the coven, she lifted one shoulder in a shrug. "I do, too."

"I'll probably piss you off and drive you away."

She got the feeling he'd been misunderstood much of his life, and it made him wary. He counteracted by striking first and running for cover. Sure, he'd hurt her feelings by leaving, but he'd come back, and she appreciated that. "I'm tenacious."

"I don't want to live in town." His voice rose at the end of his sentence, making it more of a question.

Now she understood. He was testing boundaries, sure he'd be rejected. "I'd never ask you t-to change, as l-long as you do the same for me."

A flicker of a smile crossed his face. "You have an answer for everything, don't you, kitten?"

She grinned, feeling giddy at the endearment. But then her grin faded. There was still the matter of the claiming. Had he done it by accident, or was there something special between them? If she was going to consider going forward with this, she needed to know. "Why did you bite me?"

He turned serious again. "My mountain lion thinks you're my mate."

A tingle ran up her spine. "Am I?"

A muscle in his jaw twitched and he tensed as if preparing to run, then he sandwiched her foot between both of his under the table. "Yes."

His eyes held uncertainty, as if he was waiting for her to deny him. All the awful things the coven members said about shifters played through her head. They were wrong. Adrian was sweet and strong and smart. She wanted to be with him. But she also wanted to be a witch. "I don't think I can be both a witch and a shifter. It's one magic or the other."

"You don't have to become a shifter if you don't want to. You can be whichever makes you most happy."

What if being his mate was her destiny? She felt closer to Adrian than she'd ever felt to anyone. He didn't finish her sentences for her or require small talk to feel engaged. And the sex—oh the sex!—couldn't possibly get better than it had been last night.

Then she thought about how her aunt would respond to this. "The c-coven looks d-down on shifters."

Feet withdrawing, he looked down at the coffee mug clenched in his hands. "I understand." He reached into his back pocket and retrieved his wallet. "Maybe your witches know a way to reverse my claim."

She stared at him, uncertain again. Would the witches know how to nullify the claim? Even if they did, did she want to give up a future with him? He might've run away at first, but then he'd come back for her, and that felt like it meant something. Why was he giving up so easily now? *He's trying to protect himself again.*

He dropped a couple of bills on the table. "If you ever need anything, let me know."

She grabbed his wrist before he could slide out of the booth. "Stop. W-we're in this together."

Before she could say more, the café door swung open and a gravelly voice cut through the quiet dining area. "That's the ranger."

A huge bearded man in a button-down plaid rumbled toward them like a freight engine, two other large men on his heels. They wove between the tables, oblivious to the shocked expression on the waitress's face, and stopped at the edge of the booth. The man glowered down at Adrian. "I recognize you. You're that punk from high school who got sent to juvie in Anchorage."

A muscle in Adrian's jaw bulged and his golden eyes narrowed, but he remained sitting. "You must be from the Den?"

"Damn straight, and we want answers."

Even Darcy could feel the challenge in his posture.

Adrian's hands remained clasped around his mug. "Happy to give them—at the inquest."

The man bent close to speak in Adrian's face. "You murdered my sister's mate, you bastard."

Darcy gasped as the man's canines flashed below his mustache. Now that she knew what to look for, she recognized a shifter's animal straining to get out. Was he a wolf? A bear? *Oh, Goddess.* She'd been attacked by a bear. "Th-the bear?"

The man's gaze flickered to her, upper lip curled to show more teeth. "Who are you?"

Her stomach leapt into her throat and she cringed against the padded seat.

Adrian rose. "Your issue's with me, not her. Now move along before someone calls the cops."

Stepping forward until he was nose to nose with Adrian, the man growled, "My sister has two cubs she has to raise on her own because of you." His nostrils widened. "You stink like ozone. Are you working for them?"

"Who?" she choked.

One of the other men put a meaty hand on his comrade's shoulder. "C'mon, Edric. This isn't the place for this."

Edric snarled and shrugged off the hand, never taking his eyes off Adrian. "You'll pay for what you did." He shot Darcy a scathing glance. "And your witch, too." Then he pivoted and strode out of the café, followed by his friends.

After a few beats of silence, the old man at the counter turned back to his paper, and the waitress brought them their food as if nothing had happened.

Darcy waited until the waitress moved out of earshot, then whispered, "That bear in the forest was a shifter?"

Adrian grimaced and rubbed his forehead. "A rogue."

"What's that?"

"Sometimes shifters lose control of their animal. Like going rabid." His brows drew together. "They have to be killed."

Tears pricked Darcy's eyes. That poor shifter. And poor Adrian for being forced to do the deed. Her insides still quaked from the malevolent glance the bearded man had given her before leaving. "Was he a shifter, too?"

"Yes. From the local grizzly den."

"Why did he think you're working for me?"

Adrian shook his head. "I'm not sure. My boss said there's some sort of rogue outbreak going on, maybe it has something to do with witches. The bear had unusual markings on it and smelled strange." He leaned back against the booth seat and tilted his head. "If witches are involved, it might be good to have you at the inquest with me."

Her throat constricted. "B-but I'm not a witch yet. I haven't passed the tests."

He cocked one eyebrow and leaned forward, covering her hand with his. "You will. Besides, you're an eyewitness."

She bit her lip. Going into a grizzly den sounded risky, especially if they were blaming witches. But she and Adrian were mates, and she'd better get used to being around other shifters. Besides, this was her chance to be there for Adrian, just like he'd been there for her.

Still mute, she nodded, hoping the shifters didn't expect her to do much talking.

CHAPTER THIRTEEN

drian kept an eye on the door, wary that Edric might return with reinforcements. No one wanted to admit a family member had gone rogue. It was like admitting your loved one was a criminal on death row. Which it kind of was, since the only way to handle a rogue was to kill it.

Now Adrian was second guessing himself about asking Darcy to come to the inquest. If Edric was an example of what he'd face at the inquest, things could get violent, and Darcy didn't have a shifter form to protect herself. She didn't have accelerated healing like a shifter did. Hell, he didn't even know if her claiming mark was healing like it should.

Even dark thoughts couldn't extinguish his desire for her. She was only across the booth from him, yet felt too far away. Beneath the table, their feet still touched, a secret intimacy that made him yearn for more. He wanted to touch her everywhere. She was so fucking beautiful and shy. He loved that she didn't need to fill the silence with idle chatter, loved how he could be with her and still be able to breathe. *We're in this together.* For the first time in his life, he could actually picture spending the rest of his life with someone. *With her.*

She kept glancing at him beneath her lashes as they ate. Another couple entered the café, and the gentle buzz of conversation and clinking dishes grew louder. Adrian's mountain lion itched to get away, but then his gaze would connect with Darcy's and the beast inside him would calm, as if her presence was a shield.

Darcy polished off her omelet with surprising thoroughness and nodded gratefully at the waitress when she filled their coffees again. Just like him, she enjoyed a healthy dollop of cream in her brew, and she shared a look with him over the rim of her cup as they both sipped. His gaze dropped to her shoulder. "How's your mark?"

She pulled aside the collar of her shirt, craning her head to look at the scab. "It will heal."

Voice thick, he said, "I'm sorry I hurt you."

Her fingertips traced his claim, and her eyelids fluttered as if the sensation surprised her. "It doesn't hurt. Actually, the opposite…"

Her gaze returned to his, eyes dark with her arousal, and he couldn't help smirking. If that didn't prove they were mates, he didn't know what would. He looked forward to showing her just how arousing a claiming mark could be.

The waitress cleared their dishes and Darcy glanced at her phone. "Darn."

"What is it?"

"I need to stop at the apothecary shop, b-but it doesn't open for another hour."

He realized that with breakfast over, the date was coming to an end, and he wasn't ready to let her go. "We could take a walk until then."

Her face lit up, and she nodded. As they rose from the booth, she took his hand. The casual affection felt good. *Right*. He never would've believed he might crave another person's company this much.

He allowed her to lead him from the café through the parking lot to the dirt road fronting the building. Although he could hear traffic on the two-lane highway from here, the dirt road they walked along remained blessedly empty. Side by side, they strolled toward a gray wooden sign in the ditch several hundred feet away. As they drew closer, he read *Hazel's Tea and Herbs* in white, hand-painted lettering with an arrow pointing toward a driveway.

Darcy paused and pointed, "That's the apothecary." She leaned close and gave him an exaggerated wink. "Don't tell anyone, but the owner's a witch."

He smiled back, breathing her in, thinking more about the way her hand felt in his than the witch at the end of the driveway. Running his thumb along the edge of her palm, he imagined other soft skin he'd like to be touching. If she hadn't expressed a need to visit the apothecary, he'd have swept her back to her place to get naked again. As it was, his pants felt too tight as they continued walking.

They chatted about growing up, realizing they'd both been in Anchorage at the same time while in high school. But where he'd been a troubled homeless teen, she'd been living in a very nice house on the Hillside with her mom. "How'd your mom die?" he asked softly.

"C-car accident." She shrugged one shoulder, eyes sad. "I've come to terms with it, and Aunt Willow took me in. Why were you homeless in Anchorage? I thought you said you have family in the area."

He put his arm around her waist so they walked hip to hip. Although he had to take shorter strides to match hers, she fit against him perfectly. "Mom and Dad didn't know what to do with a teenage mountain lion. Especially one that kept causing trouble."

He explained to her how they thought he needed fostering with other lions and how mountain lions weren't much like savannah lions. Although he hated to admit it, after his recent visit to his parent's house, he was beginning to think he'd been wrong about their intentions. "They were as confused as I was. If it hadn't been for Mr. Wombly, I'd probably be dead now. He was an old black bear shifter at my school. He made sure I had food and clothes, got me through school, and eventually pulled some strings to get me a job here."

"Right b-back where you started." She nodded as if it made perfect sense.

"Huh, you're right." Now that he looked back, he almost wondered if Mr. Wombly had been in touch with his parents the whole time. He'd have to ask when he saw them again. But he didn't want to think about that now.

Stopping at the side of the road near some large aspen trees, he pulled her against him. "I can't take it anymore."

She lifted her chin, mouth parted in what he believed was an invitation. Lowering his head, he kept his gaze locked with hers until their lips met. She responded warmly, sliding both arms around his waist to press herself against him. He kissed her, his fingers threading into her silken hair at the base of her neck. She was so fucking intoxicating.

He walked her backward between the trees, supporting her from stumbling until her back met the smooth bark of a trunk. Taking a wide stance in front of her, his erection felt like a living thing, surging toward her, fighting the constraints of his clothing. Her kisses were as fevered as his as she tilted her head back against the trunk.

Sweet tea and flowers and luscious female filled his senses, and he devoured her mouth in long, sure strokes of his tongue. Her hands slipped around behind him to cup his ass, grinding herself against his hard cock. She lifted one leg, the heat of her sex warm as she opened to him, and he dry-pumped her against the trunk, eliciting a soft moan from her. God, this was bliss.

He kissed along her jaw, nibbled her earlobe, brushed his mouth over her shoulder where her shirt hid his claiming mark.

She gasped, nipples hardening against his chest. "W-why is that so sensitive?"

"It's a reinforcement of the bond."

"Will it always feel like this?" She tilted her head, exposing her throat.

"Yes," he growled, loving how she yielded to him. Whether or not she ever became a shifter and gave him a mark didn't matter. She was his, and he would cherish her for as long as she would allow it. But now wasn't the time to bite her. He satisfied himself by setting his blunt teeth lightly over her fabric-covered mark.

She cried out and bucked against him. He inserted one hand between them, lifting her skirt to find the hot dampness between her thighs. "So sexy," he murmured against her shoulder as he slipped his fingers beneath her panties and into her slick folds. Dipping into her, he drew her juices up to circle her clit. Over and over he teased her while she matched his rhythm, her fingers clawing into his shoulders.

A car drove past without slowing, kicking up a cloud of dust, but he didn't pause. She was making tiny mewling gasps, obviously trying to be quiet as he brought her toward climax. When she let out a strangled noise and shuddered, he shifted his hand from behind her head to her waist, holding her up as her supporting leg threatened to give out. He wrung every last ripple of sensation from her until she sagged against him, breathing hard.

He held her, his cheek on top of her hair, his nose filled with her scent. "You are amazing," he mumbled, cock still aching, but soul satisfied.

"I th-thought mates are supposed to be able to hear each other's thoughts."

"I think you have to claim me back for that to happen. You need your animal to do that."

She lifted her chin to meet his gaze. "So I can't claim you if I'm a witch?"

He kissed the tip of her nose. "It doesn't matter. As long as you accept my claim, we're bonded."

They were bonded, soul to soul, and whether or not she was a shifter mattered as little as the color of her skin or eyes.

A naughty twinkle filled her gaze, and she dropped one hand from his shoulder to cover his erection. "I have another way to claim you."

He groaned and closed his eyes, the pressure of her hand making him want to burst. She unfastened his belt and flicked open the button of his fly. His engorged cock almost undid the zipper on its own, straining to be free, and she had him in hand within moments.

She threw her leg up over his hip, shoving aside the crotch of her panties and guiding him to her entrance.

He pumped forward, impaling her hot folds in a single thrust. She moaned, hips straining to meet his. He wrapped both hands around her ass, lifting her to seat himself more fully inside her. He pressed her against the tree trunk, body hard against her softness as he reveled in her tight heat around him. Damn, she felt so good.

He rocked back, then plunged forward again while she looked fiercely into his eyes. Slowly his rhythm built until he was pistoning into her, his hands crushed between the bark and her ass, but he didn't care. He drove forward with relentless intensity, her heels locked behind his hips. The pressure in his balls rose to intolerable heights.

She threw her head back, mouth open in a choked moan as her inner walls tightened around him. Her orgasm was his undoing. He tipped over the edge, cock pulsing and jetting deep into her core. She took all of him, her orgasm milking every last drop while he held her tight, riding out the shuddering waves of pleasure.

After his breathing slowed, he pulled away from the tree, letting her slide down off him and back to her feet. She wobbled, hands on his shoulders to steady herself. He smoothed a damp strand of hair off her flushed cheek. Her eyes widened, and she grabbed his wrist to look at the backs of his hands, scraped raw from being up against the bark. "You're hurt."

"I'll be fine. Shifters heal fast." Another car drove past, a blur of color between the tree trunks, and he closed his fly. "I'm sorry. Seducing you on the side of the road isn't what I'd call a good second date."

She shook her head and rose to her toes to kiss him on the mouth. "Technically, I'd still call this our f-first date. But who's counting?"

He smiled with genuine affection. Hard to believe they'd only just met yesterday. He'd never been this happy. Fate had definitely picked this woman for him. Lacing his fingers with hers, he said, "Let's get you to the apothecary shop and finish your potion."

CHAPTER FOURTEEN

*D*arcy's heartbeat felt like it might never slow down again. She'd never been into risk taking, but the thrill of doing something like that in public sang through her blood. As if the thrill of being with Adrian wasn't enough already. The coven insisted shifters were barely more than beasts, but he could be as gentle as he was forceful. He'd kept his hands between her and the tree trunk, and she knew he'd wanted to bite her again, but he hadn't.

She leaned her cheek against his shoulder as they walked. He felt so good. Smelled so good. Goddess, she'd wanted to bite him back there. To put her mark on him and let the entire world know that he was hers and she was his and nothing could change that. But she couldn't do that without becoming a shifter, and she'd worked too hard to become a witch to give up now.

They reached the apothecary shop just as Hazel, the owner, was flipping the sign on the front door to OPEN. The single story log cabin looked as if it had been here since the Gold Rush, but was well-maintained, with marigolds in the flower boxes at the tiny windows and wildflowers growing from the sod-covered roof.

Hazel smiled and pushed open the door when she spotted Darcy. "Good morning, Darcy. You're out early."

"M-morning, Hazel." Darcy felt her voice shrinking, even though Hazel had never been anything but kind to her. "I need p-pearl dust, please."

"Of course." Hazel gave Adrian a curious glance but didn't linger, heading into the store.

Earthy, herb-scented air rushed over Darcy as she led Adrian inside, moving past shelves overflowing with books, glass jars, teacups and teapots, mortars and pestles. A few exquisitely woven grass baskets sat next to a pair of hand-sewn mukluks in a case that also held semi-precious crystals and jewelry made by a local artist.

Adrian paced slightly behind her, cautiously looking at everything they passed. She squeezed his hand in assurance. "This'll only t-take a sec."

The back corner of the store held a huge cabinet with shelves and drawers, the area sectioned off by a wooden workbench and some thick rope. From the rope hung a piece of paper that said, *Please Ask For Assistance.* Hazel stepped over the rope and opened one of the cabinet doors, pulling down a scale and a glass jar.

A scrawny husky mix with one blue eye and one hazel eye poked its head around the counter. Darcy held out her hand to the dog. "Hi, J-jake." Jake was Hazel's familiar, but he'd always seemed like a plain old friendly dog to Darcy. He even liked belly scratches and the occasional liver treat. Suddenly, his tail went down and his ears laid back. He barked once, sharply.

Hazel's smile tightened as her gaze moved from her dog to Adrian and Darcy's clasped hands then up to Adrian's face. "Shifter, huh? I don't see many of you in here." She measured pearl dust into a small brown bottle. "Making something special?"

Darcy shrugged, for some reason feeling as though Hazel'd caught them having sex in the alley. "Just something t-to help me with my test tomorrow."

"Ah," Hazel nodded, uncertainty still in her eyes, and handed Darcy the bottle. "Your aunt mentioned you're trying to join the coven. You don't need to join one to be a witch, you know."

Aunt Willow insisted respectable witches had covens, but Darcy would never say that to Hazel. She'd heard that Hazel'd had a falling out with hers. *Like my mom.* She wondered why, but it would be rude to ask, so she just nodded. "Th-thank you."

After paying for the dust, Adrian drove her home, taking her through the neighborhood where he'd grown up and pointing out his old school, his parents' house, and places he'd played as a child. The last time he'd mentioned his family, he'd seemed resentful, but now he seemed less bitter. She wondered what had changed. "Your family sounds nice."

He pursed his lips and nodded. "They're not be as bad as I once thought."

She took his hand into her lap and stroked the back of it. "Can I meet them?"

Turning his palm up, he grasped her fingers and shot her a smile. "Someday. I have a few issues to work out first."

Did Adrian worry about introducing a witch as his mate? Aunt Willow came to mind, and she wondered how the witch would react to meeting Adrian. *Not well.* Shifters and witches did not mingle, let alone mate. She decided to drop the matter until they'd both had time to adjust.

He walked her to her door, and she was relieved to find the terrible smell from her botched potion had dissipated. She turned to him shyly. She really should start working, but she wasn't ready for him to leave. "W-would you like to come in?"

He feathered his fingers along her cheek and kissed her nose, her mouth, then pressed his forehead to hers. "I'd love to. But I have to go to work, and I know you need to make your potion." His voice was huskier than usual as he added, "I had a great time with you this morning."

"I d-did, too." She wrapped both arms around his waist and hugged him tight. "Can I see you later tonight?"

He hugged her back. "Yes. How about we actually eat those steaks tonight? I'll be back after I do some paperwork for my boss."

She realized she was grinning like an idiot against his chest. *He wants to come back.*

He kissed the top of her head and put his hands on her shoulders to push her upright. "Now go get that potion made so the rest of the night can be mine. I have naughty plans for you."

Tingles jetted through her at his promise. She nodded and held up crossed fingers. "Wish me luck."

His eyes crinkled, and he wrapped his hand around her crossed fingers, bringing them to his mouth to kiss the tips. "You got this. Third time's the charm, right?"

She nodded and watched him trot down the stairs back to his waiting pickup. Floating on air and full of confidence, she returned to her apartment and assembled her ingredients, absolutely certain he was right.

CHAPTER FIFTEEN

Adrian drove back to his cabin as if in a dream. His mountain lion was happy. He was happy. He couldn't imagine things being any better. Darcy helped make him feel like he belonged.

He drove up the steep, winding dirt road, glancing at the gorgeous view that opened up on his left. He'd never really appreciated how pretty the land in the park was. He returned his eyes to the road, thinking of his run-down cabin. He should fix it up, maybe buy some new furniture. The house had no plumbing, but he could look into fixing that. Maybe an outdoor bath house. He could clear a few trees and put it where it looked directly out on this amazing view. Once he'd checked in with Randall, he'd head back to town and order lumber.

He pulled up to the cabin and frowned. A white pickup was parked outside. In the shadows of his screened porch, a bulky figure sat on his rickety chair. Adrian cut the engine and got out, stopping about ten feet from the base of the steps. *Edric.* The brawny bear shifter's cold eyes regarded Adrian as if the ranger was the one intruding.

"What're you doing here?"

"Gathering evidence." The chair creaked as the shifter rose to his feet.

The hairs on the back of Adrian's neck prickled, and he turned. Edric's cohorts had surrounded him from behind. They were still in human form, but his thighs tensed as his mountain lion surged inside him, demanding to be let free. Ready to brawl. He kept his shift in check. Three grizzlies wasn't a fight he could win, and they'd be on him before he could shift and run. *I should've been more cautious.*

He crossed his arms, mostly to try to hold in his mountain lion, and turned back to Edric. *Remain calm. Do your job.* The Den had the right to inspect the scene. The rank stink of the three bear shifters made Adrian want to sneeze. "I'll take you to the site."

"Already been there." Edric clunked slowly down the wooden porch steps. "I'm thinking maybe you're the one gone rogue. You got no Den, Pride, or Pack to keep you in check. Living up here all alone, it'd be easy to go a little crazy. You took it out on my brother-in-law."

Adrian's spine stiffened. Being accused of going rogue was a serious threat. And Edric was right, Adrian had no one to back him up if the inquisition turned that direction. No Alpha to vouch for him. Not even Randall's testimony would carry much weight. "I'm a mountain lion, not a fucking pack animal. We're designed to be alone."

Edric sneered. "Where's your witch, pussycat?"

Adrian edged sideways and bared his teeth at both the insult and the threat. Darcy couldn't be dragged into this mess. These bears were looking for a scapegoat. Perhaps it had been a mistake asking her to the inquest. "I told you, keep her out of this."

Footsteps behind Adrian let him know the other two were keeping pace with his movement, flanking him. *Fuck.* What the hell did they want?

Edric lowered his chin, eyes flashing. As if that was a signal, four hands grappled Adrian's biceps. He thrashed, twisting and snarling, but it was three against one. Edric landed a hard fist into Adrian's stomach, doubling him over. Damn bears could pack a punch. Sucking in a breath, he straightened and threw his head back, aiming for the nose of the man on his left. The man dodged, but unbalanced enough to allow

Adrian to lash out at Edric with a foot. The big man grunted and clutched his groin.

"Fucking lion hits below the belt," one of the men said, jerking Adrian's arm up painfully behind him.

Something hard cinched around his wrist, and the next thing he knew, they bound his hands. He struggled, knowing it was futile. "You have no right to restrain me."

Huffing, Edric straightened. He looked a little green around the gills, but it hadn't diminished his fury. He grabbed Adrian by the throat and brought his face close. "You'll pay, little pussy. Believe me, you'll pay."

Adrian choked for breath, stars pressing the edges of his vision. And then the world went dark.

CHAPTER SIXTEEN

*D*arcy held her breath as she squeezed a single drop of *Populus tremuloides* syrup into the thumb-sized vial. The sparkling gold elixir brightened and a scent similar to wintergreen wafted toward her. She stared a moment longer, waiting for something to go wrong. The potion continued swirling, unchanged.

"I did it," she breathed.

Corking the vial, she wrapped it in velvet and placed it in one of the inner pockets of her purse. For a few long moments, she stared at her handbag, as if she might wake up from a dream at any moment. But her eyes were grainy and tired, her hands sore from using the mortar and pestle, and her shoulder still ached a little from Adrian's bite.

She was not dreaming.

This was the best day of her life.

She lifted her arms, threw back her head, and twirled across her living room to a song only in her head. *A witch, a witch, I'll prove I'm a witch!*

Collapsing backward onto her sofa, she thought of how pleased Aunt Willow would be when she aced the incantation tests. A small pang seized her heart as she remembered how her mother'd insisted she'd never have the talent and shouldn't even try. She shoved the thought aside. *Focus on success.*

Closing her eyes, she envisioned herself as a coven apprentice. The image flitted out of her grasp. She was so *tired*. Even the eloquence potion wouldn't do much good if she fell asleep over the spells. She cracked open one eye and looked at the sky outside her front window. Evening was still a few hours away. She should take a quick nap before Adrian returned. She'd barely shut her eyes before she sank into blissful slumber.

When she woke, twilight bathed her living room in purple half-light. She sat bolt upright. *What time is it?* It didn't get dark this time of year until around midnight. She rose and stumbled to the kitchen, coming to a full stop when she saw the time on the microwave clock. *Two?* As in two a.m.? She retrieved her phone from the kitchen table, double checking. The time was correct. Had she missed Adrian? There were no missed calls on her phone, no texts. She hurried to her front door and flung it open, hoping to find him waiting there.

No Adrian.

Where was he? Had she misunderstood how late he'd be? *Or maybe he changed his mind.* She slowly closed the door and stood staring at it in confusion. Then she grabbed her phone and dialed the number he'd programmed into it over breakfast. It went to a generic voicemail. Doubt lanced through her. Was it really his number? "H-hi, Adrian. It's D-Darcy." She gulped, trying to control her stutter. "I hope you're all right. Please call when you get this."

She hung up and stared at the screen, hoping he might dial back immediately. When he didn't, she tucked her phone into her back pocket and began cleaning up her kitchen. By three-thirty, he still hadn't called or shown up. She dialed again, but didn't leave another message. Her gut churned. Something was wrong. Their connection was real. No way had he stood her up. If only she could talk to him in her head.

He'd said he lived in a cabin near the trailhead. It shouldn't be hard to find. Taking a quick shower, she dressed and grabbed her purse and keys. When she pulled into the ranger's cabin, she breathed a sigh of relief. His truck was here.

She got out and rushed to the front door. No one answered her knock, and when she tried the handle, the door swung open. "Adrian?"

No answer. She stepped inside, glancing around the small front room. He wasn't here, and the back room with its king-sized bed was empty, too. She hurried back outside, calling his name. Where could he be?

This had to have something to do with that shifter in the café this morning. She didn't know how to reach the bear shifters, but she did know where Adrian's parents lived. Perhaps they would know.

The sun was rising when she reached the long driveway with the overflowing nasturtium planters and a State Trooper's car in the driveway that Adrian had showed her earlier. *Goddess, it's fucking early to knock on someone's door.* But what choice did she have? If the bears had decided to take revenge on Adrian, every second counted. She took a deep breath and jabbed her index finger against the doorbell.

After a long few minutes she heard footsteps inside. The door flung open to reveal an older man with short gray hair wearing a white tee shirt and boxers. He rubbed his eyes. "Are you in trouble, Miss?"

She swallowed, mouth gone dry. "I-I-I'm l-l-look-looking for Adrian."

The man straightened and his grizzled eyebrows drew together. "He doesn't live here anymore. Who, may I ask, are you?"

Barely able to catch her breath, she managed to squeak out, "His m-mate."

His expression changed to understanding, and he pushed open the screen door. "Please, come in."

Darcy took half a step back, shaking her head. "I d-don't mean to bother you. I just need to know how to reach the bear shifters."

"Why do you need to talk to them?"

She stammered out the story of the shifter in the café. "Adrian w-was supposed to come to my house for dinner. And he's n-not answering his phone."

Another male voice rose from somewhere behind the older man. "You're certain he didn't just run away?"

The older man looked over his shoulder as a guy about Adrian's age came into view. His torso was just as ripped as Adrian's and there was a similarity to the shape of his nose and eyebrows. Definitely Adrian's brother.

Darcy shook her head. "He w-wouldn't do that."

Adrian's dad scratched his stubbled cheek, looking thoughtful. "I suppose it can't hurt to call the Den and see if they know anything." He gestured for her to come in. "You're welcome to wait inside while I do. I'm Kyle, by the way, Adrian's father."

"D-Darcy." Pulse thundering in her ears, Darcy stepped inside.

The screen door banged closed behind her, and Adrian's dad retreated down a hallway. The living room was small, with a fireplace on the far wall flanked by a well-worn recliner. A sofa and matching love seat sat opposite each other. *I'm in a shifter's home.* A wolf pack, she thought, eyeing the younger man.

He looked her up and down. "Coffee?"

She nodded, not trusting her voice.

He pointed with his chin toward the afghan-covered couch near the front window. "Have a seat. I'm Kepler."

"Hi," she managed as she moved to the couch.

Left alone, she listened to low mumbling from down the hall where Adrian's dad had gone. A drip coffeemaker gurgled from the kitchen, followed by the rich scent of dark roast. After a few minutes, a woman in a bathrobe emerged from the back where Adrian's dad had gone. Her dusty blonde hair was mussed, her face lined with worry. She offered a hand. "I'm Alice, Adrian's mother. What's your name, dear?"

"Darcy B-blackwell."

"Good to meet you, Darcy. It turns out Adrian is at the Den." Her already concerned face grew tighter. "He has a meeting with them this morning."

"T-today?" Why would Adrian schedule the inquest without telling her? She got the sickening feeling things had gone terribly wrong. "He wanted me at the meeting, too."

"Of course," Alice said. "His mate should be there."

Adrian's dad returned from the back, this time fully dressed in a State Trooper's uniform at the same moment Kepler returned with two mugs of coffee. The younger man shot a curious look at his father and handed him a mug before carrying the other to Darcy. "Adrian's in trouble again?"

Kyle hooked a thumb over his shoulder. "Both of you get dressed. We need to get to the Den immediately."

A strange feeling rippled the air, almost like a scent Darcy couldn't quite place, and Kepler and Alice hurried away. Sipping his coffee, Kyle paced in front of Darcy. "I don't know if I can get him out of this one."

She kept her fingers wrapped around her mug, even though it was scalding her fingers. "Th-this one?"

"My son had a reputation as a troublemaker growing up. The Den thinks he's gone rogue."

Adrian's description of rogues went through her mind. *They have to be killed.* She shot to her feet, sloshing hot coffee over her hands. "No!"

"He said you're his mate." He paused his pacing and took a deep breath. "But you don't smell like a shifter. Or a human. What are you?"

"I'm a witch." She braced herself, uncertain how he'd respond.

He rubbed his forehead with his fingertips. "He didn't mention that. This complicates things."

"How?"

"There are rumors there's a witch behind the rogue infection." He met her gaze, eyes filled with worry. "It might be better if you don't come to the inquest."

"But I'm an eyewitness. The b-bear attacked me."

He frowned. "They'll assume you're lying."

"What happens if they find him g-guilty?"

Kyle's gaze slid away. "There's no such thing as shifter prison."

In other words, they'd kill him. And it sounded like the odds were against him. Darcy might be a witch, but she was Adrian's mate, and his only eye witness. *Your testimony's no good if they don't believe you.* Her gaze fell to her purse lying on the sofa. *The eloquence potion.* It would allow her to perform the coven's incantations without stuttering tonight—or she could use it to make her testimony for Adrian infallible.

She set her coffee on the end table and shouldered her purse. "I'm c-coming."

CHAPTER SEVENTEEN

Adrian licked blood from his lip and looked out over the assembled crowd of shifters. The back room of the bar the Den used for meetings was standing room only. He was honestly a little surprised to be here alive. He'd been certain Edric and the boys had intended to take him to the middle of nowhere and kill him. But after roughing him up and trying in vain to torture a confession out of him, Edric said he wanted his sister to have the satisfaction of seeing Adrian's face when he died.

Now, handcuffed to a heavy wooden chair, Adrian faced a host of at least thirty shifters, mostly bears, but including a smattering of wolves and one moose who worked at the Forest Service. The dead shifter's widow and two small children sat front and center. The poor woman's eyes were swollen and red, and one little boy lay on her lap while the other clutched her hand. Adrian's heart went out to them, but his mountain lion was clawing to escape the choking musk of the Den.

The dead shifter lay in a huge casket not fifteen feet from him, muzzle pointed toward the ceiling, front claws crossed over its belly as if it were a human. He'd never been to a funeral for a shifter in animal form before, but the sight was eerie as fuck. Between Adrian and the casket, the Den's Grayback stood at a podium. Adrian had already given his description of the event, leaving Darcy's name out of things by saying he'd come upon a hiker under attack, and by the time the fight was over, the hiker had fled.

The Grayback called Randall to the stand.

Randall took a seat at the front, facing the room. The werewolf had dressed in a dark blue suit, his light brown hair neatly parted and cheeks cleanly shaven. He frowned at Adrian's disheveled clothing and bloodied lip. Adrian shrugged. It wasn't as if Edric had given him a chance to make himself presentable.

The Grayback pounded his gavel to silence the murmuring crowd. "Please state your name and relationship to the accused for the record."

"Randall McIntyre. I'm Adrian's supervisor with the Forest Service."

"And what do you know about the murder of the bear shifter, Wilson Rhodes."

"I wouldn't call it murder. Adrian reported a rogue shifter had been killing and abandoning animals within the park's boundaries. Between the local news taking an interest and the recent increase in rogue activity, I felt we needed to get ahead of the situation, so I gave him the go-ahead to exterminate it."

The crowd buzzed loudly, and the Grayback banged his gavel against the podium. "What proof did he provide that this was the shifter that had been killing animals?"

"He said there were bear tracks around the sites, and he smelled it."

"Do you have any of this in your reports?"

Randall glanced at Adrian. "Not evidence about this bear, specifically."

Adrian's stomach churned. Randall had always been on him about filing reports, taking photos, creating a paper trail.

The Grayback cleared his throat. "Is it possible the accused was making the kills himself and looking for another shifter to blame?

Randal shook his head. "I've known Adrian over a year now, and I've never seen any indication of him losing control of his animal."

"Answer the question, please. Yes or no."

"Well, I suppose, yes, but that's pretty far-fetched if you ask me."

"Do you know why the accused attacked Wilson in his animal form?"

"My ranger said he came upon the bear attacking a hiker."

The Grayback nodded once. "Thank you, that will be all."

People at the back of the room rumbled as Randall returned to his seat. Adrian didn't like the worried lines on his supervisor's face, but he was glad to have Randall here. If nothing else, the werewolf could tell Adrian's family what had happened. *And Darcy.* Adrian's heart ached thinking of her. She might never know what happened to him if this played out the way he expected. But at least he'd kept her name out of things. She'd be safe from shifter retribution.

The widow took the stand, describing her mate as stable and loving. Following her, a line of bears vouched for Wilson's stability. The Grayback tapped his gavel and looked down at Adrian. "That concludes the assessment of the deceased's character. Do you have anyone else to speak on your behalf, Adrian Stone?"

Before Adrian could even shake his head, a woman's voice rose from the back of the room. "I'll represent him."

Darcy? His heart fell. How did she find the Den? Now they'd know who she was. The throng of shifters parted, allowing Darcy to step forward. Behind her, his parents, Kepler, and even his older brother Jonas followed.

Growls filled the room, and Edric jumped from his seat. "It's the witch he was with at the café!"

"Order!" The Grayback cracked his gavel.

Darcy's gaze remained steady on Adrian as she advanced, head held high as she passed rows of bristling shifters. Flashes of fur and fangs appeared in the crowd, but she didn't bat an eye. Even without an animal to call on, she was ferocious, and damned beautiful.

"Who are you?" The Grayback asked.

"I'm his mate." She turned to face the room. "And I'm the hiker Wilson attacked."

A collective gasp filled the room.

"She's lying." Edric stalked forward. "This is the witch I mentioned. She's probably the one turning shifters rogue."

"Stay the fuck away from my mate," Adrian snarled, struggling against the cuffs binding him to his chair. His mountain lion was right at the surface, fighting to break free, but if he shifted now, he'd only prove he was unstable.

"Edric, sit down or I'll have you removed," the Grayback ordered. He turned to Darcy. "Miss, this is a shifter matter. Witches have no business here."

Darcy pulled the collar of her blouse down, revealing the scabbed claiming mark on her pale freckled skin. "I may not be a shifter, but Adrian claimed me, and that means by shifter law, I can speak for him."

Adrian frowned. There was something different about her. Not just her sudden knowledge about shifter law, but a glow, an eloquence that made her words ring true. And she smelled like ozone. *She isn't stuttering*, he realized.

The widow rose, tears streaming down her cheeks. "My Wilson would never kill for sport, let alone attack a hiker. You must've provoked him."

"Those white patches on his fur weren't there before he took that witch's job," Edric added. "He was hexed, I'm certain."

Darcy faced the widow, her eyes tight with sympathy. "My deepest condolences for your mate. I understand the loss you're feeling right now. However, I assure you, I had no interaction with your mate prior to his attack. Adrian only stepped in to protect me. If he hadn't, I'd be dead right now, and you would be holding a different kind of meeting, possibly with a lot of press. Adrian's quick action spared shifter kind from discovery by humans. You should be giving him an award, not abusing him and threatening his life."

The audience mumbled, and Adrian felt the animosity in the room shrink. To his surprise, several onlookers bobbed their heads in agreement. A flush crept into his face. He was not used to attention of any kind. It was one thing for Darcy to defend him, but she couldn't possibly think she could turn him into a hero. She glanced his way, and the moment of shared contact let him know that's exactly what she was doing.

Darcy was on fire, not only in the steadiness of her voice, but the set of her shoulders as she faced the room. "My mate has full control of his animal, which I'm certain he's already proven by the look of him." Darcy focused on Edric. "Did he lose control while you were beating him?"

The big man sat with his arms crossed, face a deep red-purple. His eyes flashed with the power of his animal, but he shook his head no.

The Grayback said, "Please respond out loud. Did the accused at any point lose control of his animal during his capture or interrogation?"

"No," Edric rumbled.

"Thank you for your honesty," Darcy said, moving to Adrian's side and addressing the Grayback. "I know I'm new to your community, and I'm not even a shifter. But I am his mate. I know him to the bottom of his soul. As such, I vouch for him, and I respectfully request you release him immediately."

"We vouch for him, as well," Dad said from where he still stood in the audience, followed by the rest of his family's agreement.

The Grayback rubbed his nose, looking from Adrian to Darcy. "You smell strange for a witch, I'll admit. But as his mate, your testimony will be considered. Let the Den council make their judgement."

After a few moments of muttering, a tall woman with wildly curly black hair stood. "We find the extermination of Wilson Rhodes to have been lawfully executed."

The audience rumbled, some in agreement, others with arguments. The Grayback said, "Release the accused." He leveled a look at Edric. "And let no one set paw upon him out of turn, or face the full punishment of the Den. Am I understood?"

Edric mumbled, "Yes, Alpha."

One of the bears released Adrian's cuffs, and he rose, gathering Darcy in his arms and crushing her hard against him. She squeezed him back just as fiercely.

He looked up to find his family approaching. His father patted him on the back, and Kepler was nodding and grinning as he surveyed Adrian's arms around his mate. "Well done, bro."

Adrian looked down at his mate. "No, well done, Darcy."

She flushed and beamed. "I love you."

"I love you, too. Now let's go home."

CHAPTER EIGHTEEN

*D*arcy kept hold of Adrian's hand as they exited the bar, taking him to her car and depositing him in the passenger seat. She knew he'd said shifters healed fast, but he honestly looked like shit, and she wanted to clean him up and make sure he was all right. His parents and brothers stayed behind to keep an eye on the bears, just in case they changed their minds, but she didn't think that would be a problem. Her eloquence potion had worked like a charm.

"What happened to your stutter?" Adrian asked as she started the engine. Goddess, his voice sounded as ragged as he looked.

She pulled into the street and headed toward her house. "I took the eloquence potion."

"It worked? That's great!" He leaned back against the headrest, then jerked upright again. "Wait, you said it was temporary. What about your test?"

She shook her head. She'd thought about that a lot on the drive to the Den. "I'm dropping my application."

He turned to look at her. "I don't understand. Passing that test means everything to you."

"Not everything." She shot him a smile. "I realized I wanted to join the coven to please my aunt. To make up for whatever my mom did to upset her. And now I'm mated to a shifter—which I wouldn't change for the world—and the coven will never accept that." She turned on her signal as she slowed for the turn off the highway. "Why would I want to belong to a group that can't accept me as I am?"

"But how are you going to learn witchcraft?"

"I don't need a coven to study magic. Hazel isn't with a coven. And I m-made that potion all by myself." She swallowed, feeling the potion's effects fading. Gripping the steering wheel, she kept talking, wanting to get it all out before her speech went back to normal. "You've shown me that I don't need a coven to be whole. I only need to be sure of myself. The same way you're sure of yourself. You make me feel strong. Capable. And I love your family. I know there were some problems between you guys, but they came through when it counted."

He chuckled. "Whoa, that's a lot of words, kitten. Slow down and take a breath."

She pulled into her driveway, knowing he was poking fun to hide his fears. It's what he did. But she would not let him off so easily. Before Adrian, she'd been alone, an outsider looking for a way in. She'd believed she wasn't worthy. He gave her confidence just by looking at her, by giving her space to form her own words and opinions. Because of him, she'd discovered the best and strongest part of herself. "I love you, Adrian. I don't need a coven because I have a family—you. And nothing else matters but you."

He looked into her eyes, Adam's apple bobbing with a swallow. Reaching behind her neck, he leaned in close until their foreheads touched. "I love you, too, Darcy. I'll join a pack if that makes you happy."

"I don't need you to join a pack. I just want you to be friendly when you can and n-not be afraid to ask for help."

He nodded. "That I can do."

Knowing the time for words was over, she kissed him with everything she had and then some.

CHAPTER NINETEEN

Aunt Willow was displeased with Darcy's decision, to put it mildly. They sat across from each other in the café. "I pulled a lot of strings to get you this interview, Darcy. Why would you pass up an opportunity like this?"

"M-my stutter." Darcy clutched her coffee cup with both hands.

"Pfft. I know you've been putting together an eloquence potion." Aunt Willow stirred her tea, the spoon tinking against the ceramic. "If you need more time to make it, I can try to reschedule your tests."

"No." The words Darcy needed to say felt like a lump in the pit of her stomach. "Even if I p-pass the tests, I'll n-never meet the coven's standards."

"You may never be good at casting, but you can be an asset to the coven in other ways. Your herbs, for instance. We always need herbs, and Hazel charges an arm and a leg for her components." Willow reached across the table and put her red-tipped fingers on the back of Darcy's hand. "Witchcraft runs in your blood. Don't just ignore it. You need to be with your own kind."

The affirmation was a little backhanded, but it made Darcy feel good, nonetheless. Aunt Willow wasn't big on compliments. It gave her the courage to repeat a question she'd asked a dozen times. "Why did Mom leave the coven?"

Willow's face darkened, and she removed her hand. "None of that matters. I've let it go. The coven has put it behind them. Let it be enough that they're willing to take you back."

"You p-promised them I'm not like Mom. How can I not be like Mom if I don't even know what she did?" Darcy felt sick to her stomach. Mom hadn't talked about her early life, and the few things she'd let slip out had made Darcy believe Mom's family didn't love her. The day Darcy met her mother's sister, she'd braced herself to be snubbed. But Aunt Willow had put her arms around her and cried. She'd given seventeen-year-old Darcy a place to live and even tried to teach her spells, which Mom had refused to do.

After a moment of consideration, Aunt Willow leaned forward. "Loyalty. Integrity. Truthfulness." She pushed her chair away from the table and rose. "As long as you maintain those things, you will never be like your mother."

The lump in Darcy's throat made it difficult to speak as her aunt turned to go. Willow was the only family she had, and Darcy wanted to please her. But she also wanted to be accepted as she was, and that included Adrian. Aunt Willow had reached the café door by the time Darcy blurted out, "I met my fated mate."

Her aunt turned slowly, eyebrows drawn into a frown. "Witches don't have fated mates."

"I d-do." She pulled aside the collar of her shirt, exposing the healing mark of Adrian's claim.

Aunt Willow's face twitched in an array of emotions before she shook her head. With a sigh, she said, "Congratulations," and left.

Darcy sat for long moments, back stiff and tea growing cold. Well, what had she expected out of the encounter? Now at least Aunt Willow knew. The pressure to join the coven was off. *What do I do now?* Without someone to teach her, she may have set herself an impossible task. Maybe she should just give in and become a shifter. But much as she loved Adrian and his magnificent mountain lion, she wanted to be a witch.

She had ever since she could remember. Aunt Willow was right that witchcraft ran in her blood.

She rose from the table and paid the bill, then headed outside to her Subaru with heavy footsteps. Only yesterday she'd walked this same path with Adrian, feeling light as air. She glanced down the street toward the trees where they'd made out and her gaze fell on the apothecary sign. Hazel was always nice to her. Would she consider taking Darcy as an apprentice?

Licking her lips, she turned away from her car and walked the short distance to the shop. The bell rang as she entered, and Jake looked up from his bed near the register, blinked at her, then lowered his muzzle back to his paws as if unconcerned.

Hazel called from the back, "Be right out."

Darcy wandered toward the rack of loose tea, reading off the names without really comprehending them. Her mind churned over what to say. Hazel had left her coven, and hadn't joined Aunt Willow's when she moved here. Did that mean she didn't want to associate with other witches? Then why would she run a shop that sold spell supplies? *She sells tea, too.* Darcy picked up a cellophane baggie of spruce tip tea.

When Hazel spoke from behind her, Darcy nearly jumped out of her skin. "Hi, Darcy."

Spinning to face the shop keeper, Darcy stuttered, "D-do you have any b-books on spell casting?"

Hazel's eyes seemed to sparkle, and Darcy thought she saw the ghost of a smile fleet over her lips. "Of course. You seem to have an interest in herbs. How about one on potions?"

Darcy nodded mutely.

Hazel bent and opened a cabinet below the jewelry case and removed a leather-bound book the size of her palm. She handed it to Darcy.

Darcy licked her lips and ran her fingers over the embossed flower on the front. The book looked like someone's diary rather than anything magical. Inside, tiny handwriting filled the pages. She read a few lines to herself. *Potion making basics. Herbs both grown and harvested. Choosing the right vial.*

She looked up at Hazel and smiled. "How m-much?"

"Consider it a loan." Hazel glanced toward the door and leaned forward. "The coven doesn't like these books to be shared, so don't tell anyone you have it, all right?"

Tears pricked the back of Darcy's eyes. "Why are you being so nice?"

Hazel's lips thinned and she hesitated a moment before answering. "I knew your mother. She was a lot older than me, but I remember the way the others ran her off. It isn't right for them to make you suffer for her choices."

"What did she do?" Darcy stared wide-eyed at Hazel. Maybe she'd finally get some answers after all.

Hazel sighed, "She had an affair with Willow's husband, who was also the coven leader's son. It was a huge scandal."

Shock made Darcy's breath hitch. Her mother had never talked about her father, said he'd been a one-night-stand. "W-was he my father?"

Hazel shook her head. "No, he died before you were conceived. The coven found out about the affair after he left everything to your mother."

Suddenly, Darcy understood how Mom had afforded the big house in Anchorage on her income selling jewelry. She still didn't know who her father was, and probably never would, but that didn't matter. At least she understood why Aunt Willow acted the way she did, at least a little. "Thank you for telling me."

Hazel smiled. "If you need any help with that book, let me know. Most of the spells in there require little if any incantations."

"Are you offering to teach me?"

Hazel rubbed her fingertips over her mouth, looking once more toward the door. "Your aunt will hate me for it, but yes. I'll teach you. But only if you come to work for me. I can't run this shop by myself." She winked. "And Jake's terrible at running the till."

Darcy laughed and hugged the book against her chest, her heart so full, she was certain it might burst. "Deal. Thank you."

"Now go study that while I figure out what I'm going to do with you."

Nodding, Darcy left, silently singing to herself, *I'm finally going to be a witch!*

CHAPTER TWENTY

Adrian crouched against the soft, mossy floor at the edge of the clearing and waited as tiny footsteps passed by his hiding spot for the third time. He let out a soft purr and twitched his tail against the nearby branches. The feet stopped. Over his head, leaves rustled, revealing a cherubic face with blonde curls and her mother's ice-blue eyes. His two-year-old daughter squealed in delight. "Foun' you!"

Extending his front paws out straight, Adrian arched his back in a stretch while Lu's chubby hands reached for his neck. She wrapped both arms around him and climbed onto his back as if he was a pony, giggling as he rose. This was a game she never tired of playing, and he was happy to oblige. His wanderings these days kept him close to home, close to his family. One day, his daughter might discover she had an animal, and he would show her the deeper forest. Or, like her mother, she might become a witch. Either option was beautiful to Adrian, as long as she was part of his life.

With the girl on his back, he strolled toward the cabin. Fresh laundry hung drying in the sun, and Darcy had just finished making a batch of soap for the apothecary, filling the air with fresh sandalwood and floral essences. The cabin took up more of the clearing since he'd added two more rooms, including a separate building for Darcy's herb drying and a small garden plot full of fragrant plants and flowers. She and Hazel had branched into Internet orders for the shop, and Darcy's potions and lotions—both magical and non-magical—had become a big hit with their clientele.

Lu slipped from his shoulders and went running toward the front porch. The rickety chair had been replaced with a porch swing, and she clambered onto it, the chain rattling.

He shifted back to a man and hurried up the steps to help her before she fell off and hurt herself. Darcy emerged from inside carrying a box of soaps. Her gaze slid down his body to his crotch, then she met his eyes with a lewd eyebrow wriggle. His cock swelled in response. He reached for a nearby pair of shorts to cover himself. "Damn it, woman."

She smirked and set the box down next to several others, waiting until his shorts were in place before wrapping both arms around his waist. Her eyes said I love you without her needing to speak a word.

He kissed her nose. "I love you too, even if you are going to scar our daughter for life with your effect on me."

Lu now sat on the bench swing, bumping her back against the swing ineffectually as she tried to make the seat move. "Swing!"

Letting go of his mate, Adrian sat, and Darcy took the opposite side, sandwiching Lu between them. Adrian put one arm along the backrest, kneading Darcy's shoulder lightly. She rubbed her cheek against his forearm and smiled. Together, they pushed the swing back and let it pendulum forward while their daughter laughed with joyful abandon.

EPILOGUE

epler sat in his office at the Trooper station and read the police report for what had to be the hundredth time, mentally grumbling about the sloppiness of the photos. *Not sloppiness, ignorance,* he reminded himself. The rookie who'd sent him the intel wasn't from his office. Hell, he wasn't even with the State Troopers, just a beat cop in Kenai. But Kepler had to give him credit for taking initiative.

Zooming in on the image on his computer, he tried to get a better look at the white streak in the victim's hair. The report didn't state that the dead woman was a shifter, but the similarity to the rogue cases he'd been investigating in the Wrangell-St. Elias area for the last three years couldn't be denied. He picked up his phone and tapped in the number Officer Cal Bennet had included in the email with the report.

A deep voice answered, "Bennett."

"Hello, this is Kepler Stone with the state's Major Crimes Unit. Is this a good time to talk?"

In the background, Kepler heard the ticking of a turn signal, then Bennet said, "Stone, I'm glad you called. My only contact down here keeps blowing me off."

"I appreciate you coming to me. I assume the victim in these photos was a shifter?"

"Yeah. A wolf. I keep an ear out for shifter crimes, and this matches the rogues in Wrangell about a year ago."

The trail Kepler'd been following had gone cold, which had been both a relief and frustration. At least no more shifters were dying in the area. But the outbreak could happen again unless they found the cause. *It* has *happened again.* "Tell me what you know."

Cal described the death, which had been attributed to hypothermia. "There wasn't any sign of a struggle, and as far as I know, no other shifters were involved, but you know shifters don't die of hypothermia. Plus, the crime scene smelled like ashes, and the victim's white hair was on the exact same spots as the ones in your reports. I think this case is related to yours."

"Seems likely." The most recent theory was that a witch was behind the outbreak of rogues, but the Head of Covens said she needed a fresh sample in order to determine what type of magic was being used. "This could be just the break we need. Can you get a tissue sample?"

"Body's been cremated. The family didn't want things drawn out."

"Shit." That meant this was a dead end unless another rogue turned up. The last thing he wanted was more deaths. Kepler rubbed his temple, torn between hoping Cal was mistaken and wanting another lead. "Make sure you get a sample to me if another one shows up."

"I can try, but the only way I find out about these things is through the grapevine," Cal said. "I've tried to get on the state task force, but I don't have the credentials. There are no shifters on the investigation team in the Major Crimes Unit down here."

Fuck. A shifter with jurisdiction needed to be at the scene if this happened again, and Kepler knew in his gut this wasn't the end of things. He opened Google and looked at the map of the small Alaskan town on the banks of the Kenai River. "Looks like I'm transferring to Kenai, then."

Cal said, "Great, let me know when you arrive and I'll show you around."

"Thanks." Kepler hung up the phone and began the paperwork for his transfer. Mom and Dad would be sorry to see him leave, but it was time he broke away from the Gakona pack. His wolf had been chafing under the new pack Alpha, Gray. The guy wasn't bad, but Kepler wasn't ready to swear allegiance just because his family had.

He only hoped the pack Alpha down south wasn't an asshole...

BEWITCHED SHIFTER

Music from the bar shook the sidewalk under Ashlyn's feet as she waited for the bouncer to check her ID. She'd let her new hair stylist talk her into "mermaid hair," and the pink and blue color seemed to make people think she was younger than her twenty-five years. That, and the fact that she was carrying cupcakes.

"They're mojito flavored," she told the bouncer, feeling stupid. *Who brings cupcakes to a bar?* "For a bachelorette party."

"Ah." The bouncer returned her card with a wink and waved her in. "They came in a while ago. Have fun."

"Thanks." She smiled and stepped inside. Since moving to Kenai a couple of months ago to take over her cousin's bakery, she'd come to appreciate how friendly the locals were. Even this bachelorette party was proof of that. Between baking and catching up on the mess cousin Lana had called bookkeeping, she'd barely had time to meet anyone. Muffy, a local bride-to-be, had come into the bakery looking for a quote on a wedding cake and, after learning Ashlyn was new in town, had invited her to the party.

Ashlyn wasn't usually one to take invitations from complete strangers, but she needed friends, and Muffy seemed nice. At least the party would get her out of the house.

Pausing just inside the door, she scanned the crowd for Muffy's familiar face. Multi-colored lights flashed over a tiny dance floor packed with people, and patrons hovered around high-topped tables nearby. A long bar extended through the center of the room, and the delicious aroma of fresh Alaskan halibut and steak fries drifted from the kitchen in the back. Her stomach growled. She'd been too busy for lunch today, and sugary cupcakes weren't going to cut it, especially if she was going to be drinking.

Laughter caught her attention from several semi-circular booths along the wall. A group of women in low-cut blouses held shot glasses in the air, and she spied Muffy's dark, artistically tousled tresses beneath a sparkly plastic tiara. Nerves tightened her belly. She wasn't shy, but joining a clique of women who already knew each other was always awkward. Too bad Cousin Lana was busy on her fishing boat or Ashlyn would've made her come along.

Straightening her shoulders, she headed over, looking at Muffy's white sash proclaiming her soon-to-be hitched status. *Cliché.* But she kind of liked cliché. It felt stable. Predictable.

The bride-to-be spotted her and rose, leaning across the table and waving her manicured pink fingertips in a shooing motion at her other friends. "Scoot over, let Ashlyn in. Ashlyn, this is Jen, my sister. She's visiting from Idaho. I'm trying to convince her she should move here." She pointed to the auburn-haired woman Ashlyn settled next to, then toward the other women at the table. "And these are my friends Bev, Christy, and Alison."

The women greeted her with smiles, and Ashlyn felt a warming welcome flow through her. She hadn't realized how much she missed hanging out with friends. She didn't know these ladies yet, but they seemed really nice, and the penis-themed gag gifts scattered across the table promised they had a sense of humor. *Maybe they'll even appreciate my bad jokes.* But first, she'd bribe them with cupcakes.

Ashlyn held out the pink pastry box. "I thought you might like some treats."

"Oh, you're so sweet. You shouldn't have!" Muffy set the box aside and pushed a shot glass at her. "Here, drink. You need to catch up!"

The sharp scent of tequila wafted from the glass. Last time she'd had tequila, she'd turned into a bitch and alienated everyone at the party. Not that Ryan, her ex, hadn't deserved every ounce of her alcohol-fueled anger, but she definitely could've handled the break up better. "No thanks. Really."

"Oh, come on! The bakery is closed tomorrow!" Muffy wiggled her shoulders in time to the music, gravity-defying breasts staying perfectly in place. "Live it up a little."

Ashlyn reached for the laminated menu buried beneath the gag gifts. "You do not want to see me on tequila. Besides, I haven't had dinner yet."

"We have appetizers on the way." Muffy splayed a hand over the menu, pressing it flat against the table. "Don't worry."

Jen leaned closer, auburn tresses cascading over bare shoulders. "Just do the one and she'll leave you alone."

"At least until the next time someone says you know what!" Bev—a blonde who Ashlyn thought might've been in the bakery a time or two—gave an exaggerated wink.

"What words are we not allowed to say?"

"Oh, she's sneaky!" Jen laughed. "Trying to trick us into saying them out loud."

"I told you you'd like her." Muffy leaned over to drape a string of Mardi gras beads over Ashlyn's head. "Jen made a list. It's somewhere in there." She gestured to the baubles strewn over the table. "But everyone has to do at least one shot to start."

Ashlyn was a lightweight, and any amount of alcohol would go right to her head. On the other hand, a small buzz *would* help her relax. She tipped the shot glass back. The tequila burned an oily trail down her throat, followed by a moment of vertigo. *Whoa, that was fast.* She scrunched her eyes and shook her head. "Ack!"

"Yeah!" several of the ladies at the table cheered.

Ashlyn accepted a piece of paper titled BACHELORETTE BINGO as another round of shots arrived. The waitress set a glass in front of her and Ashlyn said, "Thank you."

That was apparently one of the things they weren't allowed to say, and the surrounding women started chanting, "Drink! Drink!"

Stomach twisting, Ashlyn looked over her shoulder, hoping for the promised appetizers. The waitress had moved to another table, but food had to be arriving soon, right? *You didn't come out tonight to be a party-*

pooper. Taking a deep breath, she lifted the glass and downed it.

She knew right away she'd made a mistake. Stomach revolting, she shot to her feet. "Excuse me."

"Are you going to the bathroom? Wait for me," Muffy said.

Ashlyn didn't wait. The tequila was coming up, and she'd prefer not to spew all over her new friends. The bathrooms had to be near the back, right? She elbowed through the crowd of sweaty bodies to reach the rear of the bar. No bathrooms, only a door to the kitchen and an emergency exit. Tequila rising in her throat, she shoved against the exit door.

Blessedly cool night air flooded over her, and she only managed to stumble a few steps outside before she doubled over and heaved into the dirt alley. After a couple of spasms, her stomach was empty. She rested with her hands on her knees, panting. Glancing upward, she noticed the aurora borealis was out, ribbons of green light roiling behind wisps of clouds. This was the first time she'd seen the lights since moving here, and she wished she was in a better condition to enjoy them.

The alley remained quiet but for the muffled beat of the music from inside as she took a few deep breaths. Ugh, she hated throwing up. And the smell—it'd been gross out here before she'd barfed. Now it was disgusting. At least the door didn't appear to have been hooked to an alarm.

Straightening, she wiped her mouth against the back of her hand and turned to the bar. She collided into the solid chest of a man. *Fuck.* The bouncer must've come to check on her. She raised her chin. "Excuse me, I was..."

A pair of glowing purple eyes met hers.

She gasped and stumbled back. She'd heard of tequila giving people hallucinations, but she'd never had any herself.

The man opened his mouth, exposing unnaturally pointed teeth. She backed up another step. Her heart was about to pound its way out of her chest. His mop of hair had a white streak down the middle, and her mind immediately conjured images of Frankenstein's Bride.

Knowing it was a bad joke, but unable to stop herself, she murmured, "It's alive!"

In a move almost too quick to follow, he reached for her.

She screamed, trying to remember anything from the self-defense class she'd taken in high school. But that'd been almost ten years ago. Like claws, his fingertips jabbed into her arms, yanking her toward him. His face descended to her shoulder, and pain seared through her.

Did he just bite me?

Agony surged through her. Pain. Anger. Fury. Her entire being seemed to explode in a shower of sparks and fur. *Fur?* Her lips curled back from her teeth.

The next thing she knew, her mouth was against his throat. The taste of iron coated her tongue.

Not iron. Blood.

What the fuck was happening? She wasn't in control. Her head twisted, jaws refusing to let go. She felt the tear of flesh and heard an awful gurgling as the man's hands pawed uselessly against her. The light in his eyes shifted to green, and she swore he whispered, "Thank you."

Then the glow faded to darkness.

Kepler arrived on the scene as the nearby Orthodox church bell began chiming midnight. He climbed out of his Jeep and retrieved his forensics kit from the back. Red and blue police lights reflected off the bar's sheet metal roofing. Tourist season was nearly over, but a swarm of onlookers pressed against the police tape blocking the alley.

He pushed through the crowd, ignoring the irritated looks, and ducked under the police tape. The officer watching the line nodded as he passed.

Near the bar's dimly lit rear exit, blood darkened the packed dirt between the dumpsters. The air stank of bad seafood, vomit, and garbage. Kepler forced his shifter senses down, breathing shallowly as he took in the scene. A lanky man with curly hair sprawled on his back near the rear exit, throat torn open like a package of hamburger.

Kepler paused next to a bloody paw print the size of a melon. Bear attacks weren't unheard of in the town on the banks of a river known for its salmon runs, but this wasn't the print of a bear. It was a wolf, and a big one. *A shifter.* He knew that even without verifying the scent.

Near the bar's back door, Cal, the local police officer, broke from conversation with a State Trooper and strode over, broad freckled face unusually grim. Cal was also a wolf shifter and had been the one who'd contacted Kepler when the rogue outbreak showed up in Kenai. Both outsiders to the local pack, they'd become fast friends in the three months since Kepler'd transferred here.

Cal pulled a tube of vapor rub from the breast pocket of his police uniform and offered it to Kepler, speaking in a low voice. "Victim's a shifter. And he has those freaky white marks we've been looking for."

Kepler shook his head, declining the vapor rub. Much as he hated the scent of a crime scene, his nose often detected clues that might otherwise be overlooked. It helped him excel at his job, and he'd already earned grudging respect within the good ol' boys club that dominated the Major Crimes Unit. He bent to get a closer look at the body. "Any idea who took him out?"

"Nope." Cal shrugged. "We're telling the press it was probably a bear attack. You think you can bring me in on this one?" Cal wanted to join the forensics unit, but lacked formal training, and Kepler didn't yet have the clout to get him a position with the human-dominated state law enforcement agency.

"I'll take it up with Finch, but you know how it is. We have to maintain jurisdiction. How's class going?" Kepler'd helped him sign up for an online course.

"I fucking hate homework," Cal complained. "Are you sure there isn't a way to test out?"

"The test won't use your shifter senses, Cal, you know that. It's all about chain of custody procedures, documentation—"

"Yeah, yeah, I know." Cal waved off the familiar lecture. "I've been studying. Go do your thing. I'll keep the humans occupied. Just let me know how I can help."

Nodding, Kepler pulled out his camera and started taking photos. The white streak definitely indicated the man had gone rogue, which meant that whoever had killed him was of secondary concern, at least to the shifter community. What or who was causing shifters to turn rogue was Kepler's primary mission. Back in Diablo Falls, the rogue outbreak had been blamed on a witch's hex, although that hadn't been proven before the outbreak ended. Steeling himself for an onslaught of sensory input, Kepler dragged in a breath, sniffing for clues. Blood. Garbage. Wolf shifter. *Mate.*

He shot to his feet and backed away. *Mate?* Not the dead shifter, but the other wolf who'd been here. The one who'd most likely made the kill. Wildflower honey and musk. A scent that made his inner wolf come to attention and demand action.

He realized he was panting when Cal offered the vapor rub again. "Change your mind?"

"I'm fine." Kepler rubbed his palms against the front of his slacks uncomfortably. All shifters longed to find their perfect match, their destined mate, but this situation was about the least romantic he could've imagined. He didn't have time to deal with a mate, especially not one who was also a suspect. "You don't smell anything unusual, right?"

"No, why?"

The back door to the bar swung open and a young woman wearing a plastic tiara emerged, phone in hand. Cal turned, one hand up to stop her. "Hey, you can't be out here."

The woman looked at the body with wide eyes. "My friend is missing and I'm worried about her."

"Well, she's not out here." Cal hurried over and ushered the woman inside.

Kepler turned back to the crime scene, gaze following the bloody paw prints circling the body. They led toward the other end of the alley. His wolf was urging him forward. Yearning to meet this woman. His human mind kept a tight leash on the beast inside him. He couldn't let hormones cloud his investigation of the crime scene.

Heart thundering against his ribs, he walked down the alley, watching every footstep to be sure he wasn't missing any clues. The prints faded quickly, but the scent of honey and female grew stronger.

He froze at the corner of a dumpster, nostrils twitching. She was here. *Right here.* His hormones were screaming at him. He called softly, "Hello?"

From inside the dumpster came a soft, breathy sob.

Throat tight, he cracked open the lid. A pair of glowing blue eyes met his.

"Don't come any closer," a woman choked out.

He lifted the lid higher, exposing a naked, amber-skinned woman cowering in one corner of the container, surrounded by crushed takeout boxes and empty alcohol bottles. Flowing pink and blue hair tangled across her round, anguished face, the bright colors completely at odds with the grim surroundings. She seemed familiar, but he couldn't place her. She likely just felt familiar because his wolf insisted they were mates. "Are you okay?"

"I said stay back!" She bared her teeth, glowing blue eyes flashing. Drying blood marred her smooth skin, and her shoulder had a fresh crescent of puncture wounds.

He glanced down the alley toward the body, putting together the pieces. *That mother-fucking rogue attacked my mate.* His wolf was going crazy. *Protect her.* He extended his free hand toward her and spoke in his most soothing tone. "It's okay. I'm not going to hurt you. What's your name?"

Her delicate bare shoulders heaved with rapid breaths. "You don't understand. I killed him. Stay back."

Shit. Her wolf form must've taken over to defend her from her attacker. "It's not your fault. My name's Kepler. Detective Kepler Stone."

She stared at him a long moment, wariness fading from her eyes. "Detective Stone?"

"Yes." He leaned into the dumpster, hand still extended. She seemed to recognize him, but he'd met a lot of people since moving here and wasn't surprised. "Let's get you out of here before the humans start asking questions."

Wariness flared in her eyes again, and she shrank deeper into the corner. "Humans? What are you talking about?" She choked on a sob. "I don't know what's happening to me."

His blood turned to ice. Was she not a shifter? He inhaled deeply, sorting through the other smells to focus on hers. His wolf insisted she was both shifter and his mate. Definitely wolf. Something like ashes. Vomit. Perhaps she was suffering a form of post-traumatic stress amnesia. Every protective urge in his body surged to full strength.

Uncaring of who might be watching from the other end of the alley, he removed his shirt and held it toward her. "What's your name?"

"Ashlyn," she whispered. With a trembling hand, she accepted the shirt. "Ashlyn Reed. I run the bakery."

He blinked as understanding flooded over him. He'd stopped by the bakery a couple of times to pick up a dozen bear claws to share at the office. Why hadn't he scented her as his mate then? Hell, he hadn't even realized she was a shifter. None of this was making any sense. A human shouldn't be able to become a shifter without visiting the hidden glacial spring, and he doubted that's what'd happened here.

He glanced toward the bar's back entrance, where Cal and the Trooper were once more in conversation. The

Trooper was human, and part of Cal's job was to keep him engaged while Kepler investigated. Most humans didn't know about shifters, and the Shifter Council wanted it kept that way. But what about Ashlyn?

She was choking back sobs and fumbling to put an arm in the shirt he'd given her. Her entire body trembled like leaves in a storm. Until he could figure this out, he needed to protect her. Protect his mate. "You've obviously had some shocking experiences tonight. Let me take you somewhere safe so we can talk, okay?"

With a shaky breath, she nodded and rose, giving him a glimpse of her naked body. The mating urge was strong, and he felt his body react, despite the sordid environment. *Rein it in,* he told himself, keeping his lips secured over his emerging fangs and his eyes cast down to hide their unearthly glow. The last thing Ashlyn needed was a horny mate she didn't even realize existed.

As her bare feet settled to the dirt, she looked up at him. "I—I'm not supposed to say thank you," she said with a hiccup, then started to laugh.

He had no idea what that meant, but she was obviously not in her right mind. He had to get her away from the scene and calmed down before asking questions. Before the Trooper or any other humans spotted her, he swept Ashlyn up in both arms. No way was he putting Ashlyn into human law enforcement custody.

He could trust Cal to come up with an excuse for his disappearance.

Heading toward the far end of the building, he circled the parking lot toward his Jeep. Ashlyn clung to his neck, her wildflower honey scent laced with tequila, garbage, and the ozone-like odor of magic. *Does that mean she might be a rogue, too?* His steps faltered as he examined her pink and blue tresses in the light of the moon. No indication of a white spot.

Relieved, he buckled her into the passenger seat and jogged around to the driver's side. He started the engine and turned toward home. Once he had her safe, he could plan out their next steps.

Ashlyn remained silent as he drove, staring out the windshield and clutching the front of the shirt closed. He pulled into his driveway, grateful for the tall wooden fence between his yard and the neighbor's. As he turned off the Jeep, Ashlyn seemed to come to life. "Shouldn't you take me to the hospital?"

"Shifters don't need hospitals." The words were out before he thought them through.

"Shifters?" she whispered, eyes round. The smell of adrenaline flooded the Jeep.

He ran a hand over his hair. *Idiot.* He needed to be more subtle. She didn't know what she'd become. What her world was going to be like from now on. "You're going to be okay. I promise. Let's go inside so I can explain."

She blinked at him, as if tempted to believe him, then glanced out the window. "Where are we?"

"My house. You can clean up, then I'll answer all your questions."

Her eyes narrowed. "Why don't you take me to my house?"

"I can protect you better here." He let a thread of his Alpha power infiltrate his words, hoping to reassure her he could keep her safe and also to compel her to obey. He generally didn't use his power because it confused other shifters, making them think he was looking for a pack. Kepler preferred to run as a lone wolf, but now that he had found his mate, that was likely to change.

He opened his door and went around to open hers for her. Too late, he spotted the neighbor's chihuahua taking a crap on his lawn as it had every day since he'd moved in three months ago. The little fucker had a complex and was in rivalry with the "big dog" next door—aka Kepler's wolf. The chihuahua started barking.

With fluid dexterity, Ashlyn shifted into a gorgeous cream-colored wolf with an amber ruff. Canines bared, she leaped past him, lunging for the dog.

Kepler tackled her just before her jaws snapped over the smaller animal.

The chihuahua scurried around the fence, unharmed, but yipping in terror.

Twisting free, Ashlyn faced Kepler, front paws set wide. Then her wolf lifted her muzzle and howled, voice resonating with power.

His veins turned to ice. *She's a fucking Alpha?* She didn't even know what a shifter was, and her animal was an Alpha, the most difficult form to control. The ice became daggers through his heart.

His mate was in real trouble.

They both were.

CHAPTER THREE

Ashlyn's entire body vibrated in the aftermath of the howl, a song with meaning she didn't understand. She saw through the darkness with more than her eyes—the air smelled sharper and the sounds from nearby houses buzzed like static on a phone line. She hadn't been able to restrain the urge to put the yipping ankle-biter on the lawn in its place. To punish it. Dominate it.

Then Kepler had crushed her against the damp grass, and she lost interest in killing. Now she wanted something else. Something just as primal. His hard muscles, sexy golden eyes, and woodsy clean scent made her want to lick him all over. Good God, she wanted to shove her nose in his crotch!

Kepler shook his head as if dizzy and demanded, "Change back."

Power pulsed through his words, a heaviness that made the hackles on her neck and shoulders rise. His golden eyes glowed with unearthly light. A violent desire to prove she would not be controlled swelled inside her, and her muscles coiled to lunge.

"I said shift," Kepler said again, more guttural this time, a sound she felt in her bones.

Grudgingly, her beast relinquished its hold. Ashlyn conformed back to her familiar human self, crouched on hands and knees against the cool, dewy grass, nighttime breeze caressing her bare skin. She was naked again, the shirt he'd given her scattered in pieces all over the lawn. For some reason, that didn't bother her now. It felt… natural. She blinked, staring down at her hands splayed on the damp grass. What the hell was happening to her?

To her surprise, Kepler dropped to his hands and knees, touching his nose to hers. Despite her confusion and terror, he seemed exponentially handsome right now. Rough stubble covered his chin, not quite a beard but perfectly trimmed in a way that made her think about how it would feel against her inner thighs. She licked her lips, tilting her chin to bring their mouths closer.

His breath fanned her face. "We have to go inside."

Next door, the neighbor's porch light came on, spilling light over the tall fence. She stiffened, remembering the chihuahua. "Did I hurt that dog?"

"It's fine. Come on." He rose, dragging her to her feet.

Numbly, she followed him onto the porch. He shielded her from the street with his body as he unlocked the door and ushered her inside a small kitchen with a breakfast nook.

Whatever adrenaline had kicked in earlier was fading fast, and her arms and legs began to tremble. He'd used a word—shifter—in reference to her situation. She would never have believed him if she hadn't just experienced the change a second time. *Am I possessed? Infected?* She was so confused.

Resting her weight on one hand against the counter, she breathed deeply and blinked, staring at an empty egg carton next to a sink holding a few dishes. She didn't want to cry, exactly, but her eyes felt watery. *Weak.*

Kepler put an arm around her waist, supporting her against him. "Come on. Once you're cleaned up, you'll feel better."

God, he felt so good. So normal. He guided her through a sparse living area to a bathroom with outdated fixtures and a hamper overflowing with laundry. Her skin reeked like garbage, blood, and sweat, but he was wearing a musky cologne that made her mouth water. Sex ought to be the last thing on her mind right now, but she couldn't help it. The scent was one that probably got him laid all the time.

The thought of him with another woman made the beast inside of her snarl and rise to the surface, but she used every ounce of willpower to keep it suppressed. Kepler had helped her get it under control once, but that didn't mean he could do it again, no matter how distracting his cologne was. Plus, the last thing he'd want would be some chick he just pulled from a dumpster.

He picked up a stray sock from the floor and dropped it into the hamper before jamming the lid closed, then leaned into the tub and turned on the shower. He urged her toward the water with a hand at the small of her back. "There you go."

The only thing grounding her at the moment was his touch, and she couldn't force herself to step away. She stared at the running water as if hypnotized.

Heaving a deep breath, he toed out of his shoes and stepped into the shower, pulling her after him. "I've got you."

He yanked the plastic shower curtain closed, and she dimly noticed he hadn't removed his pants. But his chest was bare, and his skin against hers felt so good, so stable, so *human*. Facing him, she let the water sluice over her scalp and down her back.

He picked up a bottle of shampoo with his free hand and massaged a masculine smelling lather into her hair, his touch more gentle than she expected. Picking up a bar of soap, he rubbed it between his palms then carefully cleansed the tender bite on her shoulder. One at a time, he soaped her hands, taking care to lavish each finger with attention.

She closed her eyes and let him. Although his touch wasn't intentionally sexual, his warm masculine presence permeated the small space, and a heat was growing between her legs. His fingertips smoothed the grime from her cheeks and chin. The broad pad of his thumb brushed her lips. On instinct, she opened her mouth, flicking her tongue against his wet skin.

He exhaled sharply before pulling free. "Don't let her control you."

Is he talking to himself? She opened her eyes, but he turned her around with firm hands and smoothed soapy palms down her back to the top of her buttocks. His thumbs brushed the base of her spine, fingers circling around her hips, then he rubbed down the outsides of her legs. Despite his avoidance of any erogenous zones, the pressure of his touch ignited her desire. In fact, his careful evasion only made her want him more. She had no idea what was wrong with her, but she'd lost control. The funny thing was that she didn't care.

She placed both palms flat on the tiled wall in front of her and arched her back. Behind her, his breathing roughened. She waited, abdomen tightening as she anticipated his next move.

Slowly, his hands made a return path up the backs of her legs, bypassing her ass to return to her back. "You're making this difficult," he grated.

A primal urge she didn't understand rumbled through her body like thunder. Backing up a step, she rubbed her ass against him. The impressive length of his arousal pulsed hotly through his pants. She moaned. God, he felt so big. So ready. She slid a hand down between her thighs, finding her folds already slick. Her finger slid between them easily, gliding over the sensitive bud. She rocked into him in time with her finger.

A low groan escaped him and his hands dug into her hips. "Stop."

"I need you." Had she just said that? She'd thought Detective Kepler Stone was sexy from the first time he'd walked into the bakery, but she wasn't usually this brazen. After the night she'd had, however, nothing could surprise her. Imagining him slamming into her was a much better thing to focus on than the other things that had happened.

He leaned forward, hard abs against her back, and cupped her breasts. Her nipples sharpened to aching points. She rubbed herself harder, the pressure inside her building. Even so, her own touch wasn't going to be enough. She needed filled. She needed Kepler.

Turning in his embrace, she reached for his belt, struggling with the water-logged leather. She hadn't been with a lot of guys, and she'd definitely never been this close to one with an honest to God eight-pack. The bulge in his pants promised it would live up to the rest of his body. His fingers encircled her wrists and pulled her hands up his strong chest to embrace the back of his neck. Pressing his forehead to hers, he met her gaze, the gold glow in his eyes hungry. Voice gravelly with desperation, he whispered, "You need to slow down. This means more than you realize."

She didn't know why, but she wanted to cry. Her loneliness since moving to Kenai faded, and in this moment, she had the distinct feeling she would never be lonely again. This moment was important. *Connected.* She angled her face until their lips brushed. "I want to be with you."

Kepler inhaled deeply, chest swelling against her naked breasts, and his hands fell to her hips. He leaned in, claiming the kiss she offered. She slid one hand from behind his neck and cupped his cheek, his whiskers rough against her palm as their lips explored each other. God, he was good, the perfect balance between gentle and firm, and she felt clumsy compared to him. He sucked gently on her top lip, pivoting them under the spray until her back rested against the tiled wall.

She lifted one leg, hooking it over his hip, and he leaned in, rolling the hard line beneath his fly against her center. She moaned against his mouth. Kepler pushed his tongue between her lips, dipping shallowly past her teeth. Ashlyn gasped and tilted her head, accepting his entry. He plunged his tongue deeper and harder, each stroke of his tongue mimicked by a gentle roll of his hips. Crushing her against the tile, he kissed her into senselessness, his erotic movements turning her insides to liquid heat.

His hand slid between her thighs. When he found her waiting heat, he buried his face against her neck, nibbling along the edge of her throat in a way that made her gasp.

Tilting into his touch, she clutched the bulging muscles of his shoulders while he worked her. His expertise made her dizzy as he ran his touch along her slick folds. One finger dipped inside her and her inner walls clenched around him. He growled and sucked hard on her neck. He'd probably made a bruise, but she liked it.

She hung on while he pushed in and out of her with his finger, drawing her toward climax. She was close. Frustratingly close. But she needed more.

She reached for his belt again. "I want you inside me."

This time, he didn't stop her. He pulled back enough to let her fumble with his buckle, his fingers continuing the aching rhythm that left her gasping for breath. By the time she had him free, her eyes were rolling back with pleasure. Still, she was determined to take this all the way. Take *him* all the way. She wrapped her fingers around his searing shaft and guided the head to her entrance. The man was enormous, pulsing and thick and hot.

Kepler exhaled, and she looked up to find his eyes on hers. The glow behind them was like a furnace, its flames ready to consume her. He bared his teeth and grated, "I can't stop."

"I don't want you to."

One large hand slid up the back of her thigh, lifting her against him. Wrapping her other leg behind him, she locked her ankles. With a snarl, he slid into her. His girth filled her, stretched her. So big. Almost too much, but it felt amazing to finally have him inside her. He held there, pinning her against the tiles, buried deep inside her. Her hands clawed into his shoulders, and her insides fluttered around him on the verge of ecstasy. She threw her head back and moaned, "More."

Easing out slowly, he adjusted his grip under her ass and brought his chest against hers, leaning forward to claim her lips. His tongue plunged into her mouth in time with his next stroke. She tightened both legs around his hips, drawing him deep. His next stroke was harder. Faster. Surer. Then he was driving into her, pressing her back against the cool tiles, his mouth moving along her throat, stubble rough against her sensitive skin as he nipped and sucked. She braced her shoulder blades against the wall, finding it hard to breathe against the pressure of her building climax.

She exploded with blinding intensity and screamed his name, shuddering with the contractions of her inner walls. He slammed deep inside her again, snarling as she tightened around his thick shaft. His sudden release filled her with jets of warmth, his body bucking and shuddering against her. Her fluttering aftershocks almost made her pass out. Against her shoulder, she felt the light pressure of his teeth.

She thought of other teeth. Another bite she'd experienced only a short while ago. Yet Kepler's teeth didn't frighten her. He made her feel safe. Protected. She wanted—needed—him to bite her. She slid her hand to the back of his head and drew him closer. "Do it."

Kepler's jaw clenched, the pressure of his teeth insanely close to piercing her skin. It hurt, but she wanted it to. She wanted him to cover the horrible experience in the alley with a better memory. "Please, Kepler."

"No," he said under his breath, then louder, "No!"

With a suddenness that felt like a vacuum, he broke contact.

She stumbled as her feet hit the tub basin. He had stepped out of the tub and was backing into the corner between the sink and the wall. His features were dissolving in a shower of sparks.

"Get out!" he roared. Then his voice lowered to a long, echoing howl.

CHAPTER FOUR

For the first time in years, Kepler lost control to his wolf. As his body transformed, Ashlyn's face paled. She scrambled toward the edge of the tub, one hand grasping the shower curtain for support. The plastic tore free, sending her crashing to the bathroom floor, half in and half out of the tub.

I shouldn't have given in to her advances. Should've maintained control of his wolf's urges. But Ashlyn had been so damned hot, so willing, so *wet*. He'd told himself he'd only go far enough to please her. But now his wolf was demanding more. He wanted to *claim* her. To cover the scar that bastard rogue shifter had put on her shoulder. To bind her to him as his mate. He should've taken her to the pack right away, not tried to protect her himself. He was too close to the situation to remain objective. But all he could think at the moment was: *Mine.*

The running shower splashed down Ashlyn's back and puddled onto the linoleum, a haze of shifter magic swirling across her beautiful amber skin.

Don't shift, don't shift, he begged her in his mind. His wolf pricked his ears, tongue lolling in anticipation. If Ashlyn shifted, they'd probably both lose control and run through the streets in a mating frenzy, hunting chihuahuas together. His wolf thought that sounded fun. Kepler chomped down on his own tongue, tasting blood. *Not fun. Deadly*, he reprimanded, hoping the potential danger to his mate might force his beast to relinquish control. Not only was she a newly turned shifter—which should be impossible without visiting the Source—she'd proved she was capable of killing. Who knew what could make her do it again?

Ashlyn thrashed, tangling herself in the shower curtain. Her wolf must be shredding her inside, trying to get out. He remembered the willfulness of his own wolf during puberty, when all he wanted to do was fight. To establish dominance. It was the natural order of things, each animal searching for rank among its kind. As an Alpha himself, Kepler could've broken away to form his own pack. But he'd reigned his wolf in, forced himself to behave. *Until tonight.*

How was he supposed to assure Ashlyn she could handle being a shifter when he couldn't even control his own beast?

Her icy-blue eyes flashed, and he caught a glimpse of her cream-colored wolf, fur darkened to a buff gold by the water. But then her human form solidified once more. Her teeth were bared with effort, knuckles white as she clutched the plastic curtain while the magic continued to swirl around her.

His chest swelled with pride. Her wolf was Alpha, but it seemed the human part of his mate was just as fierce. His wolf's urge to claim her grew stronger, and he took a step forward. *She will bear us strong pups.*

Years ago, Kepler had discovered that his wolf was naturally competitive. He used that weakness now. *Her control shames us, wolf. She does not wish to join you like this.* His wolf stopped moving and considered that. *We must prove our worth to her before she accepts us.* Kepler slowly, painfully, mastered his beast, concentrating on conforming his limbs to their human dimensions until he crouched naked in the growing puddle of water on the linoleum.

Ashlyn gaped at him with eyes round as full moons, her pink and blue hair plastered darkly against her scalp. Her shoulders began shaking. Was she crying? Laughing? He couldn't tell, but she was obviously hysterical.

He pulled a loose towel from the nearby hamper and wrapped it around his hips before easing toward her. The remains of his slacks lay in sodden scraps over the bathroom floor. Taking her face between his hands, he looked into her eyes. "You did well. You controlled her."

She panted and shuddered, her voice emerging as a squeak. "You're… you're one, too."

Kepler blinked in surprise. He'd assumed she'd known he was a shifter. Her wolf should've told her that right from the start. But she was new to the supernatural world. "Yes."

"I thought this only happened in movies with bad hair and fangs." Her voice shook.

He couldn't help the smile tugging at his mouth. *Sense of humor, even under stress.* She was strong. "I'd like to think we shifters are sexier than those in movies, but there is a kernel of truth in those myths." He reached up and turned off the water, then pulled a clean towel from the bar on the wall, wrapping it over her torso. "Your wolf is really strong, Ashlyn. Stronger than most. She's what we call an Alpha. You're going to have trouble controlling her."

Ashlyn pinned one arm over the towel and kicked free of the clingy shower curtain before struggling to her feet. "This can't be real. I bet I'm going to wake up in the morning with a monster hangover." She choked off another bubble of semi-hysterical laughter. "Where are my clothes?"

She thinks she's hallucinating. "It's real." He stood. "Your clothes are in pieces back in the alley."

Her eyebrows drew together, and she stared at the scraps of his pants scattered across the bathroom. He could see the shallow rise and fall of her breathing as she clutched the towel around her naked body. Then she stood taller, seeming to find her resolve, and stepped past him toward the door. "I'm going home."

He threw out an arm to bar her way. She'd kept remarkable control of herself a few minutes ago, but that didn't mean she was good to go. There were a million triggers out there, from chihuahuas to other shifters. "You can't go until we figure out how this happened, and definitely not until I'm sure you have control of your animal."

The Alpha in her eyes flashed blue. "You can't tell me what to do. I must be drunk. I'm not in control of my faculties."

"You're not drunk, Ashlyn. This isn't a dream." He shoved her toward the mirror over the sink, pressing his chest against her back to hold her steady. She struggled as he jabbed a finger at the mirror. "Look at yourself. Really look."

She met his reflected gaze, then turned her attention to the bite on her shoulder. It had almost healed, and she ran her fingertips over the crescent of angry pink scar tissue, confusion filling her eyes.

"Shifters heal faster than humans," he said close to her ear. "Don't look at that. Look into your eyes."

She lifted her chin slowly. The glow of her Alpha flashed in her eyes, proof the animal was hovering close to the surface, eager to emerge at the slightest weakness. She stiffened, her skin heating under his hands. *She's going to shift.*

"No." Kepler spun her to face him. "Do not let her control you."

She trembled and bared her teeth. The glow in her eyes subsided. Gulping a breath, she shrugged his hands away. "I killed that man, didn't I?"

"He attacked *you*." His hands clenched into fists at the thought of it. Born of violence and into violence, his mate would forever bear more than the scar on her shoulder from tonight, and he hated that. "That shifter was a rogue. An outlaw. Your wolf only acted in self-defense."

She swallowed. "What's going to happen now?"

He hesitated, realizing he didn't know. The Council should be informed. Ashlyn wasn't supposed to be a shifter. *They'll lock her away to study her. Or kill her outright.* He growled out loud, swallowing the sound when she shrank away.

Taking a step back to give her space, he inhaled through his nose, calming his wolf's instincts. Ashlyn had no pack, no family, no ties to anyone except him. *My mate.* Which she probably didn't even comprehend. Humans didn't experience pairing the same way shifters did. "I'm going to protect you."

A sarcastic chuckle shook her. "From what? Seems like my wolf has protecting me covered."

"I've been tracking rogue shifters for over two years now, and this is the first time something like this has happened. I don't understand how you're now a shifter."

"I got bit, remember?"

He shook his head. "Contrary to popular myth, a bite doesn't turn you into a shifter. You're either born as one or become one after drinking from the Source."

"Oh. Maybe someone slipped some of that stuff in my drink."

"Impossible. The magic only works inside the glacier cave. And the cave only opens when it chooses. I'm not even certain the cave can be found unless the aurora is out."

"So this isn't an infection. It's magic." She turned back toward the mirror and examined herself. "Can we break the curse?"

The pit of his stomach twisted. She'd called it a curse. She didn't want her wolf. *Of course she doesn't.* But if she went back to being human, what did that mean for him? Shifters were only granted one destined mate. Even so, he would never want her to live a life she didn't choose. He swallowed his selfishness and shrugged. "If this is a hex, then it may be possible. Do you know any witches?"

She gaped at him from her reflection. "Witches are real, too?"

He smiled grimly and nodded. "And vampires, dragons, mermaids, gargoyles—all the myths and legends are, in one way or another, true."

Her chest heaved with rapid breaths, gaze locked with his for a few heartbeats. Then she stepped away from the sink, lifting a black tee shirt from the top of the hamper and pulling it over her head with one hand. The shirt fell almost to her knees over the towel which she let fall to the floor. "I need to go home."

Damn. All he wanted to do was peel that shirt back over her head and carry her to his bedroom. But now wasn't the time to play at being mates. Once they had this mystery unraveled, he'd talk to her about that. "You need to stay with me until we know what's going on. If your wolf breaks free, the local pack won't ask questions or give you a chance to explain. They'll exterminate you."

"The... pack? As in, wolf pack? Are there a lot of you?"

He forced a smile and spread his palms. "A few," he answered, thinking of the various packs scattered across the state. He hadn't registered with any of them, but he'd never been much of a joiner. His Alpha tendencies got in the way, and he didn't want to maintain a pack of his own. It would get in the way of his job. Plus, he liked being a lone wolf. "There's a lot you need to learn now that you're a shifter."

Her lips thinned, and she shook her head. "I really do need to go home. My cat needs to be fed."

"You have a cat?" It wasn't unheard of for shifters to own pets, but an Alpha wolf owning a cat was going to be interesting.

Her face paled. "Oh my God. Will my wolf try to hurt Mr. Mew?"

He put a hand on her shoulder. "Your wolf will probably be fine with it. It's the cat's reaction I'm worried about."

"I've had Mr. Mew since I was in high school."

"Let me get you a pair of sweats, then we'll both go. I'll make sure you don't do anything to hurt your cat."

The witch sat ensconced in the corner near the DJ station, her spell of shadows making her all but invisible as the police cleared the bar. She didn't need to see the body in the alley to know who it was. The shifter's death was her fault, just like all the previous deaths. Why did she keep trusting that things would turn out different? Her previous coven leader had been right—she was in over her head and every time she tried something new, she seemed to sink even deeper. This entire project had gone spectacularly wrong from the moment she'd sent her familiar to investigate a reported hellmouth in Arizona.

Uncertain what to do next, she stared into a half-empty beer bottle someone had left behind. She could summon the agathion using any common glass vessel, and a part of her took satisfaction in seeing him inside the swill left behind by some drunk. Unlike their full-blooded djinn cousins who came to Earth to prey on hapless human souls, an agathion could not come all the way through to manifest a physical form and was generally considered harmless.

Except this one.

Right now, the tiny form of the man inside the bottle gripped her familiar in one hand, stroking the auburn fur between the ferret's eyes. Or should she say eye? The monster had plucked one of Hamilton's orbs from its socket the first time the witch had dared refuse one of his demands. Her familiar was trapped because of her, and she'd do whatever it took to free him.

She prayed the monster wouldn't punish Hamilton because of tonight's disaster. Her hex had barely lasted a few hours this time. Keeping her voice low, she gritted between her teeth, "You promised you'd keep this host alive."

"My dear, you worry too much." Violet sheet lightning feathered the agathion's skin. "This has been a most splendid evening. Far better than I expected."

Sickness at his cavalier attitude mixed with guilty relief that perhaps the agathion was finally satisfied. "Does that mean you'll let Hamilton go?"

He tilted his head. "Silly thing." His glowing eyes felt as if they might laser cut his way out of the bottle. "We're not finished. I need you to track down a newborn shifter."

Her blood turned to ice. Hexing adults was distasteful enough, but an infant? Out of the question. "I draw the line at babies, you monster."

She made eye contact with Hamilton and swallowed past the lump in her throat. The mental thread she and her familiar usually shared had been disrupted by the agathion's magic, but she knew Hamilton would support her in this decision, even if it meant his death.

The agathion laughed, his voice crackling to match the storm on his face. "Not a child, a newly transformed shifter. The one I made in the alley. She will be my key."

The witch glared into the bottle. The agathion wanted to inhabit a human much the way a shifter's animal did, which would let him walk free like other djinn. She'd only balked a little when he revealed his desire. After all, there were already djinn walking the Earth. What was the harm in one more? But she was fine-tuning his hex on the lives of these shifters, and the death toll was mounting, as was her guilt.

"You said this shifter would be the one."

"I have finally discovered the missing element. This time the hex will be permanent."

Chewing her lip, she thought about refusing. The monster reached for Hamilton's other eye, and she shook the bottle. "Fine. But permanent or not, this is the last one. I do it, and you let Hamilton go."

The ferret wriggled between the agathion's slender fingers, and the monster pressed his face against her familiar's whiskered cheek. "But we've grown so fond of each other, haven't we Hamilton?"

Her familiar twitched the tip of his tail, the only form of support he dared offer, but she knew it for what it was. He was ready for this to end, too, one way or another.

"I mean it," she insisted. "After this, we're done."

The agathion's lips parted in a sharp-toothed smile. "If you succeed at this, I'll no longer need your services. Now, hurry and find her. The hellmouth is strongest while the aurora is active, and I don't know how much longer it will last."

She set the bottle on the table. "I need you to say it. I find this shifter, and you let Hamilton go."

"Find her and hex her, and I will release your pet."

Her mouth tasted like ashes. One way or another, this was going to end badly. Even so, she nodded. "Where do I start?"

*A*shlyn watched Kepler disappear through a doorway she assumed must be his bedroom. Emerging a few minutes later wearing jeans and a red tee shirt with a computer buffering icon and the words *I'm thinking,* he held out a neatly folded pair of gray sweats and clean tee shirt.

"Thank you." Her hand brushed his as she accepted the clothing, and she felt the urge to *bite* him, for Christ's sake. Her teeth ached for it. She breathed deeply and tried to clear her head, confused by the urges roiling inside her. If she wasn't thinking about biting Kepler, she was thinking about fucking him. The primal way he'd driven into her had been the most amazing sexual encounter she'd ever experienced. Did shifters feel sex in a different way?

Shoving her legs into the sweats, she cinched the drawstring tight around her waist and rolled the pant legs so she didn't step on them. When she exchanged the hamper tee shirt for the clean one, she felt a twinge of regret, but the clean one still smelled vaguely of Kepler, which she found calming.

"Ready," she said.

Kepler picked up a set of keys from a table in the hall and led her outside to his Jeep. They backed out of the driveway and, after she gave him her address, they maneuvered the dark streets in silence. She glared at her hands as if she could see through her skin to the wolf's paws beneath. *This can't be real*. But despite how normal her hands looked at the moment, she knew the beast inside her was there, waiting to break free.

At the curb outside her apartment building, Kepler climbed out of the Jeep and went around to open her door for her. A silly part of her wanted to tell him she'd had a lovely evening, as if they'd just come back from a date. Accepting his supportive hand, she slid from the seat, bare feet hitting the chilly dirt that was supposed to be a lawn but that never managed to grow more than weeds. The sweet scent of the crushed plants reminded her of chamomile.

She led him onto the cracked cement path bordered by huge spruce trees and followed it to the unsecured entry stairway. There, she paused and looked upward at her door. "Are you sure I won't hurt Mr. Mew?"

Tender concern softened Kepler's masculine features, and butterflies took wing in her stomach. He put a gentle arm around her shoulders. "I won't let you hurt your cat." His gray eyes didn't have the glow she'd seen when he shifted, but they still felt warm on her. The air between them filled with tension, like the weather before a thunderstorm. Inside her, the wolf rose toward the surface. *Bite him. Mark him.*

Trembling, she shrugged off his arm and climbed the stairs to her apartment. Only at the door did she realize she didn't have her purse or keys. Not even her phone with her landlord's number in it, not that she'd want Gerome to see her like this.

Kepler's presence felt warm behind her. "What's wrong?"

"I'm locked out."

"Ah." He moved to the door handle and examined it. "I've learned a thing or two being a criminal investigator. Let me try."

Within a minute, he had the door open. "You should really use your deadbolt."

She was hardly listening as the familiar scents from inside her apartment washed over her. The light sandalwood from her essential oil diffuser was strongest, but beneath that she could smell the overripe bananas on the counter and the acrid smell of Mr. Mew's litter box. Her geriatric cat was nowhere in sight, but he could usually be found curled up next to the radiator in her bedroom.

Thankfully, she felt no urge to hunt down her pet, at least not to kill him. Her head was a jumble of denial and rationalization, but the wolf inside her seemed content, at least for the moment.

"Mr. Mew?" she called, stepping inside and moving slowly toward her bedroom.

Kepler followed close behind, a calming presence as she flipped on the bedroom light. Mr. Mew wasn't in his usual spot, but her nose told her he was nearby.

"He's under the bed," Kepler said.

Heat crept up Ashlyn's face as she realized her purple vibrator lay among the rumpled white sheets. Had Kepler seen it? She cut him a glance from the corner of her eye, noting the whisper of a smirk on his face. Damn, of course he had. She flipped the blankets over the sex toy before bending to look under the bed.

A whiskered orange face looked back at her from near the headboard. "Mr. Mew? It's me. Come on out."

The cat growled and scrunched himself against the wall. Her stomach churned. He usually came right to her. "I think he knows I'm different."

"Maybe he'll come out if you feed him?" Kepler said. "I don't know much about cats."

It was worth a try. Ashlyn ushered Kepler out of the bedroom toward the kitchen and opened a can of cat food for Mr. Mew. The fishy scent made her mouth water. *Gross.* But she'd been hungry since before the party, and now her stomach felt like a black hole.

She plopped the food into the cat's dish and turned back to her almost empty cupboards. All she had on hand were five mojito cupcakes that hadn't fit in the box for the party. She peeled back the paper on one and took a huge bite, unconcerned about the frosting she could feel stuck to her lips. The sweet mint frosting and lime flavored cake tasting nothing like a real mojito, but she stuffed the rest of the cupcake into her mouth. "I'm so hungry," she said around the cake.

Kepler frowned. "I'm sorry, I should've offered you something to eat or drink at my house."

At the kitchen door, Mr. Mew appeared, pausing with one paw forward. She smiled at him and he gave her a reproachful look before edging along the far wall toward his dish. At least it was progress. She couldn't blame him for needing time to get used to her.

She went to the sink and filled her coffee maker while making a point of not looking at Mr. Mew. "Would you like some coffee?" She glanced sideways at Kepler, who was watching her cat. "I also have tea and cocoa."

"Coffee would be nice, thank you."

As the smell of coffee filled the kitchen, she grabbed the other cupcakes and moved to the small table in the corner near Mr. Mew's dish. Her cat kept a wary eye on her as he ate, but didn't run away. She blew out a shaky breath, relieved that things might be returning to normal. *Other than the fact you're now a supernatural being.* And there was a sexy wolf shifter standing in her kitchen.

Kepler was still watching her cat. Hopefully not with hunger. After all, he was a wolf like her. Hoping to distract him, she held out a cupcake. "Want one?"

"Thanks." Kepler sat across from her and took it.

Ashlyn shucked a second treat from its paper and took a huge bite, unable to refrain from being impolite. She was so damn hungry, it was insane. Maybe being a wolf required a lot more calories. *Hmmm.* Eating as much as she wanted would be a nice perk if it was true.

Kepler carefully peeled back the paper and swept his strong tongue over the frosting.

She stopped chewing, hunger forgotten as she imagined that tongue—Kepler's tongue—licking her instead. Her nipples hardened against her tee shirt and heat pooled between her thighs. Even the way his fingertips held the cupcake was sexy and made her yearn for his touch. Fuck, she could smell her own arousal, which made her more horny. What was wrong with her?

She swallowed her bite, realizing she must look like an animal wolfing down food, then giggled, realizing how true that was.

Kepler tilted his head, his eyes deep pools she wanted to fall into. "What's so funny?"

"I'm wolfing." She cackled, feeling a little insane.

His eyebrows pinched, then he seemed to get it and chuckled before taking a huge bite of his own cupcake. "Mmmhmm."

Damn, he was sexy. She wanted to lick the frosting off his lips. And anywhere else he might like to put it…

She set her half-eaten cupcake down just as the coffee maker beeped. She was going to ignore it, but Kepler rose. She watched his gorgeous ass as he filled two mugs. Her hands itched to grab it, and it took all her willpower to resist.

He brought the mugs back to the table and set one in front of her before reclaiming his seat. She was about to tell him to forget the coffee when he said, "So. I'm sure you've thought of a ton of questions."

Her mood broke, all her worry rising to the surface. This pendulum of emotions and desires was wearing her out. Taking a breath, she said, "You said something about a witch. If this is a curse, can we break it?"

Quiet filled the room for a few moments as he seemed to think about his answer. "I honestly don't know," he said. "Tell me everything that happened leading up to you being attacked."

She told him about the bachelorette party and feeling sick. "I thought a bouncer had come to check on me. The next thing I knew, I had blood all over me and the guy was dead."

"You'd never met him before?"

"I don't think so. But a lot of people come into the bakery, so it's possible."

"He didn't say anything?"

"Oh, wait, he did. He said thank you." She recalled the look of gratitude in the man's eyes before the life faded from them. "He… thanked me for killing him?"

Kepler frowned and sighed. "When something, usually a traumatic event, causes a shifter animal to go insane, we call them rogues. They become violent, rabid, sometimes suicidal."

"How awful." Ashlyn's throat ached.

He nodded. "Rogue shifters are rare. But about two years ago, there was an unexplained surge of cases. The only way to handle a rogue is to kill them before they hurt someone. My brother actually had to put one down that threatened his mate."

Something about the way he said "mate" flushed her entire body with heat. She sipped her coffee to cover her burning cheeks.

"Doctors eliminated the possibility of infection," he continued. "That left magic as the most likely cause, but we were never able to track down the witch responsible. And there were never any reported cases of an attack creating a new shifter."

"Never?" She tried to recall what he'd said about shifters earlier—they were either born or had to drink water from a glacier. "Are you sure someone couldn't have put some of that glacier water in my drink?"

"It's been tried, believe me." He shook his head. "The water becomes normal water if it's removed from the cave."

She swallowed, realizing he wasn't offering her any solutions. *I'm a freaking werewolf, now.* What did that mean for her? "If we can't undo this, if I'm no longer human, can I ever go back to my normal life?"

Kepler nodded. "There are plenty of shifters living out in the open among humans—myself included. Nothing needs to change for you as long as you keep your wolf under control."

"How do I do that?" She gripped her mug with both hands, letting the hot ceramic grow uncomfortable against her palms. "Lock myself up during the full moon?"

He chuckled. "The full moon thing's a myth. Shifters can assume their animal form at any time."

"You mean I'm going to feel like this all the time?" She groaned and covered her eyes with one hand. "I was hoping it was like PMS or something."

This time he outright laughed. "Sorry, I shouldn't laugh. But your sense of humor is adorable." His phone buzzed, and he reached into his back pocket to retrieve it. He grimaced and tapped the screen. "I have to take this. Hey, captain."

Although Ashlyn could clearly hear the voice on the other end, she wasn't listening. *He thinks I'm adorable.* The wolf inside her felt all wiggly. *You like him, don't you?* she asked. The wolf grew even more wiggly, which made sense, she supposed. Kepler was the only other shifter she knew.

"I'll be in the office soon." Kepler hung up and shook his head, gaze full of apology. "If I don't get some reports filed, there will be all sorts of questions we don't want to answer. But I don't want to leave you alone."

She glanced toward Mr. Mew, who was now cleaning a front paw with long strokes of his tongue. Apparently, a full belly had persuaded him that he didn't need to hide from her. "You can go. I think I'm okay."

Kepler took a deep breath and let it out slowly, his gaze locked on hers. Then he nodded and rose. "I can't believe how well you're handling… all this." The hint of a blush tinted his cheeks. "You're a remarkable woman, Ashlyn."

Heat flooded her face, and she smiled. God, she liked him.

He moved to her side of the table, placing a finger under her chin. "But don't leave the apartment, okay?" His voice was edged with concern. "There are lots of things that could trigger your wolf, and I'd feel better if I was around to help until you get used to her."

She gripped his wrist, liking the sound of him sticking around. "How long do you think you'll be gone?"

"A couple of hours, tops." His full palm now cradled her jawline. "I have to pop over to the Soldotna office to file paperwork. I'll be as quick as I can." He bent and brushed her mouth with his.

The feather light touch sent a fire through her that pooled between her legs. She had to force her fingers to let go of his wrist as he pulled away. She'd use the time he was gone to clean up her apartment. *Especially the bed*. Because when he came back, she had plans.

CHAPTER SEVEN

Kepler drove the dark, empty streets faster than he should've, but he didn't like leaving Ashlyn on her own. She'd handled her wolf well, at least after the first couple of changes, but that didn't mean she had complete control. *What will happen when she meets another shifter? Or a vampire?* One of the shifter packs in Fairbanks ran a tour company that specifically catered to the blood-sucking supernaturals and their love of long winter darkness, and he'd already noticed an influx even this far south.

"She'll be fine," he muttered out loud as he stomped on the gas, taking advantage of a straight stretch of road. The office was only forty minutes away, but might as well have been hours. Days, even. His wolf felt all bristly inside him, making it very clear he didn't want to be separated from his mate, especially when she was as yet unclaimed. *Claiming her might not even be an option.* His wolf didn't like that thought. But Ashlyn had been very clear about wanting to return to being human. There was a good chance she'd also reject having a mate.

He hadn't done a very good job explaining what it meant to be a shifter. She knew about the animal form and rapid healing, but he hadn't told her she'd gain mental telepathy if she joined a pack or that she could potentially live for hundreds of years. Was that even possible to become human again? A shifter's animal form was as much a part of them as their heart or brain and living without it was unheard of. But then, Ashlyn hadn't acquired her animal in the usual fashion. For all he knew, her condition was temporary.

This situation was bigger than he could handle alone, but he wasn't comfortable handing her over to the pack or Council as if she was just any shifter. He needed advice, preferably from someone who not only understood shifters but also magic. Digging out his phone, he voice-dialed his brother's house. Adrian answered after the second ring, "Hey, Kepler, how's the new job?"

"Fine, fine. I actually need to talk to Darcy. Is she around?" Kepler's sister-in-law was a witch, much to the distaste of his parents' pack. But after she stood up for Adrian at a wrongful death hearing, Kepler had welcomed her to the family with open arms. He'd never been one to look down on other supernaturals, anyway.

"She's making breakfast for the kiddo," Adrian said. "Let me get her."

After a minute, Darcy said, "Hi, K-kepler." Her stutter had gotten better since he'd first met her, but still came out when she was uncertain. "Is everything all right?"

"Do you know of any spells that can turn a human into a shifter? Or mimic a shifter's ability, even temporarily?"

"Hmm," she took a breath and spoke slowly. "If a witch has a familiar, she can mentally communicate with it and sometimes see through its eyes. Does that count?"

"No, I'm looking for something that actually changes someone into an animal."

"There are legends about skin walkers—witches who can change into animals—but that magic was banned centuries ago along with raising the dead or other types of necromancy."

"But it could be done. Could the witch target someone else with the spell? A human?"

"I'm not sure. I never studied it in detail. What's going on, Kepler?"

He sighed and slowed for an empty school bus that was trundling its way toward the sports center. "Last night a rogue attacked a human. Now she's a shifter."

"Oh my God. That's really bad. Dangerous c-creatures are attracted to skin walker magic, things that have not walked on Earth for millennia. Every time a skin walker shifts, it opens a hellmouth—not one like your Source, where the spirit animals regulate access or the ley lines where the witches keep watch, but a chaotic portal. Uncontrolled. It can give monsters a chance to slip through."

His throat tightened. "Monsters like what?"

"D-demons, for one. Dragons. Djinn."

He laughed uncomfortably, knowing that Ashlyn would probably make a joke about the three evil D's if she heard that list. But this was no laughing matter.

Darcy continued. "If this human is being targeted by a skin walker, every time she shifts, she attracts these creatures. You need to bring the local coven in on this investigation. They might be able to use the new shifter to trace the magic back to its creator. What's the name of the pack leader up there? I'd be happy to make introductions."

"I haven't told the pack." And now that he knew about this spell, he was even more reluctant. Their knee-jerk reaction would be to kill Ashlyn and eliminate any risk that the curse might spread.

"Kepler! Why not?"

"They'll kill her before her new ability can cause any damage or spread to others." His entire body flushed with rage at the thought.

"Oh." Darcy let out a shaky breath. "Well, considering what's at stake—"

"No!" A growl rose up the back of his throat. "You don't understand. She's my mate."

"Oh. Shit."

"Yeah, oh shit." He made a hard right into the empty parking lot in front of the Trooper offices. His captain's Bronco wasn't in its usual spot, so at least he could file his report without needing to make small talk with the human. "Thanks for the advice, Darcy. I need to go."

Cutting the connection before she could say anything else, he parked in front of the station and headed inside.

As he skulked past Regional Director Finch's doorway, a deep voice barked out, "Stone! Where the fuck have you been? Get your ass in here."

Kepler let out a slow breath. He'd hoped to slip by without being noticed, but should've known the grizzly shifter would be lying in wait. The guy treated his office like a den, and Kepler wondered if he ever left his desk.

Stepping inside, Kepler said, "I can explain, sir."

"Well, start talking." The brawny director tapped the surface of his desk with one thick finger. As usual, his dark brown hair looked like he'd been running his hands through it, and his eyes were bloodshot. "Officer Bennett reached out to me from the Kenai P.D. and told me this is a shifter case. Why am I hearing it from him before I hear it from you?"

Closing the door behind him, Kepler clenched his jaw. *Dammit, Cal.* Probably trying to rack up brownie points. "I was detained by another matter. I'll post an official statement that this was a bear mauling."

Finch grunted in discontent. "Why do people always have to blame a bear?"

Kepler shrugged apologetically. "Sorry, sir. This is Alaska and people always assume it was a bear."

"Hmph. And what other matter took precedence over the investigation?" Finch rested his elbows on his desk, fingers steepled. As the Regional Director and the only other shifter in the office, Finch acted as the liaison between law enforcement and shifter leadership.

"A personal issue. I have it under control now." Kepler put a hand on the door to go.

"Wait." The director's voice carried the weight of an Alpha command. Kepler's spine stiffened, and he turned back to Finch to find the man's dark eyes boring into him. "You're acting mighty strange. Anything you want to get off your chest?"

For a moment, Kepler considered telling the director everything, but his wolf wouldn't allow him to speak. Finally, he managed to say, "The dead man fits the description of the other rogues I've been chasing. We might have a new lead, that's all."

"So your absence has nothing to do with the naked woman you helped flee the scene?"

Shit. Cal must've seen her. Kepler pulled out the chair facing Finch's desk and reluctantly took a seat. It had been too much to hope that he could keep Ashlyn a secret, but he still might be able to shield her from the pack. In an even voice, he described how he'd discovered Ashlyn hiding in the dumpster, the obvious victim of an attack. "Her wolf took down the rogue. She was traumatized, as anyone would be, and her animal was feeling protective. I felt that removing her from the scene would help calm her down."

Finch folded his hands on his desk and leaned forward. "So, where is she now?"

Of course Finch already knew she wasn't in pack custody, which was where Kepler should've taken her. "I took her to my house." He swallowed thickly, feeling strange about the next words on his tongue. "She's my mate, sir."

"Goddammit, Stone." Finch's eyes flashed with grizzly rage. "Anything else you want to tell me about this?"

There was only one thing that might excuse his lack of protocol, one thing another shifter would understand. "This was the first time I've met her, sir. I think the mating hormones muddled my thinking." The admission made him seem weak, but he'd do whatever it took to protect Ashlyn. "But I have it under control now."

A flicker of understanding crossed the grizzly shifter's features. "Ah, I see." He unclasped his hands and relaxed back into his desk chair. "What an unfortunate turn of events. You know I'm going to have to relieve you of duty on this investigation. The pack can take over from here."

Kepler's muscles tensed. The pack didn't know Ashlyn, or if they did, they knew her as the human owner of the bakery. How was he going to explain her sudden shifter ability? They were already riled about the rogues. They'd probably exterminate first, investigate later. "This isn't something you can hand over to untrained personnel, sir. I've been chasing this rogue outbreak for years."

Shuffling through some papers on his desk, Finch scribbled on one and thrust it at Kepler. "Believe it or not, Stone, I know what I'm doing. I've worked with the pack on rogue cases before."

"This isn't a normal rogue—"

"Enough." Finch held up a palm to stop Kepler's argument. "I'm relieving you of duty for the next few days. Take the time and get to know your mate. Oh, and report to your Alpha. I'm sure he'll have questions."

Gritting his teeth, Kepler resisted the urge to remind Finch that he hadn't joined the local pack. And he had no intention on stopping his investigation or handing Ashlyn over for questioning. No matter what Director Finch ordered.

With Kepler gone, Ashlyn finished off the cupcakes and went to her bedroom to tidy up. Mr. Mew was hiding, and a pang of loneliness rolled through her. Would her cat ever like her again? The bedside clock said it was just after five in the morning. Normally, she'd be at the bakery already, pulling the first batch of scones from the oven. Luckily, today was Monday, the one day a week they were closed. If she didn't get things resolved by tomorrow, she'd have to call her cousin and let her know they'd be closed an extra day. Not that Lana would care, since she'd be out on her fishing boat, anyway, but she was technically still a partial owner until Ashlyn paid her off.

Ashlyn pulled Kepler's tee shirt up to her nose and breathed deeply. His scent lingered in the fabric, and her wolf found it calming. Was it possible to miss someone you'd just met? She couldn't stop thinking about the way he'd touched her in the shower, so gentle, then so passionate. She hoped he wouldn't take all day to return.

He has responsibilities, Ashlyn, she reminded herself. A job, friends, maybe even a girlfriend...

A growl slipped up her throat, and she swallowed it down. That thought hadn't occurred to her, but a man as sexy as Kepler had to have women throwing themselves at him all the time. The fast-forming intimacy between them felt special to her, unique, but that didn't mean he felt the same way. The rational part of her brain told her he wouldn't have gone to so much trouble for her if he didn't feel the same way. That he'd come back the moment he could. But the wolf inside her was demanding she go out and find him.

And her wolf was strong.

She'd found herself at the door twice before she even realized what she was doing, and now looked down to find she'd donned her coat. *No, wolf, we need to stay inside.* She peeled off her coat and purposefully put it back in the closet. Kepler had said her wolf was an Alpha and that she'd have trouble controlling it. She rolled her shoulders, trying to shrug off the prickly sensation she'd come to associate with the urge to shift. If only she could hear Kepler's voice—but she'd left her phone at the bar with her purse. Not that they'd exchanged numbers. Her wolf paced restlessly inside her. *What if he doesn't come back?*

"Stop acting like a foolish teenager, Ashlyn," she told herself and stomped to the kitchen. Perhaps more food would calm her and her restless wolf. She was staring into the refrigerator thinking about Kepler when the doorbell rang.

Her heart nearly leapt out of her chest. *It's him!* She hurried toward the door.

The bell rang again, and a female voice called, "Ashlyn? Are you in there?"

Muffy? Ashlyn's excitement plummeted into dread. She crept forward and peeked into the peephole. The bride-to-be still wore her party garb, although the tiara was missing, and she held Ashlyn's purse in one hand.

Kepler'd said not to go anywhere, presumably so she wouldn't hurt someone again. Panic sent icy tendrils through Ashlyn's veins, and she shoved down the memory from the alley. *Pretend not to be home.* But she needed her phone and keys.

Outside, Muffy dug into the purse and retrieved Ashlyn's keys. She extended them toward the lock.

Oh, shit, she's coming in! Ashlyn scrambled for the door handle, uncertain if she meant to let her friend in or try to keep her out. But it was too late. The lock clicked, and the door swung open.

"Hello? Ashlyn?"

The door stubbed painfully against Ashlyn's bare toes. She backed out of the way on instinct. No hiding the fact she was home now. She couldn't even go hide under the bed with Mr. Mew.

Muffy's blue eyes filled with relief, and she flung her arms around Ashlyn's neck. "You're okay!"

Ashlyn tentatively patted Muffy's back in return. No urge to rip out her friend's throat, thank God, but she wrinkled her nose at the strange, almost ozone-like scent of Muffy's perfume. She'd never noticed that before. Her wolf was extra sensitive, it seemed.

"Yeah, I'm fine." She pulled away, clearing the raspiness from her throat. "Sorry for ditching like that."

"You went into the alley and never came back." Muffy held out Ashlyn's purse and keys. "They said someone was murdered out there. Did you see what happened?"

Nausea rolled through Ashlyn as she accepted her things. How was she supposed to answer? "I… I talked to a policeman," she started, liking that she was technically speaking truth. "He said not to discuss it with anyone."

Muffy glanced over her shoulder before stepping inside and closing the door. She narrowed her eyes and whispered, "You saw it, didn't you?"

Ashlyn swallowed and crossed her arms over her chest. Why did the air suddenly feel so stuffy? "I can't—"

"It's okay." Muffy took another step forward, bringing the ozone smell with her. "I know it wasn't a bear. It wasn't a natural animal at all. You're not going crazy."

Relief made Ashlyn feel weak in the knees. Even her wolf felt it, giving her a soft whine of curiosity. There was only one way Muffy could know. "Are you a shifter, too?"

"Hell, no." Muffy cringed, nose wrinkling as if she'd caught a whiff of garbage. Then her eyes widened, and she made a strange gesture with her fingertips. "Wait, you're a shifter?"

Now Ashlyn was really confused. How did Muffy know about shifters if she wasn't one, too? "I really shouldn't talk about this."

Muffy frowned. "But I vetted you before the party."

"Vetted me? For what?"

"Witchcraft."

Ashlyn could barely take a full breath. Kepler'd said he thought there might be a witch involved in this. Was

Muffy a witch? More importantly, was she responsible for what had happened? Ashlyn's wolf was remarkably quiet, but alert, as if poised to pounce if Ashlyn called on her. "Are you saying you're a witch? As in, cauldron-stirring, hocus pocus, abracadabra witch?"

Muffy laughed. "I don't know a single witch who says hocus pocus. Or abracadabra, for that matter. Yes, I'm a witch. When I met you at the bakery, I saw a spark of magic in your aura. We were going to ask if you wanted to join our coven."

Ashlyn's mouth fell open. Things were getting even more strange. "You thought *I* was a witch?"

"No, just someone with potential. Some humans don't realize it when they have the gift. We were going to offer to train you. But now this..." Muffy waived a hand to indicate Ashlyn's body.

"Do you know what happened to me?"

Muffy frowned and her gaze slid past Ashlyn to scan the apartment. "Your mate didn't explain things?"

Ashlyn frowned. "My mate?"

"The man who changed you."

The pain of the stranger's bite, his clawed grip on her shoulders, blood filling her own mouth... Ashlyn blinked against the memories. The inside of her mouth seemed too full of teeth, and her skin prickled with the need to shift.

Muffy's eyes narrowed. "You poor thing. You have no idea, do you?"

Ashlyn shook her head, every muscle in her body at war. She spoke between clenched teeth. "That man in the alley bit me, and now I seem to have become a werewolf."

Frowning, Muffy tilted her head. "Did you change right there in the alley, immediately after being bitten?"

Ashlyn nodded.

"That can't be right." Muffy took a step back, and Ashlyn's wolf detected a whiff of fear. "Shifters aren't supposed to have the ability to make new ones so easily. If they did, the entire planet would be overrun by the beasts."

Kepler'd said basically the same thing. Which meant this had to be a spell, like he thought. But she didn't think Muffy'd had anything to do with it. Even Ashlyn's wolf agreed. She took a breath, uncertain how Muffy might take her next question. "Is it possible a witch did this to me? A hex or curse or whatever?"

"That's what I'm afraid of. I need to take you to the coven right away." Muffy opened the door and stepped outside. "Come on."

A sliver of hope took hold in Ashlyn's chest. "Can you make me normal again?"

"Newly turned vampires can be cured within a short time frame, but I don't know about shifters—or whatever it is you've become." Muffy sighed. "We need to take this to my coven leader. The sooner, the better, before the magic becomes permanent."

Ashlyn stared down at the purse she was clutching. Shifters. Witches. Vampires. She wasn't sure how much more she could take. All she wanted to do was go back to her busy days at the bakery and evenings snuggled up with Mr. Mew and a good book. *What about Kepler?* She couldn't let her unexplained feelings for him cloud her judgement. She'd just met him. If they were a good match, he'd like her whether she was a shifter or not. And if there was a cure, Muffy might be her only chance to get it.

"All right." Ashlyn's mouth twisted in a half-hearted smile. "Take me to your leader."

Kepler forced himself to obey the speed limit as he joined the morning traffic on his route back to Ashlyn's apartment. He knew he couldn't handle this investigation alone, but who could he trust? *Cal.* He wasn't part of the pack, and although Kepler wanted to be angry with him, he knew Cal didn't deserve it. The police officer had only been following protocol when he'd sent his report to Finch. Besides, Cal would be able to keep Kepler abreast of the investigation now that Finch had booted him off the case.

He dialed Cal's number, about to hang up when a sleepy voice answered, "Fuck, Stone, what is it? I'm off duty."

"Sorry, but I need your help."

"I handed my report over to the MCU already."

"I know. I just spoke to Finch." Kepler took a steadying breath and explained the situation, including what his sister-in-law had told him about skin walker witchcraft.

"So is she a shifter or not?"

Kepler scowled. That was a decent question. "Fuck if I know."

A long pause filled the air before Cal asked, "Are you sure she's your mate?"

Kepler took a deep breath, trying not to be angry with his friend. "My wolf's not lying." Maybe it'd been a mistake to bring Cal into this. The other shifter wasn't part of the pack, but he did have a duty to protect the shifter community. He might decide to take the skin walker theory to the pack, which would only send them on a witch-hunt—literally. Kepler said, "Listen, if you're not willing to help, that's okay, just keep quiet until I get things worked out. You know how the local pack is. If they believe she's a danger, they'll exterminate her and ask questions later."

"Have you claimed her already?"

"Whether I've claimed her or not doesn't matter. She needs to be protected until we can investigate," Kepler ground out.

"Calm down, man. I'm asking valid questions. Are you certain she's not in on it with the witches or anything?"

That was something he hadn't considered, but the suggestion made him angry. "Jesus, Cal, she was shocked and terrified, not deceitful. Besides, I didn't smell witchcraft."

"Sorry, but I had to ask. We don't know enough about these rogues to rule anything out. For all we know, she's the vector spreading the outbreak. She could be making shifters think she's their mate."

Kepler's blood turned to ice. No, that couldn't be right. What he felt for Ashlyn was real. Gripping the steering wheel hard enough to make his knuckles turn white, he said, "My wolf would know the difference."

Obviously sensing he needed to tread lightly, Cal said softly, "Maybe I should meet her, too. See what my wolf thinks."

Much as Kepler hated to admit it, Cal made a good point. If the other shifter met Ashlyn and felt the same draw Kepler did, then perhaps the mate bond wasn't real after all. The thought of introducing another male to Ashlyn made Kepler's hackles rise, but he gave Cal her address. "Call me when you get here."

"Roger that." Cal hung up.

Kepler pulled up to the curb outside Ashlyn's apartment, jumped out of the Jeep, and loped toward the building, every inch of him burning to see Ashlyn again. To lay claim on her before Cal arrived. *That might be exactly what the witch wants*, he reminded himself. Outside her door, another scent permeated the hallway, one every shifter knew well. Ozone. A witch had been here. Skin crawling, he knocked.

No one answered. *Shit*. He tried the handle, but the door was locked. Glancing around for onlookers, he used his shoulder to force the door open with a loud crack.

Inside, everything looked and smelled the same. No sign of a struggle. He checked the kitchen, noting the empty cupcake wrappers in the garbage, then strode to the bedroom. The bed was now made, and Ashlyn's cat stared at him from where it was curled up on her pillow. Wherever she'd gone, it seemed to have been willingly.

He followed Ashlyn and the witch's scents outside to the street where the trail faded. They must've gotten in a car. To continue tracking, he'd need his wolf's senses, but he risked being seen if he shifted here. Heart thudding against his ribs, Kepler glanced up and down the street.

Headlights approached, and Cal pulled up in his police cruiser. "What's wrong?"

"She's gone. And a witch was here."

Cal's nostrils flared. "Shit."

"Fuck it," Kepler muttered and shimmied out of his shoes and clothes. He was going after her, and he didn't care who saw him.

"I'm with you," Cal said, unsnapping his uniform shirt.

Within moments, Kepler's wolf let out a satisfied howl, breaking the silence of the morning, and started running.

CHAPTER NINE

Ashlyn clutched her dead phone in her lap, wishing she'd thought to leave a note for Kepler. Or anyone, for that matter. Her cousin only checked on her every few days at the bakery. Muffy didn't have a car charger, but offered to let Ashlyn use her phone. Unfortunately, Ashlyn hadn't memorized her cousin's number.

Muffy pulled onto a narrow dirt road plastered with bright yellow leaves. Pale mist muted the red and orange underbrush beneath the gray skeletal tree trunks. "Where are we going, anyway?" Ashlyn asked.

"Our coven leader, Tessa, runs a school out here. The solitude means there's less chance of mortals stumbling onto spell practice." Muffy patted Ashlyn's hand, palm cool against Ashlyn's skin. "She's a nature witch, a really good one. I'm sure she'll know how to help."

After following the road for what seemed like forever, they reached a tall, wrought-iron fence. Muffy entered an access code that made the gate roll aside. It automatically slid closed behind them as they pulled up to a large gray house with white trim. A series of raised garden beds held a few late-season flowers, and the grass paths between them were perfectly mowed and clear of the leaves that carpeted the lane and driveway. Fancy beveled glass panels on the front door glowed with warm yellow light from inside the house. Yesterday, Ashlyn would've thought the place was charming. Today, all she could think about was the witch in *Hansel and Gretel*.

Muffy cut the engine and got out, closing the car door with a solid thud. She hurried up the wide wooden steps toward the front door.

Ashlyn took a few calming breaths. Her wolf was curious rather than hostile, at least for now. Kepler'd warned her it would be hard to control, and meeting another person—another witch—made her nervous.

But she needed answers.

She opened the car door, letting the cool autumn air wash over her.

An older woman in jeans had opened the front door, her long silver hair in a braid over one shoulder. Wearing Xtra-Tuff boots, she reminded Ashlyn of her cousin if Lana was thirty years older. *Only a lot less friendly.* The woman scowled at Muffy and cut a look toward the car as Ashlyn climbed out. Ashlyn caught the tail end of her sentence as she approached. "…here was unwise."

Muffy looked over her shoulder at Ashlyn and signaled her to hurry and join them. "I couldn't leave her there alone. If the shifters discover her, they'll probably kill her on sight."

Ashlyn came to a stiff halt halfway up the steps. Kepler had mentioned a pack, but she'd thought they would only hurt her if she couldn't control her wolf. She stared at the witches a few steps above her, relieved she felt no urge to harm them. "Kill me? Why?"

The older woman studied Ashlyn. "Shifters are little more than animals." Her upper lip curled with what Ashlyn could only consider disdain. "They destroy what they don't understand."

Kepler's handsome face flashed in Ashlyn's mind. He hadn't tried to kill or even hurt her. He said he wanted to protect her. *He's special, though.* Her wolf agreed. When Kepler told her not to leave the house, she'd assumed it was so she didn't hurt anyone else. But what if it was to protect *her* from other shifters?

"Ashlyn, this is Tessa, our coven leader." Muffy grabbed Ashlyn's arm, pulling her the rest of the way up the steps. "Tessa, we have to help her."

Tessa sighed and pulled the door closed behind her. "Fine, let's have a look." She moved past Ashlyn down the stairs. "Bring her to my conservatory."

Muffy nudged her to follow, keeping close behind Ashlyn as they walked the grass path between the garden beds, wisps of mist swirling in their wake. In the backyard, a small greenhouse with crenelated iron ridges and gables sat among late-flowering yellow shrubs. The glass walls were fogged over, masking the interior from view, but the moment Tessa pushed a sliding door aside to let them inside, the smell of warm soil and fresh sap hit Ashlyn. Three rows of potting tables took up the entryway, but then the space opened into what looked like a fairytale.

A huge, smooth-barked tree grew in the center of a circle of stones, and the ground beneath was a carpet of golden, lavender, and blue wildflowers. Tessa crunched over the gravel between the tables and stepped into the circle.

"How does this all fit into the greenhouse?" Ashlyn asked.

Muffy answered, "It's a sanctuary of sorts, a safe place to access strong magical energies. I can't really explain to someone who hasn't studied magic." She nodded in encouragement and nudged Ashlyn forward. "Go on."

Hesitantly, Ashlyn stepped over the stones and onto the wildflower meadow. A breeze caressed her cheek and running water trickled somewhere in the distance. The greenhouse walls faded from view, leaving her surrounded by nothing but meadow as far as she could see. Ashlyn glanced over her shoulder to where she'd left Muffy, but it seemed as if everything on the other side of the circle of stones no longer existed. "Can Muffy still see us?" she asked.

"Yes." Tessa bent and dipped her fingers into a tiny pool of water set among the gnarled roots of the tree. She flicked droplets into the air where they hovered like diamonds. Ashlyn gaped, unsure she was seeing right as Tessa repeated the motion until a sheet of droplets hovered in the air between them.

Amazed, Ashlyn asked, "What are you doing?"

"Casting a scrying spell. I need a closer look at your aura before we try to cure you. Take a deep breath," Tessa commanded. "This won't hurt, but you might find it a little disconcerting."

Muffy'd mentioned looking at her aura when she came into the bakery. Ashlyn inhaled deeply, stiffening as the sheet enveloped her. Although she could still see the meadow clearly, the thin film of water made her feel as if she'd just plunged into a cold ocean current. Her heartbeat pounded in her ears, and pressure buffeted her from all sides, throwing off her equilibrium. In her head, her wolf flailed as if trying to reach the surface.

Tessa green eyes deepened to almost black and her mouth moved, but Ashlyn couldn't hear what she said, only strange pinging and warbling that reminded her of flexing sheets of metal.

A howl rose above the metallic noise, her wolf no longer curious, but terrified.

Ashlyn couldn't exhale. Couldn't inhale. Couldn't move. Between herself and the witch, what felt like a chasm opened into another reality. A landscape of colors and shapes beyond anything that existed on earth. The scent of ash drifted from the breach, and a coldness reached for her, sharp as glass. Her mouth gaped to echo her wolf's cry.

Then the water that bound her evaporated. She collapsed to the ground, every muscle shaking as she tried to process what happened. Directly beneath her paws, the carpet of wildflowers had been rendered to blackened ash. Above her head, she heard voices, but they made little sense. *Unstable. Shifter. Hellmouth.*

Every instinct Ashlyn's wolf possessed knew that chasm had held death. Worse than death. Damnation. She had to get away. The pinging and warbling she'd heard lingered at the back of her mind, no longer the sounds of sheet metal, but more like an approaching storm. She couldn't get it out of her head.

Then somewhere in the distance, a wolf howled. The sound struck a chord deep in her chest. Steadied her. Brought her paws back to Earth. *Kepler.*

Lifting her muzzle, she let loose a cry that made the tree's leaves shiver overhead. Her wolf was in control. Her wolf would protect her. Her wolf would take her back to Kepler.

She lunged from the circle, the foggy greenhouse walls re-materializing around her. Without slowing, she crashed through the greenhouse siding. Glass penetrated her thick fur, cut fiery lines into her flanks, but she kept going.

Kepler, I'm coming.

Kepler and Cal stuck to the trees when possible, the afternoon fog helping them stay out of sight of traffic until the trail left the highway. Panting, Kepler turned onto a narrow, leaf covered lane. Ashlyn's scent had almost disappeared as the overpowering ozone smell of witchcraft grew stronger. There was more than one witch involved.

This is coven territory, Cal's voice flooded his head.

Kepler almost stumbled. Only mates or pack members could communicate while shifted. Kepler sent back, *You talking to me?*

Been listening to you count witches for the last ten minutes.

Kepler had experienced whispers of his Alpha power like this before, an inkling of what leading a pack might be like. He'd always pulled away and shielded himself, wanting to avoid any such ties so he could focus on his career. Now he was grateful for backup. *We may have a fight on our hands.*

Bring 'em on, Cal growled, never breaking his stride. His russet coat blended well with the dark autumn foliage, unlike Kepler's own pale gray. *Fucking witches.*

Ahead, a tall wrought-iron fence loomed from the mist surrounding the damp gray tree trunks, forming a palisade of spears. The carpet of leaves under Kepler's paws cushioned his footsteps as he approached the gate. Magic radiated off the barrier, a ward he was certain would be painful or maybe even kill him if he tried to leap over.

He sat on his haunches and growled.

What do we do now? Cal asked.

My mate's in there. Kepler shifted to his human form and took a step toward the entrance. "Guess I'm going to knock."

You're naked, man, Cal said, remaining in wolf form as he moved to block Kepler's path. *They aren't going to let you in.*

Kepler couldn't care less that he was naked. All that mattered was getting to Ashlyn, or at least stopping whatever the witches were planning to do to her. For the first time, Kepler regretted not being part of a pack.

Not having immediate access to backup. "Go for help. I'll try to stall whatever the witches have planned for Ashlyn until you get back."

Without waiting to see if Cal complied, Kepler approached a keypad near the gate. Beyond the fence, running footsteps caught his attention as a big, amber-ruffed wolf appeared from the mist. *Ashlyn!* She was safe and alive. The wolf raced toward the gate with determination in her gaze. Kepler guessed her intent a moment before her body coiled to spring, his stomach flipping in alarm. "Ashlyn, no! It's warded!"

She cleared the fence in a graceful leap, but at the apex, her body convulsed in a shower of sparks. Her fur dissolved, and her limbs lengthened. She hit the ground in human form, sliding to a stop on her side against the wet leaves.

Kepler rushed over. "Ashlyn!"

She lay in a fetal position with her eyes closed, sides heaving and pink and blue hair tangled with leaves and twigs. Long scratches along her ribs seeped blood. He reached for her, furious the witches had hurt her. Her eyes flashed, and she bared her teeth, struggling to sit upright.

It took him half a second to realize her gaze wasn't on him. It was on Cal.

He spun to find the russet wolf with his paws braced wide, lips pulled back from his canines in a ferocious growl. The dark guard hairs on his ruff stood on end.

Kepler held both palms up. "Cal, it's okay. This is Ashlyn."

No words of response entered Kepler's head, only a snarl and a snap of teeth.

At least this answered the question about whether Kepler's mating instinct was unique to him or not—Cal obviously felt no attraction to Ashlyn at all. Holding one palm up at the wolf, Kepler moved forward, infusing his voice with Alpha power. "Stand down, Cal."

Cal's yellow eyes flashed. Then, in a flurry of copper sparks, he shifted back to human form. He thrust a finger toward Ashlyn. "She's not a shifter."

"What're you talking about? You just saw her wolf, Cal."

"Can't you smell it?" Cal whispered roughly. "She's wrong, Kepler. All wrong."

Kepler turned back to Ashlyn. She sat with her back against a tree, both arms wrapped around her knees. The ozone scent was strong on her, as well as her amazing natural wildflower honey scent, but laced beneath was something more primal and raw. Blood. Wet leaves. An odor like burning coal. What spell smelled like that? He didn't know enough about witches to guess. "That's just the witches you're smelling, Cal. It will fade."

Somewhere on the other side of the fence, a car engine rumbled to life. A woman's voice floated through the fog, "Call everyone. We have to find her."

"Let's get out of here," Kepler whispered, taking Ashlyn by the elbow. "Can you walk?"

Although the cuts on her side had already begun to heal, Ashlyn blinked at him as if he spoke a foreign language.

Letting out a worried breath, he lifted her. She looped her arms around his neck as he carried her into the woods.

Cal followed sullenly behind, pushing through the undergrowth. After they'd put some distance between them and the fence, Cal asked, "Isn't that the woman from the bakery?"

"Yes."

"She's… something's not right. Not normal. We need to tell the pack. Hell, we need to bring the whole Council in on this one."

Kepler grit his teeth. "Not until I know they won't hurt her."

"What if she hurts you?"

Kepler rounded on him. "Does she look capable of hurting anyone right now?"

Cal stopped, concern darkening his freckled face. "You're under her spell."

"She's not a witch."

"She's also not a shifter."

"Fuck you, Cal. She's my mate."

"You haven't claimed her."

Kepler's teeth lengthened, pressing against his lips until his words slurred. "I'll claim her right here and now if that's what you need to prove she deserves protection."

"I'm not saying we shouldn't protect her. I'm saying we can't do it alone." Cal took a step back, his eyes flashing copper. "I'm going to tell the pack." In an explosion of sparks, he shifted and disappeared into the fog before Kepler could say another word.

Exhaling a long white plume of air, Kepler continued hurrying the opposite direction. A part of him knew Cal was right. They needed help. The strange smell on Ashlyn wasn't fading, and he knew in his heart what that meant. *She's been cursed.* But with what?

Ashlyn's arms tightened around his neck. "What's claiming?"

Kepler stopped walking, realizing he and Cal had been speaking about her as if she wasn't there. "This wasn't how I wanted to have this conversation."

"You said I'm your mate." Her voice had a sexy rasp to it that made his balls ache.

Looking into her eyes, he was glad to see the glazed look had gone away. She was so beautiful, amber cheeks flushed and lips slightly pursed. They were far enough from the witches' compound to take a breather, so he set her gently on her feet, keeping a hand at her waist to make sure she stayed upright before speaking.

"Every shifter has a perfect mate somewhere in the world," he said. "When we meet him or her, our wolf knows. It's fate. We can choose to accept the bond or reject it, but our wolves will always desire each other."

She stood motionless for several heartbeats, the forest's silence like a held breath. Finally, she asked, "Is that what I'm feeling?"

Relief flooded through him. *She feels it, too.* He wanted to pull her close and kiss her, to run his hands through her hair and breathe in her honey scent. "Yes. We're mates."

Her eyes flashed blue, and he knew her wolf was giving approval. Hex or not, her wolf was real. Their connection was real. He lowered his lips to hers. She responded by putting both hands around his neck and kissing him back.

After a lingering moment, she broke the kiss to look at him again. "The witches were going to try to remove the curse, but I don't want to anymore. Especially if it would send my wolf to that place."

He frowned and pulled her hands from his neck so he could step back and look at her, still holding her wrists. "What place?"

"The coven leader was investigating my aura. But the spell she cast…" Ashlyn shuddered and hugged her arms around herself. "I swear, she opened a portal to hell, all roiling color and chaos. They even called it a hellmouth. My wolf didn't like the magic. *I* didn't like the magic. I shifted, and we ran."

"A hellmouth." The pit of his stomach felt like he'd just taken a bullet. His sister-in-law had used that word over the phone.

He dragged in a breath, sensing Ashlyn's wolf along with the slightly off scent he and Cal had argued about. *It must be the lingering scent of the hellmouth.* The Source was in essence a hellmouth, too, a portal that allowed shifter animals to find their hosts. He'd never been there, but her description resembled the stories he'd heard.

Taking her hand, he continued walking between the trees. "Remember I told you about the glacier, the Source for shifter magic?"

She nodded.

"Normally, a shifter who finds a human mate takes the human there to discover the new shifter's animal. But when we first met, I was too clueless to recognize you as my mate." He ran a hand through his hair, thinking about his first visit to her bakery. The shop had been busy, and the scent of baked goods so pervasive, he'd obviously missed her. But her wolf had recognized him. "I think your wolf was impatient. And we know she's a strong Alpha. I'm guessing she found another way to you."

Ashlyn pulled her hand free from his. "But the rogue… are you saying my wolf caused that shifter to get sick?"

Pausing at the lip of a shallow ravine, he shook his head. "The shifter outbreak started before we met. Your wolf just took advantage of an opening." He jumped down and held out a hand to Ashlyn. She took it and leaped down beside him. As they followed the gully, he described what Darcy had told him. "The magic is forbidden by the covens because it opens a hellmouth, a portal that can allow demons and other monsters through. In your case, it let your wolf through."

She halted and covered her mouth, eyes going wide. "Cal said I'm not a real shifter. Does that mean my wolf is a demon?"

Kepler cupped her face between both palms and looked into her eyes. "You're my mate and your wolf is real, no matter how you got her."

"But am I a real shifter?"

"You're going to discover that not all supernaturals get along. Shifters, witches, vampires—they all look down on each other. It's like racism among humans. To me, it doesn't matter. You're my mate and that's all that's important." He kissed her lightly and once more took her hand to keep walking.

She was silent for a short while before she said, "Would going to the Source make me a real shifter?"

"If you already have a shifter form, drinking from the Source will swap your animal out. You'd lose your wolf and end up with a moose or something." He shook his head, thinking about recent rumors about exactly that happening to a shifter up north.

Ashlyn giggled, then quickly sobered again. "Don't make me laugh. This is serious. The witches said I was unstable."

Unstable. How many times had he been called that in his youth? His mom used to joke about how he and his brother Adrian would never find a mate to calm them down. His heart thudded against his ribcage as he realized there was another way to stabilize a shifter's animal. The mating claim. Many shifters discovered a calmer version of themselves after claiming a mate. What if that was all Ashlyn needed?

He stopped next to a fallen tree and faced her. As they'd been walking, the mist had cleared, and a flock of wild geese flew in a V overhead, their honking barely audible in the brilliant blue sky. Sunlight made the golden leaves carpeting the ground look like something out of a painting. He pushed an errant strand of pink hair behind her ear. "We could try completing the mate bond. It might stabilize your wolf."

She stepped closer and ran both palms up his chest to once more circle his neck. "If claiming involves what I think it does, then what are we waiting for?"

He restrained himself, taking one more deep look into her eyes. "I want to make sure you understand. A claim means we're bonded for life. We'll be able to hear each other's thoughts, feel each other's emotions. As a shifter, you're going to live longer—hundreds of years, maybe. With me. You'll never be able to be with anyone but me."

She leaned into him. "And you with me?"

He nodded, the desire to taste her lips making it difficult to breathe.

She lifted her chin, bringing her mouth close enough he could feel her whispered words on his skin. "Then I'm yours."

CHAPTER ELEVEN

The witch sat in her rental car and gripped the steering wheel with both hands, refusing to look at the empty bottle strapped in the passenger seat. Well, not empty, exactly. Below the edge of her sunglasses, she could see a hint of swirling lavender light within the brown glass.

"I can fix this," she said out loud, uncertain how she was going to make that happen as she stared at the big gray house ahead.

She wasn't part of this coven, hadn't had to answer the summons. In fact, she'd be in grave danger if anyone suspected her of being in league with the agathion. But the coven had somehow caught wind about the shifter she was after. She had to find out what they knew and reach the shifter first. Her familiar's life depended on it.

She parked next to a beat-up Subaru under the boughs of an old spruce tree and threw a reusable grocery bag over the growler. She could no longer dismiss the agathion like she used to, which worried her. He was getting stronger, even though she had yet to secure him an appropriate host. She locked the bottle in the car and turned toward the house.

The sun had crossed the sky and brushed the tips of the barren trees, setting the yard aglow with orange light. The air whispered to her of witches who'd recently passed through here. Now that the coven knew someone was casting death spells, they were duty-bound to purge the world of forbidden magic.

"Would help if I had Hamilton to help me," she muttered under her breath, longing for her familiar.

At the base of the steps, the breeze whispered something new. Something foreign. *The agathion's shifter?* Could the coven have captured it already?

Veering between the flower beds, she skirted the house until she reached a greenhouse. No surprise, it radiated magic. One of the panes had been shattered, leaving shards of broken glass scattered across the grass. No shifter here, but something had definitely happened.

A glance over her shoulder assured her no one was watching from the house's windows before she moved toward the wreckage. She lifted her sunglasses, squinting at the ground. Several glass shards were discolored with blood. *The shifter's?* The only reason she needed to find the shifter was to get a physical sample for the hex—blood, hair, skin, anything would do. This blood was already on glass, the perfect conduit for the agathion's power. Maybe things were finally going her way.

Maybe this could all be over soon, and Hamilton would be free.

Carefully plucking several shards from the grass, she wrapped tissue around them and placed them in her purse. Now to find a safe place to cast—

"Jen, you made it!"

Her heart nearly leapt out of her body at the sound of her name. She turned to find Muffy striding toward her from the house, lines of distress creasing her brow. Her sister grabbed her hand, tugging her toward the back door. "Thanks for agreeing to help. Come inside. Tessa has a plan."

A twinge of guilt soured Jen's stomach. Her sweet, unsuspecting sister had invited her to Alaska, hoping she'd like the coven enough to join. But everything Jen touched seemed to go to shit. She had no intention of poisoning the coven her sister had grown to love.

But she couldn't let the coven suspect she was behind the hexing. She'd just have to play along until she could break free and cast her final hex. Softening her face into a smile, she followed Muffy inside.

CHAPTER TWELVE

Ashlyn let out a slow breath, staring into Kepler's eyes. The golden glow there spoke to her wolf. His nearness ignited her passion. He was huge, strong, and *naked*, skin warm in the autumn chill. Her thighs quivered in response. *Fated mates*. Could a modern day relationship be built on something out of a fairytale?

Kepler seemed to think so. She loved how easy it was to lose herself in him. To trust that everything was going to be okay. He pulled her tight against him and secured his mouth against hers, tongue demanding entrance as if they'd kissed a million times.

She pressed herself against him as they kissed. She knew almost nothing about his life outside of the time they'd spent together, yet the emotion she felt was real and strong and pure. Forever with Kepler would be nothing shy of heaven. She wanted him more than she'd wanted anything in her life. It had been a whirlwind, but she couldn't believe how incredible it felt to love him. *I love him.*

"Claim me," she said.

Kepler's arms tightened around her, and he growled deep and low. He rolled his hips, letting her feel the hard length of his erection pinned between them. One of his hands slid over her naked ass and into the space between her thighs, fingers dipping into her waiting wetness. She gasped, arching her back to open herself up for his exploration. He delved between her folds, slipping along her lower lips with teasing slowness.

More accustomed to her wolf now, Ashlyn reveled in their heightened senses. Her wolf made her bold, more sure of herself. Releasing one hand from her grip around his shoulders, she slid her palm between them to find his shaft. Thick, rock-hard heat met her hand, and she wrapped her fingers around it, stroking upward.

His touch on her backside drew away, but before she could protest, he lowered her into a hollow of dry leaves beneath the roots of a fallen tree. The earth smelled raw, primal, matching the feelings growing inside her. This was so right, this moment with Kepler. *All things will be made right.* She had no idea if that was her wolf's thought or her own, but didn't have time to dwell on it.

Kepler knelt between her legs and dragged her ankles up over his shoulders. Her stomach dipped as she realized his intention. His tongue parted her slit, meeting her core in an explosion of sensation that made her gasp. He circled her opening once, then sucked gently on her sensitive nub.

She bucked upward with a moan. Her entire being wanted this, wanted him. His tongue flicked against her, making her body surge with pleasure. He worked her clit while she threaded her hands into his hair, rocking against his mouth. The pressure inside her expanded, racing down her thighs, tingling in her nipples. Her legs trembled, and she gripped handfuls of his hair as she climbed toward climax.

He plunged his tongue into her opening, throwing her over the edge into ecstasy. She screamed his name as he kept thrusting his tongue, thumb against her clit, extending her orgasm until she could no longer breathe.

When her muscles could take no more, he eased, letting her sink into bonelessness against the cushion of leaves. Her racing heart and ragged breathing made the world spin, and she closed her eyes. "Kepler, that was…" she couldn't finish between gulps of air.

He planted small kisses against her inner thigh, moving upward over her belly to her breasts. "You are," he nipped one nipple, sending an aftershock rolling through her, "the most beautiful," he nipped the other nipple, "woman on the planet."

She curled her fingers into his hair again, shuddering as he continued teasing each nipple, intensifying her aftershocks. Her core ached, tired yet yearning to be filled.

Wrapping her legs around his hips, she said, "I want you inside me."

Kepler moved to her mouth, kissing her deeply. The head of his cock was ready, pulsing at her entrance. He pushed into her slowly, surely, his eyes never leaving hers. She never wanted this moment to end. She tightened her quivering muscles around him.

He groaned, "You're so tight. So hot."

She lifted her hips, seating him fully inside her, feeling the pressure of him deep in her belly. He let out a shuddering breath, each of them still for a long moment, lost in each other's eyes. Lost in each other's bodies. God, she loved the way he covered her, as if he owned her. He pulled back slowly, beginning a rhythm. Increasing his tempo, he gripped the back of her neck, fire in his eyes.

She clutched his back, rising to meet his thrusts as he drove into her. When he plunged his tongue into her mouth, her teeth felt too sharp, but he didn't seem to notice. She opened wide, tangling her tongue with his, tasting him as she'd never tasted any man before. *Mine,* her wolf growled. The urge to bite him, to taste him, was growing inside her in a way she found both unsettling and exciting.

He continued kissing her, a form of claiming all its own, until the first tightening of her inner walls made her dig her nails into his back in anticipation.

Then his teeth were against her shoulder. Both her orgasm and the fire of his claim shot through her as a single sensation. She howled in pleasure, shudders coursing through her body before she clamped her mouth onto his shoulder in return. As her teeth sank into his smooth, hard flesh, he growled, thrusting hard and filling her with pulsing heat.

Locked together, they slowly relaxed, him still on top of her as she went limp against the cushion of leaves.

Kepler feathered his lips against her jaw. "Mine."

She smiled. "Mine."

His warmth felt like a protective shield. Then she felt a caress in her mind that was so full of tenderness, she wanted to cry. Kepler's silent voice sounded exactly like his regular one. *Ashlyn, can you hear me?*

I can! She'd never imagined being this close to another person, and it felt amazing. *The claiming worked!*

His arms around her tightened. *It did.* Pure joy infused his words. *We are bound. How's your wolf?*

She looked inside. Her wolf was all relaxed and melty inside her. *I don't know if she's stable or not, but she's certainly content.* She ran her fingertips along his jawline and smiled at the warm glow in his eyes. *Do my eyes glow like yours?*

He nodded. *Yes, but yours are glacier blue.*

Can humans see it? Or only other shifters?

Humans can see it, but most of them think it's a trick of the light. Even so, you should be careful using your wolf's senses in public.

She nodded, then asked out loud, "If we're both shifters, does it mean our kids will be puppies?"

He chuckled. "Don't worry. Shifter kids don't experience their first change until puberty."

She grinned back, loving that he appreciated her humor. "What do we do next?"

He kissed her gently, then rose. Shadows were taking over the forest as the sun began to set. "We should've picked a better place and time for this. There are witches after you, and Cal could return with the pack at any moment."

The cool air gave her goosebumps as she climbed to her feet, worry taking over where contentment had been. "Can we outrun them?"

He shook his head. "Not forever." The glow in his eyes brightened as he looked at her. "I was hesitant to introduce you to the pack, but I think it's safe, now. As my mate, you're protected. They can no longer kill you as an outsider. I just need to introduce you and we can explain what happened."

Ashlyn glanced down at her nakedness. "I'm a bit underdressed for a meeting."

Kepler grinned. "How about we wear fur?"

Her wolf wriggled, excited to come out and run alongside Kepler's animal. But Ashlyn's chest felt tight. She was still uncertain. "You think that's the best way?"

"I want them to see, smell, and hear your wolf. None of this questioning what you are bullshit, regardless of how you came to be. Plus, we can travel faster as wolves."

At least out here in the woods, she wasn't likely to attack someone's pet. And she had to learn to let her wolf out or they'd both go crazy. She nodded and took a deep breath. "Let me shift first, in case I have trouble."

"Go ahead." He nodded in encouragement, his eyes bright as stars. "I can't wait to run with you."

Closing her eyes, she let down the barriers she'd erected to contain her wolf. The animal swelled within her, a prickle of magic racing along Ashlyn's skin. This was so amazing, so exciting. She couldn't wait to see the world as her wolf again.

The scent of ash enveloped her, followed by a sudden headache. Her wolf no longer pressed at her awareness. Ashlyn scrunched her lids harder. *Wolf?* The image of her animal in shackles came to her, pale fur lit by abrasive, shifting colors.

Then a laugh like a roll of thunder filled her head.

CHAPTER THIRTEEN

Kepler watched Ashlyn's forehead crease in concentration and told himself to be patient. She'd done an amazing job containing the Alpha wolf inside her, but releasing it, embracing it, was new to her. It might take more effort.

Another minute passed. He frowned. "Ashlyn, is everything okay?"

Her eyes popped open, flashing purple light before settling to normal, human blue. "I'm fine."

Purple? He frowned. "What's wrong?"

"Nothing," her voice emerged husky, like it wasn't her own. "But my wolf doesn't want to shift right now. She wants us to talk."

He looked into her eyes, trying to understand her abrupt change of behavior. *We can talk in wolf form.*

Kepler? Help! Ashlyn's voice sounded far away.

He shook his head. *Ashlyn? What's going on?*

I don't know. I don't know where I am. The panic in her voice made his pulse race.

He pulled in a breath, staring at what appeared to be his mate smiling at him. The corrosive stink like burning coal had returned in force. He didn't know much about the creatures Darcy'd said might come through the hellmouth, but he knew this wasn't Ashlyn. She was possessed. Was it a demon? He'd have to play along until he came up with a plan or Ashlyn regained control.

The thing looked downward as if realizing it was naked. "Let's get accustomed to each other's human forms first."

In his head, he urged the real Ashlyn to take back control while out loud he said, "Of course. Why don't we find some clothes?"

"It *is* a bit chilly out here." Seemingly unaware Ashlyn was in communication with him, the demon stepped forward and placed a palm flat against his chest. Its veins seemed to glow through its skin with a faint, purplish light. "But you have a way of warming me up."

Trying not to gape, he covered its hand with his own. "I, um, need a little recovery time first."

The demon must've detected his distaste. Its eyes flashed purple again and narrowed. "You're smarter than I expected, especially for a beast."

Kepler bared his teeth and took a firm grip on the creature's elbow. "What the fuck are you and where's my mate?"

"I'm your new master." A smile twisted not-Ashlyn's mouth. "You should be honored to be my consort."

A consort? That must be why the thing hadn't yet run away or tried to kill him. It must need him for some reason. He shook his head and gripped its elbow harder, which seemed to excite the demon because it rubbed Ashlyn's nipples against his arm. "I am delighted by this body's response to you."

Her body shuddered and, with a force that caught him off guard, ripped away from his grip. Hands balled into fists, Ashlyn pressed them against her temples. "Keep your hands off my mate."

Anger roiled through Ashlyn. How dare that thing possessing her body touch her mate with such familiarity! With fury fueling her, she screamed her protest, resuming control of her senses. The pain of twigs and stones dug into her knees. Then what felt like an electric jolt stole her breath and she lost sensation again.

Ashlyn strained against the pressure that had squeezed her into a remote corner of her own consciousness. *How can I be kicked out of my own body?* Her wolf had shoved her aside the few times the beast had taken control, but not like this. She had no hold on her limbs or voice, and her view of Kepler was small and fuzzy.

The sound of his words came to her through a muted roar, as if she was hearing it from behind a waterfall. "Ashlyn, are you in there? Use your wolf! Fight! Push the demon out!"

A demon? Weren't demons supposed to need an invitation? Or was that vampires? She couldn't remember. Straining against the pressure holding her, she shouted, *Get out!*

A voice responded to her, tone full of disdain. *I am no mere demon. Your kind call me an agathion. It is pointless to fight, so stop struggling. We will have a lot more fun if you cooperate.*

She had to make this thing leave. Where was her wolf? Changing tactics, she searched for her animal, but the demon possessing her had transplanted it. *What did you do to my wolf?*

The demon didn't answer. Instead, it seemed to be occupied fending off Kepler's attempt to tackle her. Through her fuzzy view, she watched her body raise both hands and send twin arcs of lightning against Kepler's chest.

He flew backward, landing on his back on the forest floor where he lay unmoving against the crushed branches.

Was he dead? Panic surged through her, and she flexed, straining against the agathion's hold on her.

Her body advanced on Kepler. "I'd hoped to savor my first soul slowly, but perhaps a full meal is a better way to begin my sojourn on Earth."

Ashlyn didn't know what that meant, but it sounded bad. *Kepler, wake up!*

The agathion straddled her mate's body, splaying both hands against Kepler's chest. A trickle of pleasure washed into Ashlyn, not her own, but the agathion's as Kepler's perfect, golden energy flowed into it. "This male's life force is strong." The voice had become giddy. "Such ambrosia."

Kepler was defenseless. She had to do something. With a great burst of effort, she broke through the containment. Regained control. Stared down into her mate's shocked face.

He bared his teeth and golden sparks filled the air as Kepler's huge gray timber wolf materialized beneath her. Thrashing, he bucked her off, sending her sprawling on the forest floor.

In her head, the thunderous voice shouted, *Enough!* and a flash of purple light blinded her. Kepler and the world around her disappeared into a roiling mass of colors and shapes.

An angular face the size of a bus loomed above her, reminding her of the *Wizard of Oz*. But her sense of humor fizzled as the agathion spoke, revealing wickedly angular teeth. "I suggest you settle down and be quiet." Its lavender eyes flashed like sheet lightning. "You wouldn't want to alert the others to your presence."

The way it said *others* made her shudder. She glanced around, still unable to make sense of her surroundings. "What others? Where am I?"

"Stupid human. So unaware. So helplessly bound to your own mundane plane of existence." The face loomed closer, kicking up a gust that smelled like singed hair. "Let's just say you don't want the beings passing through that realm taking an interest in a stranded mortal soul."

Ashlyn shrank back, trying to make the billowing colors around her solidify into recognizable objects or spaces. She felt like a kite being tossed in the wind, vertigo making her dizzy. Strange pinging and warbling noises surrounded her that seemed to have no source. The only stable thing she had was the thread connecting her to Kepler. *Kepler, are you all right?*

She could feel his confusion as he answered, *I got away. What is going on?*

That thing's called an agathion. It tried to eat your soul. Ashlyn's throat felt tight. *I can't beat it. It kicked me out of my own body.*

I'm going for help.

Ashlyn knew what needed to happen. The monster controlling her body had to be killed. *She* had to be killed. *You have to kill me before I hurt anyone else.*

No, the witches did this to you. They might know what to do.

There's no time. This monster can't be allowed to reach the town.

She could feel his angst through their connection, as she was certain he could feel hers. They'd just found each other, just discovered forever, and their chance at a future was being ripped away. But there was no other option. *Promise me, Kepler.*

After a brief pause, he said, *I promise I won't let you hurt any more people.*

That was all she could ask for. Closing her eyes, she thought about her wolf. Had the agathion killed her? She remembered seeing the animal in shackles, so maybe it was still alive. *Wolf, where are you?*

A mournful howl floated above the other strange sounds. Off balance, she tried to move toward it. If she focused on thoughts of her wolf, her surroundings seemed a little more solid. The ground became what felt like rough stone, but the world—realm, the agathion had called it—made little sense to her. All of her senses seemed jumbled, what should be something she saw coming across as a taste or smell, and her sense of touch would sometimes translate as a color or sound. At least she hadn't encountered any other monsters.

Yet.

She pushed through what felt like yellow foam and paused at what looked like a vibrating tightrope over what could've been a river of magma. Her wolf called to her from the other side. Touching the tightrope with her toes, she was filled by the flavor of chocolate. *What the hell.* She felt like she was playing a child's board game gone horribly wrong.

Crossing over with more ease than expected, she was stopped by a bouncing green orb. Watching it made her eyes cross, so she closed them and kept going. Then the scent of anise brushed by her. She felt it pause and reverse direction toward her again. Something about it made her blood run cold, as if she'd gained the attention of something. Her wolf howled again, a snarling, protective sound, and she started to run.

Behind her, she could feel the anise scent approaching. *Shit shit shit. What is it?*

Ahead, a periwinkle sliver of light held steady amidst the rest of the shifting landscape. Her wolf's howl was coming from in there, calling her. She dove for it, the brush of anise at her heels, and everything went dark.

For a moment, she lay very still, unsure what had happened. *Am I still alive?*

A soft whine reached her, and she lifted her head to find a pair of glowing blue eyes watching her in the darkness.

"Wolf!" Ashlyn's voice echoed back at her, as if she was inside a vast cavern. She crawled forward over hard, rocky ground. "You're all right."

A long pink tongue met her cheek.

Hope warmed in Ashlyn's chest. Perhaps together they'd be strong enough to force the agathion from her body. Assuming Kepler hadn't killed her yet. Certainly she'd feel something when and if he did? She had to assume her body was still alive until then.

Wrapping her arms around the wolf's furry neck, she hugged her tightly. "I'm glad you're alive. Ready to help me fight a monster?"

Her wolf nuzzled her ear and whined softly.

Ashlyn ran her hands over what felt like a solid ring forged in one piece around the wolf's throat. It was connected by a thick chain bolted to the cave's wall. The only light in the cavern seemed to come from her wolf's eyes, but she saw what might be a keyhole embedded in a metal plate where the chain connected to the wall.

Remembering how Kepler had picked the lock to her front door, she reached out to him. *Kepler, can you hear me?*

He didn't answer. Her nausea returned, not vertigo this time, but dread. Had the agathion got him? Maybe it was just the cave blocking reception. She scanned their surroundings, hoping to see a door. A key. A magic button that said 'eject.' Anything.

But the surrounding blackness seemed absolute.

The wolf bent and lifted something in its jaws, depositing it in Ashlyn's lap. The thing moved.

Ashlyn recoiled, ready to shove it off, but a protective sensation washed through her from her wolf. In the dim glow from her wolf's eyes, a mangy, one-eyed ferret stared up at her. The tiny creature cowered in her lap as if expecting a blow.

"Oh, you poor thing," said Ashlyn. "Are you trapped here, too?"

The ferret nodded.

Ashlyn hadn't expected the creature to answer, but then her wolf wasn't an ordinary wolf, so she shouldn't be surprised. "Are you a shifter animal?"

The ferret shook its head no.

"Do you know the way out?"

The creature jerked its head to the right in a purposeful way, as if telling her to look over there. Then it hopped off her lap and scratched her thigh with its front feet.

Fingers buried in her wolf's ruff, Ashlyn said, "I think it wants me to go with it."

Her wolf nudged her shoulder.

Stomach churning, she rose. The ferret ran a few steps away, all but disappearing in the darkness before it turned to face her, single eye glittering like a dim star.

Ashlyn followed the ferret's hunched gait, walking carefully over the uneven stone. She had no idea how the thing knew where it was going, but it stayed only a few paces away, turning to face her every few steps. Ahead, what looked like a glowing orange circle grew brighter, eventually clarifying into what looked like a group of knee-high mushrooms.

The ferret stopped at the outer edge and stood on its hind legs, peering over the caps.

Something about the circle made her head spin. "Curiouser and curiouser. What is it? A fairy circle?"

The ferret scurried around the circumference, coming to stop at her other side. It once more stood on its hind legs to peer into the middle.

"You want me to go in there?" The idea made Ashlyn want to vomit.

The ferret scratched the top of her foot like it had her thigh.

"I guess that means yes." Sighing, Ashlyn looked over her shoulder. She could no longer see her wolf, but she could feel her comforting presence. Stepping into the circle of mushrooms might very well send Ashlyn to yet another place. What if she couldn't get back?

The ferret scratched at her foot again.

Bending, Ashlyn picked the creature up. Its fur was softer than she'd expected, its body light and bony. It squeaked as if in pain. She hadn't been rough, but adjusted her grip. "I'm not going to hurt you, but I need you to come with me."

The ferret lowered its head in what might have been resignation.

Steeling herself, Ashlyn lifted a foot and stepped into the circle.

CHAPTER FOURTEEN

No way in hell would Kepler let Ashlyn die. A witch had caused this, and a witch was going to fix it. He'd accept nothing less. He dodged trees and leaped over brush, heading straight toward the coven's gate. *Ashlyn, what's your witch friend's name?*

She didn't answer.

He slowed, searching for their mental bond. But there was nothing. Dread settled into his gut. Darcy's warning about monsters hovering around the hellmouth returned to haunt him. Ashlyn was alone on the other side. He glanced in the direction he'd come from, realizing he'd also abandoned her body to a monster. An agathion, she'd called it. *It was leave her or kill her.* He prayed the witches knew what an agathion was. Raising his muzzle, he howled in frustration but continued onward.

Despite his natural healing power, his chest still burned where the demon had touched him. He'd never felt as close to death as in that moment. If his wolf hadn't taken over, he was certain he'd be dead right now. No one the agathion came in contact with stood a chance. More was at stake than the life of his mate.

He reached the wrought-iron fence and skirted it toward the gated driveway, praying the witches had a way to exorcize the thing without hurting Ashlyn. *I should've let Darcy introduce me to the coven.* He hadn't met the local witches and had no idea if they were friendly to shifters or not. Ashlyn seemed to think they wanted to help, but he'd feel better if he had backup.

Cal, can you hear me? Desperate, he searched for the connection they'd shared earlier. *I need your help.*

Relief flooded him when Cal answered, *Glad you've come to your senses. What happened?*

Ashlyn tried to shift, but something went wrong. I think a demon came through instead of her wolf.

Fuck, man. Okay. Finch and I are almost there.

The last person Kepler expected Cal to rally was the grizzly shifter. *What about the pack?*

I thought about what you said, and you're right. We need level heads here. Plus, I'm following chain of command. Which actually meant he wanted to show off for the

Regional Director. But before Kepler could comment, Cal's voice grew more serious. *What the hell is that stench?*

Shit. Kepler suddenly realized Cal was probably backtracking his trail, which put him on a collision course with the demon. *Stop. It's the demon. Don't go back to where you left me and Ashlyn. Come to the coven house.*

The witches? Aren't they the ones who started all this?

I don't think it was these witches. But I'm hoping they have a way to get rid of the demon. Kepler shifted to human form and approached the keypad. *Whatever you do, stay away from Ashlyn until we have the witches on our side.*

Fuck, man, she'd better be worth it.

She is. He reached for the buzzer, but the gate swung open before he touched it. Of course the witches were waiting for him. Aware he was naked as a jaybird, he strode down the driveway, keeping his wolf at the surface in case he needed a quick change.

A group of women waited for him on the porch of a big gray house. One of them hurried forward with a fleece blanket, her gaze seemingly unable to stay off his junk. She flushed as he accepted the blanket, then stepped aside. He wrapped it around his waist and stared up at the coven. "You were expecting me."

An older witch at the front of the group nodded, her face stern. "Saw you on the gate camera when you ran away the first time. My name's Tessa. I lead this coven." Her attention moved past him toward the gate which had swung closed behind him. "Where are the other two?"

"Cal went to get the pack." He decided it might be best if they thought he had a lot of backup on the way. "But Ashlyn, my mate, seems to have been possessed by a demon."

Exclamations of distress rose from the group of witches. "We're too late."

"The agathion is loose?"

"This is a disaster."

Tessa raised a hand, and the voices silenced. "Thank you for bringing this to our attention. You may remain inside the compound for safety. We will take it from here."

Kepler put his hands on his hips. "I don't think so. That's my mate you're talking about."

Once more, the group murmured. The older witch raised her brows. "The woman or the man?"

"The woman, Ashlyn."

"Are you certain? She isn't one of your kind."

"Of course I'm certain." He hated the way supernaturals always divided people by bloodlines. If it wasn't pack versus pack, it was wolf versus bear, or shifter versus witch. He was done with it. "One of your kind cursed her, so I expect one of you can reverse it."

She shook her head, gaze full of regret. "We have apprehended the guilty party and she will pay, I promise. But there is no way to reverse the spell. We must destroy the host before the demon gets any stronger."

A dark-haired witch shouldered forward, glaring at the coven leader. "She's more than a host. Her name's Ashlyn, and she's my friend. I feel partially responsible for what's happened to her."

"It was in no way your fault," Tessa insisted.

"I invited Jen to visit." Muffy tapped her own chest. "I invited them both to my party. All of this happened right under my nose. I'm a terrible witch and a terrible sister. I should've seen it."

"Your sister is the witch who's been creating the rogues?" Kepler asked, his hands balling into fists at his sides. His wolf was ready to rip out someone's throat. *We need them alive to reverse the spell on Ashlyn*, he reminded his animal. "Can she reverse the hex on Ashlyn?"

Tessa glared at Muffy. "You reveal too much, especially to someone outside the coven. There's nothing Jen or any of us can do."

Muffy threw up her arms. "She wants to make this right. But you won't talk to her."

"Her suggestions are all forbidden magic," Tessa said.

Kepler advanced up the steps, forcing several witches to stumble backward as he put himself nose-to-nose with Tessa. "Let me talk to the witch who did this."

Beside the coven leader, Muffy held her ground. "It's his business, too. They're mates. I know I'd want Jonathan to do everything he could if I was in trouble."

Tessa shook her head, gaze moving between Kepler and Muffy. "Impossible."

"The witch who summoned the agathion must know its weakness," Kepler pressed. "I want to talk to her."

The front door opened and a blonde woman called out, "Tessa, there's a shifter at the gate who says he's with the State Troopers. What do you want me to do?"

Tessa rolled her eyes. "I had hoped to settle this problem internally, but I see it's already spread beyond the coven's boundaries. Let him in."

Moments later, Finch and Cal stood at Kepler's side, both naked. Finch spoke low, hands discreetly over his crotch and eyes on Tessa. "Afraid I don't have my credentials on me at the moment, ma'am."

"We have other means of verifying your identity, Director Finch." Her gaze remained shrewdly on his face, although the younger witches around her were obviously ogling the naked men. Tessa turned toward the house. "Follow me, please."

Inside, Cal and Finch were given blankets like Kepler's then they all followed Tessa to a low door. The witch looked over her shoulder. "My Circle of Protection was damaged, and this makeshift one is fragile. Please do not disturb or pass over the stones."

She descended a narrow stairway into a basement that was barely more than a crawlspace. Kepler had to duck to keep from bumping his head on the bare joists overhead, and though the space appeared dry, the air smelled earthy and pungent, like mushrooms. A few bare lightbulbs hung at regular intervals down the joists, revealing a circle of stones on top of clear plastic vapor barrier. In the center sat a woman on a wooden chair.

Kepler'd expected her to be tied up or something, but her hands rested in her lap, clutching a wad of tissues. She lifted her chin to regard the approaching group. Her long auburn tresses hung limp around her ghostly pale face, and her reddened eyes looked as if she'd been crying.

Muffy hurried forward, stopping short at the edge of the stones. "Jen, the agathion—"

"I know. Hamilton told me."

Kepler frowned. "Who's Hamilton?" He hadn't seen any male witches since he'd arrived.

"Jen's familiar." Muffy faced him, eyes worried. "The agathion was holding him hostage, forcing her—"

"Muffy," Tessa's tone held warning.

Muffy nodded, stepping back to allow the others to approach. Cal hung back, eyes wide, but Finch moved forward next to Kepler.

Stopping only when his bare toes nearly touched the stone circle, Kepler glared at the witch inside. Finally, he stood face-to-face with the person who'd started everything. Who'd evaded him for years. He had so many questions. None of them mattered now except for one. "How do I banish the agathion?"

Finch planted ham-sized fists on his hips. "And why are you suddenly helping?"

Jen shook her head, mouth a grim line. "He kidnapped my familiar and broke his promise to give him back to me after I completed the hex." She looked past the shifters toward the coven leader. "But I can't banish the agathion back to his realm because it would require me to use forbidden magic."

Tessa's arms were crossed, her face stern. "The magic is forbidden for a reason. It opens a hellmouth. Anything could come through. Besides, even if I let you try, you don't have the proper components."

"If it's the only way to get Ashlyn back, we need to do it," Kepler said and looked at Jen again. "What components? Tell me what you need and I'll get it."

"I need a physical sample from the being to be hexed. Blood, skin, hair."

"That's easy." Kepler exhaled with relief. "I'll go to Ashlyn's apartment and bring you her comb, toothbrush, whatever you need."

Jen shook her head. "Old samples won't work. We need samples from the body while it's inhabited."

Tessa added, "The agathion knows that. Even if it didn't kill you on sight, it won't allow you to collect materials that will banish it."

Kepler grit his teeth, recalling Ashlyn's glowing purple veins and how close he'd come to death when the agathion had touched him. But he refused to give up. "I think I can get close enough. It called me its consort when I was with it earlier."

Jen blinked, horror filling her eyes. "You're Ashlyn's mate?"

"Yes." He felt his lip curl in a snarl, exposing one long canine.

She visibly swallowed. "Then it may allow you near, at least for a time. The problem will be when you try to get away."

Kepler grimaced and nodded, one hand going to his chest to touch the tender scars the creature had left there. "Maybe I shouldn't try to get away. Is there some way you can have everything ready to go so I can finish the spell right there?"

Her eyes grew thoughtful. "We do have more of the glass with her wolf's blood on it. If I construct a blade, and you mingle their blood—"

"The host is human," Tessa interrupted. "She doesn't have the experience or knowledge to respond to an open hellmouth. We can't take a chance that something worse than the agathion will come through."

Kepler wasn't sure who he hated more, Jen for hexing Ashlyn, or Tessa for hindering the only means of saving her. "Ashlyn's wolf is an Alpha. She'll know what to do."

Tessa looked at him with pity. "In order to cast the spell that let the agathion through in the first place, Jen bound the wolf. Ashlyn is on her own."

His heart sank as he thought of Ashlyn all by herself on the other side. What if Ashlyn was already dead? *Ashlyn, please respond.* He tried to summon their mental bond again.

No response.

Even so, he insisted, "Ashlyn's smart. She'll know to come through when she sees it."

Annoyingly calm, Jen replied, "She may be able to free her wolf. Hamilton's helping her now."

The pinprick of hope was all Kepler needed. He turned to Tessa. "We have to try."

Tessa shook her head. "And if we fail?"

He looked first at Finch, who nodded, then at Cal, who looked a little unwell but nodded, too. They knew the stakes. They knew what had to be done.

Fighting back the chill trying to paralyze his bones, Kepler said, "If we fail, we kill her."

CHAPTER FIFTEEN

*A*shlyn stepped over the mushrooms into the circle, holding her breath in anticipation. The next thing she knew, she stood in what looked like a study. *I was right, that was a portal.* Looking behind her, she was relieved to see an open wooden door that revealed only blackness. *That must be the opening I just stepped through.* This place was so weird.

The room held a closed roll-top desk, a rickety wooden chair, and bookshelves, everything in sight a monochrome shade of orange. But what struck her most were what had to be a hundred mounted taxidermy heads on every spare inch of wall space. Some appeared to be common animals from Earth plus a few that appeared to be human, but others had grotesque horned protrusions, extra eyes, or double rows of teeth.

She cradled the ferret against her chest like a teddy bear. "What am I supposed to do in here?"

It wriggled to be free, so she set it on the floor. It loped toward the chair and jumped from it to a bookshelf and began to climb. Was this where the demon that possessed her body lived? She moved toward the desk, but her steps faltered as she caught sight of the head of a man mounted to the wall. His curly hair and contorted expression was familiar. *The shifter who attacked me in the alley.* She wanted to be sick.

The ferret latched onto a book, tipping it from its slot on a high shelf, and Ashlyn forced her gaze away from the menagerie of heads to help pull the book free. In the weird orange light, it looked almost red, and the cover felt velvety yet slick at the same time. Her gut churned thinking about what it might be made of. No writing or images decorated the front or thin spine.

Opening it, she discovered its pages were also blank. A smell like oatmeal wafted upward, and as she turned the pages, the smell changed to diesel fumes, strawberries, campfire… Each page had a smell instead of words. She frowned and looked up at the ferret. "What is this?"

It scurried back along the bookshelf and hopped to the top of the desk cabinet, scratching at the closed roll-top.

Ashlyn shut the book and moved to the desk. The tambour moved smoothly as she slid it up, revealing a desktop that looked more like a surgeon's table, with bloody instruments laid out in a neat row. Appalled, she drew back.

The ferret nudged a scalpel and looked at her.

"What do you want me to do with that?" Ashlyn glanced at the heads staring blankly into the room. No way was she removing body parts from anyone or anything.

Standing on its hind legs, the ferret used a front paw to point at the book still clutched in her hand.

"Oh, you want me to cut up the book?" Destroying the nasty thing felt right. She swiped aside the medical instruments and set the book on the desk. Picking up the scalpel, she poised it over the cover.

The ferret lunged forward and nipped her wrist.

"Ow! Why'd you do that?"

It clawed the book open, riffling pages until the book fell on one that smelled familiar. Wildflowers. Honey. *Wolf.*

Her eyes widened. "My wolf?"

With one small claw, the ferret made a cutting motion along the bound edge of the page.

Ashlyn looked from the scalpel to the page. "Cut the page out?"

The ferret backed away.

"All right…" Licking her lips, she took a breath and placed the scalpel against the page. When the ferret didn't object, she sliced the page free.

She'd expected to feel something, see something, but the page just sat there. "Now what?"

The ferret pushed the page toward her, so she picked it up. Then it hopped off the desk and ran back to the door, where it turned around to look at her expectantly. Okay, she was supposed to follow it again. Wrapping the page around the scalpel, she clutched them both in one fist.

Then she thought of something. "What about you? Is there something in here that can help you?"

The ferret shook its head and edged closer to the opening.

Feeling sorry for the tiny creature, she picked it up. This time, it didn't flinch. The blackness beyond the door was daunting, but she knew her wolf was on the other side waiting. With a final glance at the strange room, she stepped through, once more finding herself at the edge of the mushroom circle.

"Wolf, I'm coming!" she cried.

Somewhere in the darkness, her wolf whined, and she followed the sound until she could see its blue glowing eyes. At her animal's side once more, she set the ferret down and knelt on the stone floor. "I got this."

She unwrapped the page, keeping the scalpel in her other hand. Except the page was no longer a paper. It was a leaf with a long, serrated stem. *Not a stem.* She turned to the ferret. "A key."

The ferret nodded, front feet pressed against the wall where the chain was connected.

"I feel like Alice in Wonderland," she muttered and placed the key into the keyhole on the wall. "Here goes nothing."

Color exploded all around her. The scalpel fell from her grip and she closed her eyes against a sudden return of vertigo, groping blindly for her wolf. "Wolf? Wolf, where are you?"

Her wolf pressed against her, body warm and solid in the ethereal surroundings. Clinging to the animal's thick ruff, she knelt, feeling warm and giddy with success. "We did it!"

She cracked open one eye, focusing on her wolf and allowing the billowing colors to flow past her. Her elation faded a little. "We're still not in my body."

Small paws touched her leg, and she slid her gaze down to find the ferret looking up at her. In the colored light, it looked even more abused, the reddish fur patchy in places and the missing eye crusted with scar tissue. Trembling, the ferret climbed onto her lap and curled itself into a ball.

A scent like anise grew stronger, and Ashlyn's entire being prickled with awareness as she remembered how it had pursued her earlier. Was it one of the monsters the agathion had warned her about? She searched the ground around her for the dropped scalpel, but it was nowhere in sight.

Her wolf leaned against her, muscles tense and wary. Ashlyn felt like a rabbit caught in the open. She had no option but to remain perfectly still and hope whatever it was passed her over.

After the smell faded, she whispered, "Do you know what that was?"

Of course the animals couldn't answer. But they both stayed close, as if she held the power to shield them from danger. Longing for Kepler, she closed her eyes and pictured him, strong and protective. She imagined his arms around her and the warm masculine scent of his body when he held her close. *Kepler, what do I do?*

Ashlyn, I knew you were alive! Kepler's voice flooded her with relief.

We're still connected!

Of course. You're my mate.

She wished she could fall into his arms. *I freed my wolf, but I have no idea where I am or what to do next.*

Can you sense your body? We need to know where it is.

Her chest tightened. *No, I'm completely disconnected.*

That's okay. We can follow your scent. The witches have come up with a plan to get you back into your body, Kepler said. *Watch for the hellmouth. When you see it, don't hesitate, go through it.*

She tried to remember what she'd seen when the agathion had thrust her out of her body, but she'd been so confused. *I don't know what it looks like.*

I'll tell you when, but if we lose connection again, trust your wolf. Follow her lead. He hesitated, as if uncertain what to say next. *And Ashlyn? Forgive me.*

For what?

Breaking the curse is going to hurt.

Kepler rode the four-wheeler hard, losing sight of Cal's russet fur as he rerouted to avoid a fallen tree. He couldn't carry the glass knife Jen had made while he was in wolf form, and he couldn't easily track the agathion in human form, so they'd settled on letting Cal sniff out the trail. Kepler wore an old flannel jacket the witches had given him, along with a pair of cargo pants that were one size too small, the hexed knife hidden in the pocket on his thigh.

In Kepler's head, Cal said, *I think we're getting close.*

Do not let it spot you, Kepler warned for what felt like the hundredth time. He nudged Ashlyn. *We're almost there. Be ready.*

Okay. Her voice trembled.

He was about to reassure her when Cal interrupted, *Shit. It's almost to the highway.*

They had to stop it before it reached civilization. A naked woman asking for help on the side of the road would immediately attract attention, and they wanted to keep this as quiet as possible. Kepler gunned the ATV. One of his wheels caught air, and he leaned into it to keep the vehicle upright, landing hard, wheels churning up leaves and dirt behind him.

Between the gray trees far ahead, he spotted a flash of pink and blue hair. *I've got her, Cal. Pull back.*

Good luck. Cal slowed to a trot, allowing Kepler to whip past. *We're ready if you need us.*

Kepler's stomach clenched. They had to end the monster, one way or another, and if the plan didn't work or something happened to Kepler before he could complete it, Cal and Finch would move in and kill the vessel. Kill Ashlyn. Kepler wasn't about to let that happen.

"Ashlyn!" he yelled over the roar of his engine, hoping to stall the agathion before it reached the road.

The pink and blue hair stopped, and the figure turned to face him, blue eyes flashing purple. He pulled up just out of reach, letting the engine fall to an idle. The agathion cocked its head. "You surprise me, shifter."

"I thought about what you said, about being your consort." Kepler's heart thundered against his ribs and made it hard to keep his voice steady. "You're obviously powerful. Humans will fall at your feet and worship you in terror. So, I agree."

A grin split its mouth, and Kepler fought to keep the revulsion off his face as it stepped toward him. "Do you know what a consort does? What will be required of you?"

"I understand what being a consort means." The witches had discussed this in detail, directing Kepler on exactly what the agathion was likely to crave, including tastes of his soul. But if that's what it took to get close enough to save Ashlyn, Kepler was ready. Still, he wanted to offer other alternatives first. The monster was restrained to human limitations while inhabiting a mortal body. It had to be tired and cold.

"But first let's give you comfort." Kepler gestured to its naked, scratched up skin. *Ashlyn's skin*, Kepler thought, examining the twigs and leaves snarled in its long pink and blue hair. Its bare, dirty feet were also smudged with blood. "I can provide clothes, accommodations, transport, food. Whatever you desire."

The agathion took another step toward him. "Your mate is no longer in this body, if that's what you're worried about. She's dead. Even if I decide I'm done with this realm, this body will be a corpse."

Kepler pressed his lips together. The agathion must not know Kepler was still in contact with Ashlyn and that her soul was alive. Alive and ready to fight back. He nodded deferentially. "I understand. You're stronger than she was." God, he hated saying that. He shrugged. "That makes *you* my mate, now."

As if acknowledging a victory, the agathion lifted its chin. "It's good you recognize that. I accept your service." It shifted its gaze to the ATV. "What is this transport you have brought me?"

Things were proceeding better than Kepler'd expected. Sliding back on the seat to make room, he gestured to the handlebars. "A four-wheeler. I'll show you how to drive."

If the agathion was occupied steering the ATV, Kepler could use Jen's knife. The blade was nothing more than a shard of glass no bigger than his thumb with a wad of duct tape for a handle, but it had to be embedded in the body in a place it could not be dislodged, at least not until Ashlyn regained control. Once she did, he'd remove the dagger, shatter it, and break the agathion's power over her.

The agathion waved him back toward the driver's spot. "You shall transport me."

Shit. Kepler felt his eye twitch and hoped the agathion didn't notice. He should've known things wouldn't be easy. *Time for Plan B.*

Instead of sliding forward, he dismounted and went to the back of the vehicle where a tote had been strapped to the rack. "Let's get you clothes first. You must be cold. It'll be even colder riding the wheeler."

Swaggering forward, the agathion put both palms against Kepler's flanks, pressing itself against him from behind. "I believe humans have many methods of keeping warm."

Skin crawling, Kepler remained steady. He couldn't disengage without making the agathion doubt him. "I look forward to showing you many human pleasures once we've reached the comfort of my house." He pulled open the tote and removed a white cashmere sweater one of the witches had donated. "Right now, you'll enjoy these clothes. I promise."

The agathion frowned and looked past him to the tote. "Where did you acquire these things?"

Kepler shrugged, trying to remain nonchalant. His heartbeat pounded in his ears. "Stole them. There are plenty of homesteads in these parts that don't lock their doors."

To his relief, that seemed to satisfy the agathion. It took the sweater and held it against its chest. "What else have you brought me?"

Kepler reached for the knife in his pocket. He had to strike just right, or he'd kill rather than incapacitate. When the agathion leaned over to rummage through the clothing, Kepler struck. He angled the blade into the agathion's back, sliding along ribs until the glass shard lay beneath the skin like a splinter.

The agathion screamed, body contorting. It tried to remove the blade, but the handle was out of reach. Blood welled around the embedded hilt, trickling down the amber skin.

Now, Ashlyn! Come through now!

Crimson light filled the air, and all of a sudden, a small reddish ferret popped into existence. It tumbled across the ground and came to rest at the base of a tree, immediately righting itself and scurrying out of sight. He'd been prepared for monsters, but a ferret? He called to Cal, "One of you catch that thing."

It's that witch's familiar, Cal replied. *Let it go.* The russet wolf and Finch in his huge grizzly form had emerged from the underbrush.

Hell, no, Finch said and shot off into the trees. *The witch betrayed us.*

Kepler didn't have time to wonder that he could now hear Finch. The agathion had turned to focus on him, purple lightning arching from its fingertips. "Traitor! You will pay!"

Dodging the bolt, Kepler called, *Ashlyn, where are you?*

Had the witch betrayed them? Had this all been a ploy to get her familiar back? If Ashlyn couldn't get control of her body, he knew what had to happen next. He'd promised. But he didn't want Cal and Finch to touch her. Ashlyn was his. His love. His life. His responsibility. Heart breaking, he prepared to shift into his wolf.

Just as Ashlyn's body collapsed to the forest floor.

What felt like a hurricane struck Ashlyn, shredding the surrounding colors into jagged pieces and making it impossible to breathe. Kepler's voice reached her just as the smell of ash bowled her over, breaking her hold on her wolf. She tumbled end over end, dizziness intensifying until she could no longer tell up from down.

By pure force of will, she stopped her momentum and got back on her feet. Ferocious snarling drew her attention to where her wolf was locked in combat with the figure of a man. Purple lightning danced across his skin. *The agathion!* The hellmouth must've opened, but nothing around her looked like a portal.

Scrambling forward, she waited for an opportunity to jump in and help her wolf, but the fight was too chaotic. She was afraid she might do more harm than good. Her wolf's teeth and claws cut into the agathion, and he returned damage with arcs of light. She couldn't tell who was winning.

Behind her, she heard her name. Turning, she spotted a dot of gold no bigger than her thumb. It remained steady while the world around it churned. Through it, Kepler's nearness was a lifeline, drawing her toward him. The hellmouth.

Kepler, the agathion is fighting my wolf!

You need to come through now! he urged.

The agathion had her wolf by the throat. Ashlyn clenched her fists. Short of throwing random punches, she was helpless. *I can't leave her!*

The sound of the storm shifted, becoming more like sighing. The anise smell that had stalked her earlier returned. Terror spiked through her. Where was the ferret? Had something got it while she wasn't watching? *Kepler, there's something else here,* she sent. *I think it's hunting me.*

Come through now. His voice held the same tone of command he'd used when she'd first met him, his Alpha tone, and she could feel his desperation through their bond. *Ashlyn, please.*

A second anise scent, slightly sharper, joined the first. *Oh, God.* A pack? She still couldn't see anything.

Shadows flickered between her and the gold dot. What happened if the beings that smelled like anise reached the portal first?

Wolf, hurry!

Her wolf stood on top of the agathion, teeth in its throat. For a moment, she thought they'd won. But then her wolf's eyes met hers, and a single word reached her. *Go.*

The agathion thrust a hand against the wolf's chest, sending it flying. Then he raised both hands toward her. Lightning shot out, but her wolf pounced, sending the bolts astray.

Go, the wolf sent again.

The portal would soon be closed, with or without her. Ashlyn had to go without her wolf. She backed a step toward the hellmouth. Then another. Her wolf was holding the agathion off. Giving Ashlyn a chance to escape. But what would happen to her wolf once Ashlyn left? The animal had become more a part of her than she'd ever imagined possible.

Lightning crackled through the air, and two more things that looked like men popped into view. They were bigger than the agathion, and their skin glittered with what looked like a million stars. Turning purple glowing eyes toward her and the hellmouth, they ignored the fight and moved forward. Her wolf howled, begging her to go.

Chest tight, Ashlyn knew she was out of options. She had to leave.

Spinning, she dove for the portal.

She slammed back into her body with the force of a freight train. A rush of cool air met her lungs. Her cheek was pressed against the damp ground, yellow leaves filling her vision. The solid earth beneath her felt almost wrong in its steadiness, and the middle of her back was on fire. She turned her head and forced her eyes to focus, seeing her mate standing several feet away. She tried to say his name, but only managed a gasp.

He stayed back, eyes wary. "Ashlyn?"

"My wolf." Her throat spasmed, and her hands clawed at the damp leaves. "It's trying to kill my wolf."

A pained look fleeted across Kepler's face. "I'm sorry. We can't wait." Kneeling next to her, he yanked something out of her back.

It felt as if he'd just ripped every vein out of her body. She screamed in agony, stars filling her vision.

"Shit, that's a lot of blood," Kepler said, pressing hard against her back.

Through a haze of pain, she heard Cal ask, "Did it work?"

She heard the sound of crunching glass.

"Yes," Kepler growled.

She wanted to protest that it hadn't. That her wolf was still on the other side, fighting for her life. But pain was making it impossible to breathe, much less speak.

"So Jen didn't betray us." Cal sounded relieved.

Kepler muttered. "Fuck. Why isn't she healing?"

"Maybe it's not her," an unfamiliar voice said. "I have a bad feeling about this. Maybe the agathion's fooling us."

Her fingers and toes felt like ice, and her teeth chattered. *Why am I so cold?*

"It's her," Kepler's voice held an edge. "She said the agathion was trying to kill her wolf. If she lost her animal, she lost her ability to heal."

Ashlyn's heart cracked at those words. Kepler had been right about a shifter's animal being a part of them, and the emptiness she now felt hurt more than the pain in her back. Would she ever know if her wolf had won or lost?

"She was protecting me," Ashlyn whispered.

She couldn't feel the strength of her animal anymore. Couldn't feel much of anything. *Wolf, please come back.*

But as she drifted into unconsciousness, she was certain her wolf was gone.

The ATV ride was rougher than Kepler liked as he drove toward the road while holding Ashlyn limply in front of him. The wound on her back needed stitches, but shouldn't need a hospital, even for someone without shifter healing, but for some reason the bleeding wouldn't stop. He'd just reached the pavement when a truck pulled alongside his ATV.

Muffy was at the wheel and Tessa jumped out, flinging open the door to the back seat. "I thought you'd need help. Get in."

Kepler laid Ashlyn on the bench seat and climbed in beside her. Several blankets lay folded on the seat, and he pulled one haphazardly over his mate, trying to warm her. Her skin felt chilly and the blood on her bare skin had become tacky. "She won't stop bleeding. I think she's in shock."

Tessa closed the door and climbed back in front.

Muffy slammed the truck into gear and did a U-turn on the two-lane highway. Instead of buckling up, Tessa sat on her knees and leaned over the seat. "Let me see."

Cradling Ashlyn against his chest, Kepler allowed Tessa to examine the wound. Ashlyn's back glistened crimson, her matted hair stuck to her shoulders. The sharp metallic scent of her blood filled the cab, and he hated the way her eyelids fluttered, showing only the whites.

The witch made a noise in the back of her throat. "Did you puncture her lung?"

"No." Kepler knew he spoke too sharply, but he was furious. "I embedded it under her skin as you instructed. Please, do whatever it takes. Save her."

"I worried this might happen." Tessa dug into a bag on the seat beside her, bringing out some sort of poultice. She mashed some green gunk that smelled like astringent onto the bloody gash and taped a wide gauze pad over it. Then she placed her palm flat over the wound and spoke a few words in a strange language. "That should seal the wound."

"Is she going to be all right?" Kepler stroked Ashlyn's hair.

"I can't say yet. She's lost a lot of blood."

Muffy was driving them away from town, he realized, and suspicion rose in his chest. "Where are you going? We need to get her to a hospital."

"The agathion was stronger than we expected," Tessa said, eyebrows pinched. "If she can't beat it, we can't have her loose among humans."

He clutched Ashlyn tighter against his chest. "Then how do you plan to keep her alive?"

Tessa's glared at him. "I've stopped the bleeding. There is nothing more a doctor can do. She's best off in our care."

Kepler begrudgingly understood her reasoning, but it didn't make him any less angry. "I crushed the knife. You said crushing it would break the agathion's hold on her."

"That was our best guess, but none of us are overly familiar with this magic. No one practices it."

"Jen does." He gritted his teeth, thinking of the ferret running away like a coward. "She set us up. This was all so she could get her familiar back."

Muffy scowled over her shoulder at him. "Of course she hoped she'd get Hamilton back, but that wasn't her goal in the end."

"How do you know? That ferret was the first one through the hellmouth. Ashlyn almost didn't make it.

Her wolf…" He couldn't finish. He couldn't imagine having his own wolf ripped from him. Was that why Ashlyn was dying?

Ashlyn's fingers moved against his chest, and he looked down to see her lips moving. Leaning close, he heard her say, "…ferret saved us."

He had no idea if she was delirious or actually conscious enough to be listening. He hoped it was the latter. But that gave his anger nowhere to go. He slumped against the seat, breathing in shallow, angry gasps.

"What is she saying?" Tessa asked.

"She says the ferret saved her," he snarled. "That damned familiar should've been the one to stay behind, not her wolf."

Tessa's eyes narrowed, then she turned around and buckled in. "I'll question Jen about that later. Right now, let's keep your mate alive."

CHAPTER SEVENTEEN

Ashlyn woke in an unfamiliar bed, sunlight glowing through gauzy curtains. She sat up, feeling weak, but alive. Yet there was an emptiness inside her. *Wolf?*

There was no response.

In a chair next to her, Kepler slumped to one side, mouth slightly open while he slept. Her hands and arms were covered in small scratches, as if she'd been rolling around in a briar patch, and she wore a simple yellow nightgown. Her mouth felt full of cotton.

A glass of water sat on the bedside table. She reached for it, but her grip was weaker than she expected, and it slipped from her fingers, splashing water onto the wood.

Kepler woke as it thudded to the floor. He shot to his feet and took her face between his hands. "Ashlyn. You're awake."

His touch was a balm, a comfort. She gave him a weak smile. "I'm thirsty."

"Yes." He turned to the bedside table and did a double take before seeing the glass on the floor. "I'll go get you some water."

He retrieved the glass and left the room.

Alone, Ashlyn looked around again, taking a deep breath. She thought she smelled baking bread, but her senses seemed dull. *My human senses.* She'd never imagined she could miss her wolf so badly. Would Kepler still want to be her mate now? Were they even still bonded? Eyes filming with tears, she sought the mental bond they shared. *Kepler?*

I'm hurrying, love.

She let out a small sob. At least she still had that. She still had a connection.

Ashlyn, what's wrong?

She heard pounding footsteps approaching. *I'm just relieved I can still talk to you this way.*

The footsteps slowed. *Me, too.*

He rounded the doorframe, glass in hand. Tessa and Muffy followed on his heels. He handed Ashlyn the glass of water. "Here."

Ashlyn took a sip, its coolness burning her parched throat. "Thank you."

Tessa came forward carrying a tray with a steaming mug and a plate of toast. She moved to the other side of the bed and set it on the table. "Do you mind if I examine your wound, Ashlyn?"

In a flash, the memory of excruciating pain returned. Cold sweat prickled her skin. She shuddered, sending water sloshing over the rim of her glass.

"Ashlyn?" Kepler steadied her hand with his.

It's okay.

Kepler nodded, and Tessa pulled aside the collar of Ashlyn's nightgown, peeling back the bandage and running cool fingertips over her shoulder blade. "There will be a scar, but I think you're healing nicely."

"How long have I been asleep?" Ashlyn's voice felt scratchy, and she took another sip of water.

"Two days." Kepler tucked a strand of hair behind her ear. "You fought off the agathion for two days."

The last thing she remembered was coming through the hellmouth. "Is it gone?"

"Your aura is fully clear." Tessa smiled. "You're human once more."

The words cut through Ashlyn. *Human.* She slumped back against the pillows. *Not a shifter.*

Kepler pulled his chair close and sat, setting her glass aside to take her hand. "I'm sorry. I know you must be hurting without her."

Tears blurred her eyes, and she nodded.

I'm here for you always. He leaned forward and kissed her forehead. *If I could share my wolf, I would.*

Muffy stepped forward, holding a small animal carrier and looking worried. She glanced at Kepler, then back to Ashlyn. "I have someone who would like to see you, if that's all right?"

Kepler scowled.

Ashlyn looked through the wire door at a small pink nose and striped auburn fur. She sucked in a breath, reaching out. "You made it!"

The lines of worry on Muffy's face softened to relief, and she opened the cage. "This is Hamilton."

The ferret leapt toward Ashlyn, scurrying along to blankets to nuzzle her hands as she stroked his soft fur. He was still bony and light, and the scar over his missing eye looked uncomfortable, but he was no longer matted and dirty.

"God, he stinks," Kepler complained.

Ashlyn frowned. "Be nice. If it wasn't for him, I wouldn't be here. He helped free my wolf so she could…" she choked on the last words. "So she could protect me."

Kepler made a non-committal sound, eyes hard.

She turned back to the ferret. "Thank you, Hamilton, for helping me. I'm glad you escaped." Ashlyn's throat felt tight. She looked back at Muffy. "Why was he there?"

"Hamilton is my sister's familiar. You met her at the bachelorette party. Remember Jen?"

That party felt like it'd happened a million years ago. "I remember Jen, but what's a familiar?"

"Familiars are connected to their witch much the same way a shifter's animal is connected to their human, only we don't swap forms." Muffy set the pet carrier on the floor. "Hamilton went through a hellmouth and got trapped. The agathion held him hostage, forcing Jen to help him."

"That's no excuse." Tessa crossed her arms. "She can never atone for the deaths she caused."

Muffy nodded. "She knows. But she *is* sorry and wanted me to tell you that, Ashlyn." She glanced at Kepler. "She'll tell you personally if you let her."

"Absolutely not," Kepler said.

"Ashlyn, as the only living victim, you have a say in her punishment," Tessa said. "Regardless of whether you wish to speak to Jen or not, she'll be held accountable."

Ashlyn held the ferret a little closer. "What sort of punishment?"

The coven leader looked a little squeamish. "No one has been accused of using this magic in centuries, but the traditional method of execution was death by fire."

Ashlyn had never been a vindictive person, and death by fire seemed barbaric, even for Jen's crimes. "Is there another option?"

"We can find a more humane way for her to die. But her body must be burned in any case. It's the only way to ensure the dark forces she communed with can't use her to return."

Hamilton squeaked and wriggled beneath the covers next to her leg, huddling against her and shivering. Ashlyn took a deep breath. "If Jen dies, what happens to Hamilton?"

"He shares her punishment."

"What?" Her hand fluttered over the shivering lump beneath the covers. "But he was a victim, too!"

"Ashlyn," Kepler said, but she stopped him.

"Can't you strip her of her power or something? There have been enough deaths. All those shifters, now my wolf." A sob caught in her throat.

"Your wolf isn't necessarily dead," Tessa said. "Just disconnected."

Ashlyn sucked in a breath. "What do you mean?"

"Like most spells, shifter magic requires a genetic component to tie this realm with another. The magical energy—in this case, the shifter's animal—is delivered through a constricted channel. Shifters call it the Source. It's a well-guarded portal, allowing only shifter animals through. The hellmouth the agathion used was not guarded and could let anything through. Now we've closed it, you don't have a connection to your wolf."

"So you're saying she could still be alive?"

"Yes."

Ashlyn flung the covers aside. "Kepler, take me to the glacier."

He put a gentle hand on her, keeping her from standing up—which wasn't hard because her legs could barely hold her. "Drinking from the Source a second time will replace your animal."

"But I never drank a first time."

He frowned and looked at Tessa.

She shrugged. "It's shifter magic. I only know the basics."

"I want to try," Ashlyn said.

"The Source may not even open for you."

"We're mates, which means I have an animal—my wolf —waiting for me. I have to go to the Source."

Kepler sighed. "Fine, but I want to do everything right this time. First, we need permission from Councilman Riordan. Let me make a phone call."

Ashlyn nodded and leaned back against the pillows. She'd let Kepler go through shifter channels, at least to start.

But regardless of whether the Council gave permission or not, she was going to the glacier.

Kepler stood on the glacier's surface and waved to the departing helicopter. The pilot saluted and pivoted, taking off toward the cloud-covered sunset. Finch had pulled a lot of strings to let them use the crime unit's helicopter, but Ashlyn had been ready to walk, swim, or crawl to the glacier, even though he'd warned her the Source might not reveal itself.

She slid her mittened hand into his. "Think there'll be an aurora tonight?"

"I hope so." He looked at her, bundled in a down parka and snow bibs, nose pink from the cold. She'd made light of her bulky clothing, pretending she couldn't put her arms down, but he hadn't laughed. Without her animal, she was more susceptible to frostbite and hypothermia than he was. They'd brought a winter tent and a few days of supplies, but if the cave didn't open, he was going to have a hell of a time getting her off this ice.

Even if the cave did open, he hated to think what was going to happen if she ended up with some other animal than her wolf. What if her new animal no longer wanted him as a mate?

As if sensing his worry, she hugged him. "It's going to be fine. My wolf's an Alpha, remember? No way she let that agathion win. She'll find me again."

But the shaking in her voice betrayed her bravado. He wrapped his arms around her, squeezing through all the padding and fluff. "I should be comforting you, not the other way around."

Her lips smiled, but her eyes were tight with concern. "There were other things over there that might want to hurt my wolf."

He'd asked his own wolf what it knew about the other side, but it had been unable or unwilling to provide information. All he could assume was that shifter animals survived there the same way real animals survived in the wilderness. He kissed her forehead. "Like you said, she's an Alpha. She survived among those creatures for who knows how long while she was waiting for her chance to find you."

"That's true." Ashlyn laid her cheek against the front of his parka. "Besides, I think I'd feel something if she was dead, even if we are disconnected."

He nodded, knowing he'd feel the same way if he lost his wolf.

The cloudy sky had darkened to slate gray, a pale line to the south the only reminder of the setting sun. An icy wind had kicked up, driving snow into his exposed skin and biting through his clothing. If he was chilled, Ashlyn would soon be freezing. "It's going to be full dark soon. Let's set up our tent."

But she refused to release her hold on him. "Kepler, look."

He followed her gaze along the glacier's jagged surface.

Not fifty feet away, a dark hole had opened in the ice.

CHAPTER EIGHTEEN

Ashlyn trembled with excitement and self-doubt. The moment of truth was here. What if her wolf was dead? Worse, what if her wolf *wasn't* dead, and she ended up with another animal? "I'm scared," she whispered.

Kepler's arms tightened around her. "You don't have to do this. We can turn around."

His suggestion that she give up only made her more resolute. "It took me half an hour to put on my snow gear. I'm not chickening out now." She faced the cave and took a deep breath. "Let's do this."

"Wait," he said, digging in a nearby pack. He pulled out their ice cleats. "It may be slippery."

As she pulled the cleats on over her boots, her pulse rushed through her ears and a cold sweat broke out underneath her parka. True darkness had fallen, and with the cloud cover, even the snow looked black. "I can barely see the cave anymore."

"Just follow me."

He squeezed her hand and led her across the jagged ice, their footsteps crunching against the snow. When they reached the entrance, she paused in awe. Deep inside, the ice glowed with faint, blue light. *The same color as my wolf's eyes.* They stepped through, and the color began to flow like water, brightening with hints of yellow and green the deeper they went. Stones littered the cave floor, eventually forming a tunnel leading downward. Deeper and deeper into the ice they went, the living glacier creaking around them.

"This glacier sounds like it's trying to eat us alive," Kepler said, his voice muffled by ice.

She let out a nervous laugh. "This is nothing. You should see the other side of a hellmouth."

Kepler grunted. "Touché."

Eventually, the tunnel opened into a vast cave. The high ceiling danced with shifting ribbons of color more glorious than Ashlyn could've imagined. Trickling water echoed through the space. The cave floor wasn't wet, but it definitely felt warmer than it had outside. Black boulders dotted the ice, some even taller than Kepler. As she crunched toward the cave's center, the glint of falling water caught her eye. From the high ceiling, a thin trickle splattered onto a huge flat stone embedded in the ice.

Ashlyn drew up at the edge. The stone was only a few inches higher than the ice, and the falling water flowed over it to disappear into the glacier beneath. It felt like an altar, of sorts. Definitely otherworldly.

She let out a slow breath and lifted her foot to step onto the stone. "This must be the place."

"Wait," Kepler tugged gently on her hand, pulling her to face him. "A kiss for luck?"

The overhead ice aurora made his eyes glitter with the golden glow of his wolf. Through their mental bond, she sensed his worry. Leaning forward, she pressed her lips softly against his, lingering, savoring the feel of him.

Before she pulled away, he murmured against her, "I love you, Ashlyn Reed. No matter if you get your wolf back, a different wolf, a bear, or nothing at all. You're mine. Always."

She frowned, for the first time considering his stake in her actions. "Are you worried if I get another animal, we'll no longer be mates?"

His lips thinned. "The thought crossed my mind."

"Well, shit. Now I'm worried, too."

"Just don't get a chihuahua for an animal."

She laughed. "Bad jokes are my deal in this relationship, okay?"

One side of his mouth lifted in a smile. "I make no promises."

She gave him one more peck on the lips and unzipped her parka. It was surprisingly warm inside the cave. "Hold this so I don't get it wet."

"Maybe you should take it all off so you don't ruin your gear if you shift immediately."

She smirked. "You just want to see me naked."

"That, too." He smiled, but his worry still showed through.

Wanting to lighten the mood, she ran her thumbs under the straps of her snow bibs and did a little shimmy as she stripped. "I'm too sexy for these bibs, too sexy for these bibs…"

His laughter echoed through the cave, his gaze following her with a hunger she hoped would remain, whatever the outcome was. Once she was fully naked, she turned back to the water. Goose pimples prickled her skin, and not only because she was naked. What if she did get some weird animal like a chihuahua? *Stop doubting. I'm going to get my wolf back.*

She took a huge breath and leaned toward the waterfall, tilting her head to let the cold liquid fall into her mouth. After several swallows, she stepped back. She didn't feel any different. Her hands looked the same. She still had goose pimples. Then a warm spot spread in her belly. It filled her chest and ran through her limbs.

Overhead, the aurora cracked and snapped, and everything looked clearer. Smelled sharper. Kepler's warm, male scent called to her, filled her with an acute hunger, and she swore she could detect the beating of his heart. As she turned to him, a familiar, joyous howl resonated in her head.

Wolf! Tears blurred her vision. *You're alive! I knew you were stronger than that monster.*

She looked at Kepler, letting her wolf's power rise into her eyes. His worried expression shifted to amazement, then a joy to match her own. "It worked?"

"My wolf is back," her voice choked with a sob.

Whooping, he reached out and swept her into his arms, spinning her once before setting her on her feet and claiming her mouth with his. The mating fire flared within her immediately, and she kissed him fervently, tangling her tongue with his. His parka felt rough against her chest, and she fumbled with the zipper. "You are wearing way too many clothes."

He shucked out of them and yanked her body against his. His thighs were hard against hers, and she lifted one leg up around his hip. He gripped her buttocks with both hands and picked her up the rest of the way, letting her wrap both legs around him. Centered against her core, the length of his erection pulsed with a need that matched her own.

Between kisses, he kicked their snow gear into a pile, then lowered her down toward it. "Oh, no," she said. "This is my party. I'm doing the claiming here."

She gave him a playful shove, and he collapsed onto the nest of parkas, his cock a thick line against his belly. She growled and knelt, wrapping her mouth around it, engulfing him until he hit the back of her throat. He tasted salty and musky and perfect as she cupped his balls and worked his shaft. Groaning, he threaded both hands into her hair, hips bucking upward to meet her with each stroke. "God, woman, you're going to kill me. Come around here so I can taste you."

She swiveled, lifting a knee over his head to straddle him. His tongue flicked out, penetrating her slit, and he grabbed her hips, driving her down against his mouth. He worked her folds as she sucked his shaft until she could no longer concentrate on what she was doing.

Breaking from his hold, she pivoted again, straddling his hips. He bared his teeth, eyes glowing golden, and gripped her ass, helping settle her over his shaft. She was dripping wet, her folds swollen and aching for him. With a solid thrust, she impaled herself on his length, gasping as he filled her, stretched her with exquisite pleasure.

He groaned her name, hips flexing upward to meet her. Her own voice emerged as a growl to match his, "My mate."

"Yes."

Rolling her hips, she started a rhythm, plunging him in and out and ratcheting up the heat growing between them. The tightness in her belly grew and sweat slicked her skin. He moved his hand to press a thumb to her clit, and she exploded, back arching and head thrown back in a scream.

She'd barely finished when he flipped her onto her back and pinned her, continuing his thrusting as his eyes bored into hers.

"Kepler, I'm going to come again." The pressure she'd thought would subside with her first orgasm only rose higher as he drove into her, over and over.

"Mine forever." His teeth had sharpened, and she knew what he meant. What they both needed.

Lifting her mouth to his shoulder, she bit into him the same moment he pierced her skin over the claiming mark he'd made the last time they were together.

Lights flashed before her eyes, and a moment of vertigo made her feel as if she'd been thrown back into the hellmouth. Then everything settled, and there was nothing but Kepler. It was as if she could feel his heartbeat inside her own chest.

"I love you, Kepler." She settled back against the arm floor, too spent to move.

Chest heaving, he rested on his elbows above her, one hand stroking her hair as he pressed his forehead against hers. "I love you, too."

When their breathing had settled, he rose and created a nest out of their discarded clothing. Settling her on top of it, he curled up behind her, spooning his warmth against her backside. "Is it wrong I never want to leave here?"

She smiled and wiggled deeper into his embrace, loving the way his cock pulsed back to life against her ass. "I feel the same way."

Bathed in the blessed light of the Source, they made love the rest of the night.

essa's house was surprisingly silent, considering over twenty people had assembled for Jen's sentencing. Harsh morning sunlight poured through the great room's two-story windows, making everything seem sharper than normal. The plush furniture had been pushed aside, and rows of folding chairs now filled the space. A mix of shifters and witches had divided themselves along an invisible line in each half of the room.

Among the first to arrive, Ashlyn and Kepler sat in front, facing a long table where three Shifter Council members awaited the proceedings. Ashlyn couldn't take her eyes off them. She didn't know why, but she'd expected the shifter leadership to look more like animals. They wore jeans and button-down shirts and had haircuts like any other person she might meet on the street. Sitting beside them, the Head of Covens looked more supernatural than they did, with her perfectly done French knot and flawless tan skin.

Kepler leaned over and whispered in Ashlyn's ear, "Are you certain you want to be here? It's likely to be gruesome."

"Yes, I need to be here. I don't want Hamilton to suffer," Ashlyn said. "And burning Jen alive is barbaric even if Hamilton wasn't included."

"If I could give her worse, I would. She's responsible for the deaths of at least nine shifters, and almost killed you, too."

Ashlyn shook her head. "The agathion did, not Jen."

"She opened the hellmouth," he insisted. "She let him in. She's a liability every second she's alive."

Leveling him with an angry glare, Ashlyn said, "Using that logic, you should've handed me over to the pack and let them kill me."

He had the courtesy to blanch. "I sound just as bad as the pack, don't I?"

She squeezed his hand. "No, but please consider another option besides burning her to death."

Just then, Tessa appeared from a side hallway holding a pet carrier with Hamilton inside. Jen followed a few feet behind her, eyes downcast. Tessa stepped over a small circle of stones that had been placed around a bare wooden chair next to the front table and set the carrier on the floor. Jen sat on the chair and folded her hands in her lap, staring down rather than the assembled crowd. The coven leader stepped away and made a few graceful motions with her hands. Magic prickled through the room, making Ashlyn's skin crawl as though she'd been swarmed by insects.

From the table at the front, the Head of Covens rose. In what had to be an expensive suit and stiletto heels, she looked like she belonged in a New York board room rather than this makeshift trial in the Alaskan outback. "This is the sentencing hearing for Jennifer Lynn Elliot on the matter of using forbidden magic, her part in the deaths of nine shifters, and the endangerment of another. Jennifer has admitted to her crime and agreed to bow to the will of this hearing. Before we proceed, is there anything else the guilty party would like to say?"

Jen looked up, gaze connecting with Ashlyn's for a moment before she dropped it again. "Only that I'm sorry. I never expected people to die, I was trying to save my familiar. It was stupid to fall for the agathion's lies."

"May I speak?" Muffy's voice rose from the crowd.

The Head of Covens frowned, but nodded. "Please provide your name and relationship to the guilty party."

"Muffy, please don't," Jen said as a tear ran down her cheek. "Don't associate yourself with me."

Muffy ignored her. "My name's Muffy and Jen is my sister. I want to point out that what Jen did was a mistake, not intentional. It's like murder one versus manslaughter. I beg the court to consider a reduced sentence."

Councilman Riordan rose from his seat, pale eyes flashing with his wolf's power. "If it happened once, I might call it a mistake. But she let that monster kill those shifters."

"She didn't actually kill them," Muffy pointed out. "In fact, neither did the agathion. They were technically killed by fellow shifters."

The gallery erupted in protest.

"Because they went rogue!"

"Don't try to turn this back on shifters!"

"You don't come back from being rogue."

"Enough!" the Head of Covens said with a forcefulness rivaling any Alpha's.

The audience fell to grumbling silence.

"The point of this hearing is not about the why or how. It is about justice. Jennifer has admitted her guilt. The punishment for her crime is death by fire."

Beside Kepler, Ashlyn rose. "I would also like to speak."

The Head of Coven's eyes twitched in obvious annoyance, but she pursed her mouth and nodded. "It is your right as one of the victims."

"I'm not going to say what Jen did is forgivable, but I do want to point out that her familiar, Hamilton, helped me free my wolf from the agathion's prison. I don't know what part he had in the other shifter's deaths, or why they went rogue while I didn't, but Jen's magic is what saved me in the end. I think Jen and her familiar tried to do the right thing."

"Only because the agathion subverted his promise," Tessa said, her face stony with condemnation.

"What do you mean?" Ashlyn asked, looking between the coven leader and the accused.

More tears slid down Jen's cheek as she stared at the pet carrier where Hamilton had his face against the bars, staring pitifully at Ashlyn. "He promised to free Hamilton after I helped him. He did, only he didn't send Hamilton back to me. Instead, he released my familiar into the hellmouth, alone and unprotected with no way back."

Ashlyn remembered the sensation of being hunted in that dark void and shuddered. She turned to the gallery. "I know I'm a new face here, but I want to advocate for Hamilton. If I understand correctly, a witch's familiar is tied to her in a similar fashion to a shifter's animal." She glanced over her shoulder toward the Head of Covens, who nodded in confirmation. Ashlyn continued, "My wolf was willing to sacrifice herself to save me, and I would do the same for her. I might even be tempted to make rash choices if I thought it would save her. I'm sure all of you feel the same way."

She paused for a heartbeat to allow that idea to sink in before turning back toward the table. "Jen regrets her actions and is willing to pay the price, but burning her alive will also kill Hamilton. Horribly, I might add. He doesn't deserve that. As one of the victims, I ask that the court consider alternative ways to punish Jen without harming her familiar."

"I understand and appreciate your forgiveness," the Head of Covens said. "But the only way to ensure Jen no longer serves as a conduit for the agathion is the incineration of her soul."

Throat constricted with emotion, Ashlyn asked, "When I came back through the hellmouth, I was able to fight off the agathion's possession by becoming human again. There has to be a way to close off Jen's power and keep the agathion from accessing her, too—besides burning her."

"Yes!" Muffy spoke again, making all heads turn toward her. "Jen can revoke her magic. She can make herself human."

This time it was the witches in the room who gasped. Words like "living death" and "zombie" rumbled through the crowd.

The Head of Covens' cheek twitched as she seemed to consider. "That would break her bond with her familiar. Then he would not suffer her fate."

Jen's already pale face turned ashen. She clenched her hands together on her lap hard enough to make the knuckles gleam white. "If it means Hamilton gets to live, I'll do it."

"And then she won't have to die." Muffy moved toward the front table, looking frantically back and forth between Ashlyn and the Head. "She'll be a harmless human."

"I don't think you understand what you're asking." The Head of Covens frowned deeply. "Such a sentence would only prolong your sister's suffering. She'd most likely kill herself within the first few weeks rather than endure the void of losing her magic."

Ashlyn recalled how devastated she'd been when she lost her wolf. How becoming human again after experiencing the supernatural had hurt. And she had only been connected to her wolf a short time. What would it be like for a witch who'd always possessed power to lose it? "Hold on," Ashlyn looked at Tessa and back to the Head of Covens. "Will that really turn her into a zombie?"

"Not as such, but it will hurt enough to drive her insane," the Head of Covens replied.

Tessa added, "It's a witch's version of going rogue."

Jen leaned forward and set her hand gently on top of the pet carrier. "At least allow me to keep Hamilton from suffering. Afterward you can do as you like to me."

Councilman Dixon, the auburn-haired selkie representative, spoke. "You've been hiding your use of black magic for years. How can we trust you to cast anything, let alone remove your own magic?"

The Head of Covens rubbed her temple and sighed. "I along with several other coven leaders would test her, of course, and verify she had no trace of magic. We would also test her familiar and ensure it reverted to a normal animal. But I'm not recommending this sentence."

Councilman Riordan curled his lips in a very wolfish looking snarl. "I say let her taste her own medicine. Let her suffer what it means to go rogue before she dies."

Ashlyn swallowed, suddenly doubting her part in changing the sentence. Perhaps being burned alive wasn't such a bad option.

The Head of Covens signaled to a witch standing at one side of the room to approach, and whispered something in her ear. The witch disappeared down a hallway, reappearing moments later carrying a small leather pouch, which she handed to the leader. Rising, the Head of Covens approached Jen's chair, her stilettos clicking across the wooden floor. "Please bring out your familiar and rise for your sentence."

With trembling hands, Jen opened the pet carrier and removed Hamilton, lowering her face to press her lips to the top of his head as she stood. When she looked up, her eyes glistened with tears. "We're ready."

"You are hereby sentenced to revoke your magical power immediately and at your own free will, upon which, you will be remanded to your sister's custody for the duration of your life. In the event you do not revoke your power, you will be bound to a stake and burned to ash before the sun rises in the morning. Do you understand?"

Jen nodded, gulping. "Yes."

The Head of Covens opened the leather bag and brought out a small gleaming knife and two tiny vials, one brown, one green. She offered them to Jen.

Hamilton squeaked and squirmed in her arms, burrowing against her neck as if beseeching her to reconsider.

She rubbed her cheek against him one last time before setting him on the floor. "Go, Hamilton."

The little ferret cowered for a moment, looking up at her with his one good eye, then he turned and slunk out of the circle toward Muffy.

Jen took the items, staring stiffly at them for a moment. Then she took a deep breath and made a series of movements with her hands. She emptied the contents of the vials onto the blade, one after the other. Speaking a few shaky words Ashlyn didn't understand, Jen plunged the point beneath her ribs.

Ashlyn gasped as Jen sank slowly to her knees, dropping forward onto one hand while keeping the other clasped around the knife's hilt. A crimson pool grew steadily beneath her, running up to the edge of the circle of stones where it magically stopped. Light pulsed around her as if in time to a beating heart, growing dimmer with each flash until it vanished.

Taking a step forward, Ashlyn was going to try to stop the bleeding, but Kepler's grip on her arm stopped her.

"Don't interfere."

She watched in horror as Jen yanked the knife free and sagged onto her side, curling into a fetal position. The knife fell from her hand into the pooling blood, it's once-gleaming metal now corroded and black.

"Is she dead?" Ashlyn whispered.

The witches in the gallery rose in a whoosh of sound and approached the circle of stones. Forming a solid wall, they faced the circle, and a hum of magic filled Ashlyn's ears, encircling her heart until she could hardly breathe. She glanced at Muffy, who held Hamilton against her chest, tears glistening on her reddened cheeks. The ferret squirmed and writhed, but Muffy held on tightly.

Suddenly, the magic ceased, and the wall of witches parted. Jen lay where she'd fallen, shoulders shaking with silent sobs. The blood on the floor had vanished. Hamilton escaped Muffy's grasp, scurrying under the chairs and disappearing from sight.

The Head of Covens addressed the room. "It is done. Let it be known that the covens have verified that Jennifer Lynn Elliot has revoked her magic and is now a mortal human. She is no longer under the protection of our order."

A chorus of "Aye" rose from the witches, along with a few disgruntled words from the assembled shifters.

Councilman Riordan stood, his piercing gaze silencing the crowd. "The witch has served her sentence. Although she no longer falls under the protection of the witches, be warned that anyone who harms her will be held accountable for harming a human without cause."

The shifters in the gallery muttered their reluctant acceptance of his announcement. Ashlyn got the feeling Jen might not have long to live, anyway. Muffy was on her knees next to her sister, encouraging her to stand. Although Jen's eyes were open and her chest moved with rapid breaths, there was a deadness to her gaze that Ashlyn recognized. She'd felt it herself when she lost her wolf.

She almost felt sorry for the witch.

Almost.

Kepler leaned against the countertop and sipped his coffee, watching Ashlyn as she moved around the bakery kitchen with her cousin, Lana. He needed to get to work, but hated leaving his mate's side for even a few hours after everything they'd been through. Plus, she fed him muffins when he came to the bakery, so he spent his mornings there before going to the office.

Lana hefted a tray of doughnuts and carried it to the front customer area, shoving it into the glass case near the register before returning to the kitchen. He liked Ashlyn's cousin, but she put a bit of a damper on his ability to be frisky with his new mate. She kept glancing out the front windows, and he had the feeling there was more to her hanging around the bakery these last few days than having her boat dry-docked for repairs.

The bell over the door jingled, and Cal's voice carried into the kitchen. "It's just me!"

Lana's face brightened, and she tucked a loose strand of unruly blonde hair under her baseball cap before rearranging the bear claws on a tray for what had to be the dozenth time.

Kepler shot a glance at Ashlyn, raising one eyebrow in an "I told you so," fashion.

Ashlyn's eyes twinkled, and she sent, *She has a crush.*

It can't go anywhere. He shook his head. *She's not his mate, or he would've said something.*

Her face fell. *Crap.* Lana had lost her husband a while back, and Ashlyn was super protective of her.

Cal strutted into the kitchen wearing his new brown Wildlife Trooper uniform. After the hearing, Finch had finagled Cal an entry level position. Kepler'd never seen his friend this happy.

Glancing at Kepler's maroon tee shirt as he bee-lined it toward the bear claws, Cal said, "Nice shirt, man."

"Thanks," Kepler replied. The shirt said *stop looking at my wife's cookies,* and Ashlyn had giggled about it for hours after he'd put it on it.

Cal nodded at Lana as he helped himself to a pastry. "Hey, how's it going?" Without waiting for her reply, he pulled a stool out and sat facing Kepler. "So, you decide yet?"

Lana's cheeks flushed, and she dusted imaginary flour off her jeans. "Um, yeah, good. I'm good. I need to go."

She rushed out of the kitchen and through the front door, the cold smell of snow driving away the smell of baked goods for a moment.

Ashlyn frowned. "What was that all about?"

Cal looked just as confused, speaking around a mouthful of bear claw. "No idea. I thought we had a good time last night."

Kepler narrowed his eyes and stared his friend down. "You didn't."

"What? Yeah, we did." He polished off the bear claw.

Throwing her oven mitt aside, Ashlyn peeked into the customer area before rounding on Cal. "You shouldn't lead her on."

"I'm not. She came over last night to chill, you know?" He shrugged.

Kepler set his coffee aside and put his hands on his hips. Shifters often dallied with humans on a casual basis, knowing it wouldn't lead to anything permanent. But Kepler'd never really thought about how a human might hope differently. "Lana is off limits."

Cal frowned. "She's a grown woman. She's got needs the same as the rest of us."

"She's fragile, Cal." Ashlyn sighed. "Just leave her alone, okay?"

Cal's face fell, and he nodded. "Fine." He reached for a second bear claw. "But we did have fun."

Ashlyn smacked his hand with a scowl. "Paws off the claws. Those are for customers."

"I like it better when Lana's in charge." He licked his fingers. "Don't I at least get a pack discount or something?"

Cal had been bugging him since the honeymoon to register their new pack with the Council, but Kepler wasn't sure he was ready. He was still focused on spending time with Ashlyn. "Stop bugging me about the pack thing. I haven't decided."

"Let Ashlyn do it. She's as Alpha as you are." Cal licked his finger and used it to pick up crumbs from an empty baking tray. "More Alpha, maybe."

Ashlyn's scowl dissolved into a smirk. "Kepler's right about you being a suck up, Cal." She shook her head. "But I kinda like it."

Cal grinned in triumph. "See, Kep? Listen to your better half." He snagged a bear claw and scooted past Ashlyn before she could stop him. "Gotta go. Finch wants me to find out who's been harassing moose around Skilak Lake. See ya!"

Kepler looked at his phone. It was seven thirty. "I should go, too."

Ashlyn put a hand on his chest. "We really should talk."

He sighed. She was less opposed to forming a pack than he was. Covering her hand with his, he looked into her eyes. "It's a tremendous responsibility."

She wrapped her other arm around his waist, tilting her head to look up at him. "Cal's a worthy pack mate, even if he is a pastry thief. It's good to have friends who'll watch your back."

He hated to admit it, but she was right. Cal had pulled through for him, even when he'd doubted. "What about

Finch?"

She made a confused face. "Isn't it weird for a bear to join a pack?"

"My point exactly. And Finch is my boss. How's it going to work if I'm his Alpha?"

Her eyes narrowed to crescents as she grinned. "You get to tell him to give you a raise, I guess."

He laughed. "Always the jokes."

"You thought I was joking?" She raised her eyebrows. "Seriously, though, it'll all work out. I know it will. And we'll all live happily ever after."

Pulling her closer, he inhaled her wildflower honey scent. "I already am."

He'd never imagined feeling this content. He'd found his mate, nearly lost her, and got her back stronger than ever. Lowering his head, he kissed her, savoring her taste and softness. By the time they stopped, he was breathing hard and ready to plunder her right there.

She nuzzled his chin, a naughty grin lighting her glowing blue eyes. "Go to work, my love. But don't wear yourself out. I have plans for you tonight."

He grinned and kissed her forehead. They had years together—centuries. And he could hardly wait.

Dear Reader,

Thank you for reading this Aurora Shifters Double Feature! I love imagining the paranormal exists near my home in Alaska. The next book, Midnight Heat, features Ashlyn's cousin Lana and a "wolf of the sea" - a surly selkie shifter!

She's stranded on an island with her worst enemy—and he has a secret she never suspected...

Tap the cover to get it now or keep reading for an excerpt!

XOXO,
Tamsin

P.S. Be sure to check out all the Alaska Alphas books at:
< https://books2read.com/rl/aurorashifters >

The sound of fiddling pierced the cold November air as Captain Elias Sobol hesitated outside the bar's heavy wooden door. The flickering neon sign in the bar's window was making his head swim, and the air had a crackly feel that told him a storm was coming. Even his inner seal was jittery, vibrating with anticipation like that moment right before he plunged into the ocean. *It's just being in a new town.* He didn't like encroaching on another selkie clan's territory. But the entire crew of the *Utkin* was gathering to support Bobby's first band gig, and Elias didn't want to let him down.

His first mate, Jacob, pushed open the door from inside. "You coming? We've got seats up front."

"Yeah, be right there." Elias adjusted his pelt—to humans it appeared as a duster-length sealskin vest—

and stepped inside. Warmth hit his face, carrying with it the overwhelming scent of humanity and spilled beer. Despite it being past the season for tourists, the bar was packed with people, faces lit by strings of Christmas lights criss-crossing the ceiling. Elias immediately spotted Walton's sealskin hat at the front near the low platform where Bobby and his band stood belting out a fast-paced tune.

Turning, he slid sideways through the crowd, weaving between bodies like swimming through long fronds of kelp. Maybe after the band finished playing, he'd go to the beach and shift. Letting his seal out to swim would help clear his mind. As he approached the long bar, a delicious scent reached him—cinnamon and mocha with an underlying hint of what he could only describe as sex.

His heartbeat kicked up, and a single thought consumed him. *Mate.* His eyes came to rest on a short figure with brown curly hair sticking out beneath a pink winter cap. She sat on a bar stool with her back to him, but he could see her delicious womanly curves filling out the sweatshirt and jeans she wore. A true Alaska girl. He couldn't hold back his seal's low growl of approval.

She swiveled in the chair to glance at the band, revealing her profile. Her cheeks were flushed as if she'd just come in out of the cold, and her broad smile shot straight through Elias's heart. The smile wasn't directed at him, however. She was talking to a weathered man with shaggy, dirty-blonde surfer hair sitting beside to her.

Elias rolled his shoulders, shaking off the possessive aggression settling over him. Not all shifters found their true mates, but when they did, the physical attraction was supposed to be instantaneous and undeniable. He only hoped they had human things in common, as well.

He silently chided his inner seal, *You knew she was here all along, didn't you?*

His seal responded by filling his mind with lusty thoughts.

Feeling his body respond in embarrassing ways, he shook his head but couldn't help the smile tugging his lips. They said meeting one's mate for the first time was something you'd never forget. *I'd prefer she didn't remember our first meeting as me being a perv who approached her at the bar.* Elias straightened his shoulders, pulled his vest closed over his front, and nudged past a group standing between him and the woman.

His mate didn't appear to have sensed him yet, and as he drew near, he understood why; her cinnamon scent grew stronger, but it also told him she was human.

Damn. That put a kink in things. Humans weren't as in-tune with their instincts—he was going to have to woo her now and find a way to reveal his true nature later. He paused a few bar stools away, taking a moment to plan his new strategy. On stage, Bobby was playing his heart out on the fiddle, the guitarist strumming an accompanying beat while the vocalist shouted something about gambling away his heart.

Elias's future mate bobbed her head in time to the music.

I could ask her to dance.

His seal laughed at him, knowing full well Elias didn't dance.

Someone at a table near him reached out to tug his sleeve. "Hey, Elias," a woman shouted above the music. "What are you doing in Kenai? Buy me a drink?"

He pulled back and it took him a second to recognize her. He'd met her in Homer last year, and they'd spent a few enjoyable nights together, but hell if he could remember her name. He forced himself to smile but shook his head. "Not tonight, love."

The woman stuck out her lip in a pout, but he moved past without another glance. At least she'd had the right idea. *Start by offering to buy a drink.*

He was within arms length of his mate when he spotted the metallic glint on her left hand. *Married?*

He glanced once more at the man next to her. She was totally out of that guy's league. Was the ring a ploy to keep guys from hitting on her? He'd met women who did that. He started forward again. Suddenly, the man next to her grabbed her chin in one hand and kissed her. Not a peck, but a deep, satisfying, intimate kiss.

Elias's spine stiffened. Before his brain had time to catch up, he'd grabbed the guy by the back of his collar and yanked him off his stool, tossing him onto the floor.

The crowd surged back, giving the fallen man room.

"What the hell?" the guy shouted, face dark with fury.

"The lady doesn't appreciate being mauled," Elias answered, peripherally aware that the woman had risen to her feet behind him.

The guy sat up, drawing his feet under him to stand. "She's my wife, you asshole."

A lead weight settled to the bottom of Elias's stomach. "Shit."

He turned to find the woman gaping at him, brown eyes wide. Then she turned her lovely face away to look at her husband on the floor. *Husband. Wife.* The ring wasn't an act.

If there was one boundary Elias wouldn't cross, this was it; he wouldn't steal another man's wife.

Something hard slammed into Elias's cheek, rocking his head back. Stumbling, he turned in time to receive a second jab directly in the eye. Stars filled his vision, and his own fists flew up on instinct. The man was back on his feet, fists in front of him like a boxer. He jabbed again. This time, Elias dodged the blow.

Someone in the crowd yelled, "Fight!"

"Peter, stop," the woman shouted, reaching with both hands for her husband's arm.

Elias seldom started brawls—at least, not without good reason. But he also wasn't one to back down from one. Still, the guy had a right to be pissed. Elias forced his fists open and raised both palms in front of him. "I thought she was someone else. Honest mistake."

The man danced forward. "Honest my ass. Come on and fight, you pussy."

The band had stopped playing and the crowd had formed a surging ring around the area. A grizzled bouncer shoved into the open space. "Break it up, Peter." He held out both arms as he stepped between them and glared at Elias. "Both of you, take it outside."

Above the crowd, Elias felt Jacob's eyes on him and the telepathic bond he shared with his selkie crew surged to life. *Need backup?*

What a fiasco. He didn't need his crew knowing he'd found his mate. If they did, they'd do everything they could to break up her marriage, and if they did that, he may as well just steal her away right now. Keeping all thoughts of his mate out of his mind, Elias shook his head and sent back, *Nope. I'm done. Tell Bobby I'm sorry.*

Turning, Elias jetted out the door and into the cold night air, ignoring Peter's drunken taunts as he climbed into his pickup. He was halfway home before he cooled down enough to realize he hadn't even learned his mate's name.

~

Get Midnight Heat now!

ALSO BY TAMSIN LEY

Galactic Pirate Brides series

Galactic Pirate Brides Box Set (Includes first 3 books)

Rescued by Qaiyaan

Ransomed by Kashatok

Claimed by Noatak

Taken by the Cyborg

Mates for Monsters

Mer-Lovers Collector's Edition (Includes first 3 books)

The Merman's Kiss

The Merman's Quest

A Mermaid's Heart

The Centaur's Bride

The Djinn's Desire

Khargals of Duras

Sticks and Stones

Alaska Alphas

Alpha Origins

Untamed Instinct

Bewitched Shifter

Midnight Heat

Wild Child

<u>Kirenai Fated Mates (Intergalactic Dating Agency)</u>

Arazhi

Zhiruto

Iroth

****POST-APOCALYPTIC SCIENCE FICTION WRITTEN AS TAM LINSEY****

Botanicaust

The Reaping Room

Doomseeds

Amarantox

ABOUT THE AUTHOR

Once upon a time I thought I wanted to be a biomedical engineer, but experimenting on lab rats doesn't always lead to happy endings. Now I blend my nerdy infatuation of science with character-driven romance and guaranteed happily-ever-afters. My monsters always find their mates, with feisty heroines, tortured heroes, and all the steamy trouble they can handle. I promise my stories will never leave you hanging (although you may still crave more!)

When I'm not writing, I'll be in the garden or the kitchen, exploring Alaska with my husband, or preparing for the zombie apocalypse. I also love wine and hard apple cider, am mediocre at crochet, and have the cutest 12-pound bunny named Abigail.

Interested in more about me? Join my VIP Club and get free books, notices, and other cool stuff!

www.tamsinley.com

Aurora Shifters is a collaboration of Alaskan authors who decided to put our own Arctic spin on hot paranormal shapeshifters.

Tielle St. Clare moved to Alaska when she was seven years old and believes romances should be hot and sexy with a great story and fun characters. Learn more about her at www.tiellestclare.blogspot.com

Tamsin Ley was born and raised in Alaska and writes steamy sci-fi with a pinch of pixie dust. Find out more about her at www.tamsinley.com

Boone Brux has lived all over the world, finally settling in the icy region of Alaska. No person or escapade is off limits when it comes to weaving real life experiences into her books. Learn more at www.boonebrux.com

Be sure to join the Alaska Alphas Facebook Group! www.facebook.com/groups/alaskaalphas/